UNITED SENTRY

MITCHELL PEEBLES

TO: mona

Explore your fears, limits & abilities.

 FriesenPress

One Printers Way
Altona, MB R0G 0B0
Canada

www.friesenpress.com

Copyright © 2024 by Mitchell Peebles
First Edition — 2024

All rights reserved.

No part of this publication may be reproduced in any form, or by any means, electronic or mechanical, including photocopying, recording, or any information browsing, storage, or retrieval system, without permission in writing from FriesenPress.

ISBN
978-1-03-919430-4 (Hardcover)
978-1-03-919429-8 (Paperback)
978-1-03-919431-1 (eBook)

1. FICTION, SCIENCE FICTION, APOCALYPTIC & POST-APOCALYPTIC

Distributed to the trade by The Ingram Book Company

Acknowledgements

FIRSTLY, I WANT to thank my beautiful wife, Victoria, for all her support and encouragement. For listening to rants and dealing with my absences while I wrote this novel. Also, for supporting and helping me budget when the manuscript was ready for publishing! I love you.

I thank my brothers, Taylor, Kurt, and Ian, for all the years of inspiration and all the ideas we came up with for games and movies. The three of you created my imagination! Taylor, with your dangerous stunts as a kid, Kurt with our Assassin's Creed vision, and Ian with our Halo 4 (back when the game didn't actually exist) outside.

I thank all the friends who have patiently waited for this book as I continuously said that it was almost ready for years. I thank you for your continuous interest; every time I got to explain my book, I got renewed excitement. And now it's finally here!

Ultimately, I thank God for giving me the imagination and the drive to create my own world and for giving me parents who always pushed my brothers and me to pursue our passions and not to give up on difficult endeavours. You made the best environment to grow up and thrive.

ONE

RYLAND SNUCK THROUGH the bushes in pursuit of his prey, semi-automatic rifle in hand. The beast was triple his size and weight, faster and stronger. The only thing Ryland had over the creature was intelligence.

As it dodged trees, roots, and bushes to escape, the beast's matte-black skin made it look like a shadow, causing Ryland to second guess its whereabouts. However, he had already shot it once, and he knew he could outlast it.

Ryland stayed out of sight and moved as quietly as possible, hoping the hulking beast would think it had lost him. He could tell its pace was slowing, and he was grateful for it, but he could also tell it was looking for him through the thick, dense forest.

The sun was on its way down, and the forest was dark due to the dense trees blocking the light. There was no wind either, the forest being located in a valley, with a town to the north and mountains to the south.

Ryland heard the leaves in the forest canopy flutter in the wind as he took cover behind a tree. He raised his gun and aimed at the beast's shoulder, he had to slow his breathing from the run. He finally controlled his breathing and squeezed the trigger.

Three bullets pierced the beast's thick skin within centimetres of each other.

The beast took off again. Ryland slung his rifle on his back so he could run. Dodging trees and leaping over bushes, Ryland kept up with the beast as it limped. Ryland jumped and grabbed a branch, using it to swing over a tall bush. When he landed, he spotted the beast lying on the ground to his left. The forest dweller was five hundred pounds of muscle with black skin, horns growing out of its jaws and shoulders, and a short, thin tail, like that of a lion. It was a hulking, four-legged creature whose skin was so tough, a knife would have a difficult time piercing it.

Nevertheless, a woman was over it holding a knife covered in blood, as was her hand. Ryland was impressed with her knife—and her beauty.

She had brown hair, and she was wearing baggy cargo pants with a matching sand-coloured T-shirt and a brown leather jacket. An old hunting rifle was slung over her shoulder. As she stared back at him, he realized he had seen her in the town to the north.

That look, it's like Nat's, he thought. She looked only a few years younger than his twenty-five years.

"Is this yours?" she asked.

"You killed it," he replied. "Though that doesn't matter to me, just as long as it's dead."

Relaxing his stance, he stood up straight.

"Not that I was trying to take this kill away from you," she said. "I just thought I could help." Such animals were hunted for bounties.

"And who is this beautiful and skilled hunter to whom I'm speaking?" Ryland asked, admiring her beauty again. She was pretty and could hunt, which meant she was from a family of girls and had to learn to hunt, or she was from a family of all boys who had taught her to keep up.

"My name is Keira," she replied, not knowing how to react to his admiring look.

"It's a pleasure to meet you, Keira. Thanks for your help." He bowed his head. "My name is Ryland."

Her eyes flicked to his waist where a loose metal cable was intertwined with a rope embedded with metal, rock, glass, wood, and bone beads, a cross in the middle of the beads.

She nodded. "You've been staying in town. Live around here?"

"No. I... travel a lot."

"If you want, we can take this forest dweller to my place," she suggested.

"No, that's okay. I have a place not far to the east." It was a bit farther than he was letting on, but that wasn't an issue.

"This beast is heavy, and there aren't any communities nearby besides Mount Horizon," she said. "I have people that can help."

"I can handle it," Ryland said. He admired her persistence. She wasn't rude about it, just calling his bluff because she knew the area.

"I believe you can, but you don't have to. Come on, I'll show you the way." She started walking before he could reply. He rolled his eyes and smiled, then started off in a different direction.

When Keira noticed, she stopped. "Hey, what—"

"I just need to grab my stuff," he replied. She turned and followed him toward his camp.

"Mount Horizon is a nice town," he said as they walked. "It has a variety of landscapes."

"Yeah," she replied, nodding. "I like the mountains the best."

"Mount Horizon has spectacular mountains."

"Do you have a different favourite landscape you've seen?" she asked, looking in wonder.

"I like deserts, though I'm not sure why. Sand can be annoying, but deserts look like places where you can be alone and become stronger."

"Stronger? How?"

"Through the trials the desert puts you through. Deserts may seem vast and empty, but they can be very dangerous."

"Why would you want to go through trials?" Keira asked.

"To become stronger. A person should always want to improve themselves." Ryland ducked past a few branches and entered a dense patch of trees where his bivouac was located, a small tarp set under the cover of a coniferous tree.

"You live here?" she asked.

"No," he said, sliding a backpack out from under the tarp. "I just slept here for the night."

Once they got to Mount Horizon, Ryland and Keira were greeted warmly by everyone they encountered. They walked past a fountain and a big community garden in the middle of the small town, which had an elegant tree in the centre. Trees intermingled with buildings of wood and stone, lining the narrow dirt and gravel walkways. The town had an organic warmth to it, where everyone knew everyone, and the people worked to help one another. In other communities, Ryland had seen paved roads, which were used by the few vehicles people owned. The world war happened over 200 years ago and wiped out most factories, vehicles, and technology. Not many cities had cars or any transportation, and guns had been distributed equally to every city according to its population. Mount Horizon was so small it had probably received none, but some individuals would have found some guns while looting.

Mount Horizon had few streetlights, which meant it had a small amount of electrical power. The nukes had reduced humanity to several million people, and they had gone underground for a hundred years. Luckily, the areas hit didn't stay uninhabitable for nearly as long as they thought, and humanity started to rebuild.

Ryland could feel the wind a bit more now that they were level with the treetops. The land where the town was located was flat, rising toward the mountains in the west. Ryland enjoyed the landscape. The towering peaks provided an ideal vantage point, overlooking all the other landscapes with only the sun overhead.

Keira's house was to the west of the fountain. It was large enough to hold a family of six or seven comfortably. As Keira entered, she announced her presence. "Hello, I'm back!" Then she lowered her voice. "This is Ryland. He was hunting a forest dweller by himself, so I decided to help him."

Ryland looked at the far wall and saw a large glass display case filled with light-coloured sand and smooth stones. *Where did they get that much sand?* he wondered.

A man came around the corner near the display, wiping his hands with a towel, one eyebrow raised. "A forest dweller? On your own?"

"It's still out in the forest," Keira said. "Can we get some help to bring it back? And can Ryland stay for supper?"

"Take your uncle," the man said. "And yes, Ryland is more than welcome to stay for supper." Ryland assumed he was Keira's father.

Just then another man, presumably Keira's uncle, came from the left hallway. "Let's go get the forest dweller before someone else does," he said, smiling as he walked toward the door. "Keira, go get the sled."

As Keira went out, her uncle turned to Ryland. "So, you were hunting by yourself, were you?"

"Yes, sir," Ryland replied.

Once they got outside, Keira came around the side of the house with the sled, and they were off.

When they got to the site of the kill, they saw the beast, but they also saw something else, or rather, someone else. The person looked like a shadow with matte-black skin and bright red marks on it that seemed to glow.

"Who is that?" Keira asked.

"I'm not sure," her uncle replied. Ryland looked to the right and saw a group of ten men holding bow-staffs, spears, swords, and knives.

"Whoa, look over there," he whispered, pointing. Ryland pulled out his phone. In the pre-war world, everyone had one. Now only the Circle of Generals and some of their subordinates used them. Decades after the war, humanity assigned leaders all around the world to govern their countries. A century after the war, the countries amalgamated their leaders to form the COG, which governed each continent together. Ryland typed a few coordinates into his phone without Keira or her uncle noticing.

"I think a fight is about to happen," Keira's uncle said as the man with black skin ran toward a tree with bushes on either side of it. The ten men would not see him until they got around the tree.

"Is that the Blood's Shadow?" Keira asked, her voice filled with fear. Keira knew her uncle was skeptical of the group's existence, but the man's matte-black skin was strong proof.

"If it is then those men are in serious trouble," her uncle replied.

"Probably why they have ten guys," Keira said.

When the men got close to the tree, the man with black skin stepped out in front of them. The others stopped and talked to him. Keira, her uncle, and Ryland were too far away to hear them. Then one of the men in the group lunged at the man with the black skin. He took the attacker down in a matter of seconds. Then the rest of the group attacked, but the man with the black skin moved so fast that they couldn't touch him. In less than a minute, all ten men were on the ground and probably dead, except for one who was on his knees, weapon in hand. The man with the black skin walked up to him and stabbed him in the chest.

"Whoa!" Ryland exclaimed.

"Okay, we're not going over there for a while," Keira's uncle said. "Let's go back home."

"Don't you wanna see what happens?" Keira asked.

"I'll admit I'm curious but not enough to risk staying," her uncle replied.

As they walked away, Ryland looked back, and the man with the black skin was nowhere in sight. He took out his phone and typed a message, keeping his phone at his waist to avoid detection.

"I have to go," he said when he was finished.

"What?" Keira asked in surprise, turning to him.

"I have been alerted of something I need to attend to," he replied. Then their faces lit up with recognition as they realized he was a part of the COG.

TWO

Six years earlier

—

RYLAND'S EYES DIDN'T need to adjust from the cave to the outside due to the dark, damp environment. The tall trees made it even darker. His mind matched his surroundings, filled with darkness as it raced, looking for his foe, the one who had killed his partner, Nat. Ryland's knees were still red from kneeling in her blood. He tried to open his mind, relax, and keep calm, like he had been trained, but it was futile. He was out to kill. He was military. Only a few military departments were still operating after the war, which had nearly destroyed the planet.

Ryland was part of a surveillance program called Sentry, which worked for the Circle of Generals. His job was to check into more locations than the generals could, ensuring that the cities were running well and that no threats existed inside or out. At the moment he was in pursuit of one of those threats.

A few metres from the cave, he found footprints. While following them, he kept his eyes peeled, listening for any sound that might indicate his foe.

An hour went by, revealing nothing. The footprints disappeared, so Ryland searched in a circle around the cave. Finally giving up, he pulled out his cell phone to report the loss. Then he paused. He knew he had to call headquarters, but he was unable to move. This was his partner, and her death was his fault. He had left her a few weeks ago because of a fight, and now she was dead.

Finally, Ryland forced himself to press the button, establishing a secure line with headquarters.

"I have an agent down at my location," he said. "No culprit found."

They would search for him, and that meant he had failed. It wasn't that he would be punished. The other agents understood loss, as did Nick, the head of Ryland's zone. Nick was reasonable, and he knew every agent personally. There weren't many agents around the world, but even if there had been more, Nick would still have known them all. No one would blame him. Ryland was more scared of having lost his partner and what it would mean moving forward.

A helicopter came, dropped off a few soldiers, then ascended to survey the land below. Ryland was surprised to see that one of the men who had been dropped off was Nick. As he approached, Ryland remained seated on a rock by the cave entrance.

"You know how it happened?" Nick asked.

"I just found the body," Ryland replied, looking down. "We went our separate ways."

"Ah, jeez, Ryland."

"Then I came back." Ryland stood up to offer a defence, only to realize he had none.

Two men went into the cave, then came out with the body on a stretcher in a body bag. Ryland looked away.

"I'm so sorry, Ryland." Nick placed a hand on Ryland's shoulder. "We'll find the culprit."

A soldier came up and pulled Nick away. Ryland could only imagine they were explaining the scene. When Nick returned, he told Ryland he needed to take a break and go see Liz.

Liz was a friend and a psychiatrist, part of the Sentry program in a town near Ryland's area. He went to her every so often for an assessment or for help. Every agent had to ensure they were at the top of their game.

Agents had seen some gruesome things as the world was being discovered again following the war.

∎

"Void sucker," Liz said after hearing what happened. "I'm so sorry, Ryland." She handed him a warm drink. "How do you feel? Honestly?"

Ryland took a sip before replying. "I feel like crap, Liz. It's my fault. If I didn't leave—"

"You thought what you were doing was right," Liz said, cutting him off. "You can always play the what-if game." She knew the whole scenario. She wasn't just a psychiatrist to Ryland; she was also a good friend. Liz knew why he had left Nat, and considering Ryland and Nat's history, she understood his decision.

"Nick will do the service for Nat," Ryland said in a matter-of-fact tone. Due to agents being posted around the world, they couldn't take time off and attend an in-person service, so it would be broadcast over the radio for all of them to hear. There was no time off for Sentry agents, but there was life between each call.

Ryland awoke the next morning at Liz's safe house, a place he had been to dozens of times. Then he remembered being in pain the night before. He knew it wasn't physical pain, or else he would still feel it. Then his memory returned, accompanied by a fiery flood of emotions. Nat was dead. Murdered.

He sat up in bed as the pain of his emotions deepened in response to the inescapable loss. Never again would he be able to see Nat, whom he missed so much, even though he had left her only a short time ago.

As he looked around the room, his emotions settled somewhat, realizing he was at a dear friend's house.

After getting dressed, he went upstairs, the smell of breakfast so strong it made his stomach ache with hunger.

As he entered the kitchen, Ryland was excited to see Liz, but he was unable to express it. It was like something was stopping him from smiling and greeting her like he usually did.

"Morning," Liz said as she cooked something in a frying pan. "How are you feeling?"

"It's good to be here, but I still feel lost."

"Well, I'll help you find your way back to a purpose," Liz said, scraping a few eggs and some sausages from the frying pan onto a plate.

They sat at the table in the next room. Both rooms were dimly lit. The kitchen was a simple, open-concept design with all the appliances within reach of one another. The dining room was decorated with photos that Ryland hadn't seen before.

"Why does it seem that only one emotion can dominate a human heart?" Ryland asked after swallowing a bite, unable to look at Liz.

"What do you mean?"

"I'm excited to see you, Liz, but I can't seem to express it."

"The other emotion is too strong, I guess."

They both pondered the idea as they continued eating.

"Can you help with some house maintenance today?" Liz asked.

"I don't see why not. It's not like I'm going anywhere," Ryland responded, forcing a smile. He was there for support, but he didn't feel trapped. He was still in the same zone, so if he was needed anywhere, he could get there fast. Ryland and Liz were both working for the Circle of Generals, Liz as a psychiatrist and Ryland as a military survey analyst, analyzing threats to different cities to avoid another war.

Ryland tried to distract himself with paperwork from his latest mission. Laketown, located to the west, was a port city, second in size only to Grand Port in the north. It was run by a young man named Travis, whose father had run it before him. There weren't many threats, only a few gangs that would maybe start a turf war. They wouldn't get much traction in Laketown, and if they did, Ryland would be sent there before anything major could happen.

That made the paperwork simple. He would report that nothing major was happening in the city. He didn't necessarily have to report the gangs either. The COG wouldn't care until a gang threatened to take over the city itself. The COG had to worry about the big picture, and they knew every city had its small issues.

Once Ryland finished his paperwork, it was time for Nat's service. Liz joined him. Over the radio, Nick spoke about Nat as an agent and a friend. After a moment of silence, he opened it up for others to say something.

The first person to speak was Fred, of course, he was a compassionate, caring agent and was part of Ryland's recruitment class. His code name was Jovian. It was no surprise that he went first, he was a caring, 'big brother' type. He always looked out for everyone, even to the other team back in Sentry training. "Ryland, I'm so sorry. She was an amazing friend, and you two had a great partnership. I was always proud to call you guys friends and never worried about that zone." Fred was like Nick. He knew every agent's name and was friends with them, watching out for them. Although he was not a safe house agent, he had that kind of therapeutic personality.

"We'll find that void-sucking murderer, Ryland," another voice said. It belonged to Alek, an agent in a zone across the world. He had always been a problem solver.

After Alek, more voices came on to comfort Ryland or to say good things about Nat.

Following another minute of silence, Nick came back on to close the service. Ryland looked up and realized Liz was watching him. He didn't know what to say, but he was thankful for all those who had spoken.

THREE

THE FOLLOWING NIGHT, Ryland went into town, not quite sure where he was going. The town was almost like home considering the dozens of times he had been there on visits or as part of a mission.

A drinking establishment called Scandalous Bar on the north side of town was one of Ryland's favourites, though he hated himself for having a preference. It was a time for hating himself, though. The north side of town also had a strip club, which made the area more violent, with men seeking control and then losing it through drinks. The mayor's office was on the same side, probably in an attempt to slow crime down, but Ryland felt the placement was fitting considering how corrupt the mayor was.

But we're all corrupt, he thought. *The only difference is the mayor doesn't care.*

As Ryland entered, he was hit with the smell of alcohol. The dimly lit atmosphere suited Ryland's mood. He would have preferred it to be darker still. When he continued toward the bar, he smelled another scent, a woodsy pine smell.

Ryland ordered a whisky with a sour lime accent. He never drank to get drunk except for the time he left Nat—and now. The first mouthful always burned his throat, like the drink was cleansing him.

As the burn travelled down his throat, he looked around the bar and noticed a door he hadn't noticed before. It had the strip club logo above it, a silhouette of a woman bent over while looking back over her shoulder. He realized they must have moved the strip club to beside the bar.

How convenient, he thought, rolling his eyes as he returned his attention to his drink.

After a few more drinks, he got up and headed toward the door to the strip club. When he neared the door, someone made a comment. Ryland paused, then decided to ignore the man, who was clearly drunk and had thrown up already.

When he opened the door, the club smelled better than the bar, though his eyes had to adjust to all the flashing lights and colours. Ryland wondered how he hadn't heard the music when he was next door.

Surprised there weren't as many drunks in the club as the bar next door, he made his way through the crowds surrounding the dancing women on their stages when what he was looking for—but hoped never to find—walked right up to him.

"Hello, sweetie," a red-haired woman in black lingerie said, running a hand across his chest. Her hair was long and as straight as a curtain, sparkling due to the lights and the pieces glittered throughout. When Ryland left Nat, the woman had been his "usual," as she had been a couple of times throughout the years before that.

"Hey, Elease." His voice was flat, monotone.

"How are you?" She squeezed his shoulder, feeling his muscles.

"Remember that girl I told you about?" Ryland asked. Elease paused, probably jealous of Nat, but Ryland was with her now. She nodded.

"She's dead," Ryland said. Elease's face dropped.

"I... I'm so sorry," she said, sounding like she meant it. "Come, let's get a private room. On me." As much as Ryland was her man inside the strip club, he liked her for more than her body and... talent.

"I came here for pleasure, not talk," he said. She couldn't help but smirk, but her eyes were still sad.

They went to a private room. After Ryland paid, Elease started to dance. Ryland stared, not at her but at the wall behind her. He felt numb, emotionless, like all the chemicals that normally controlled his emotions had been drained out of him. Elease moved in closer, making it harder for him to look anywhere else, putting his hands onto her hips as she swung them. Ryland was always allowed to touch without permission, Elease trusted him, knowing he was military.

As she continued her routine, Ryland's passions returned. After a tease, Elease took Ryland's clothes off and brought a fiery passion out of him.

It was two in the morning when they started talking about Nat and anything else that came to mind. The night became like a love song, full of cuddles and talking about passions, frustrations, secrets, and lies.

"Are any clients abusive?" Ryland asked. This was why she trusted him. When he had seen a client abuse one of the girls the first time he came, he didn't hesitate to confront the man. When he refused to leave, Ryland broke one of his fingers.

"There is one guy. One sec." Elease got up and left. When she returned, she was with another woman. "This is Meagan," she said. Meagan had short black hair and long fit legs. Her eyes were hard and her demeanour strong.

"The guy's name is Joe, and he keeps grabbing and pinning me against the wall," Meagan said. "We banned him, but then he broke the bouncer's nose. He found me once after work in the parking lot."

"So, he isn't going to stop?" Ryland asked.

Meagan shook her head. "I don't think so. I've seen him be aggressive in town with—"

"Alright. Know where he lives?"

"On the west side of town, second street, fifth house. Near the first path."

When Ryland left the club, he started toward Joe's house, then decided to return to Liz's house instead. He would deal with Joe tomorrow.

When he arrived at Liz's house, she was up waiting for him, and she didn't look happy.

"What were you doing, Ryland? Nat just died!" She had probably followed him to the club. She seemed to know everything about him.

"Yeah, she's dead, but she's not some goddess to be worshiped now."

Liz stared at him in shock. "No, but she was a friend to be honoured."

"I tried honouring and protecting her while she was alive, Liz. Now she's dead because of it!"

"There are worse people out there to be protected from than you," Liz replied.

"Not that the agency will let me do anything about it."

"Because you need to grieve!" she said.

"I haven't felt anything since I found her dead body," Ryland said, matching her tone. "This at least allowed me to feel something again."

Liz sighed, her anger dissipating as she shook her head. "You're feeling something again, pleasure in a time of grief."

FOUR
Present day

RYLAND WENT OUT into the mountains to the west, climbing the one closest to the edge of the sparsely treed forest that bordered them. He was wearing a pair of black cargo pants that matched the dark rocks. The pants had seven pockets that were able to accommodate everything he needed. He was also wearing a forest-green sweater that blended in with the bushes. His short, light-blonde hair would have the biggest giveaway if anyone was looking for him, which was why his sweater had a silk hood. It was comfortable and easy to slide on and off.

He liked this part of the job, searching for something and making sure it didn't find him first. His muscular build gave him an advantage in any terrain. He knew how to climb, run, and jump. He was also fairly tall, so he could reach branches and ledges that others could not.

As he climbed, he felt the air get colder, and he was thankful for the sun amidst the scattered clouds, not to mention his multiple layers of clothing.

Halfway up he saw a tree growing straight up despite the angle of the mountain, which was small enough for him to hike to the summit with little effort. He turned and looked out at the clear, empty air, which allowed him to see hundreds of kilometres. The blue sky made him feel open and comfortable, reminding him of his days of relaxation with the friends with whom he would train and explore.

His thoughts were interrupted when he saw the small town of Mount Horizon, which reminded him of Keira. She stood out to him, so open and so skilled in almost everything she put her mind to. *She seems to be trying to find a reason for adventure even though her parents tell her not to do so. She doesn't need a reason. I better be careful.*

As he continued his climb, the mountain grew steeper. Always looking for a challenge, he saw a cliff to his right with a big crack in its face. He jumped and slid his fingers into the crack, his body swung underneath the rock with nowhere to put his feet. With only the first two knuckles of his fingers holding, he lifted his body enough to reach the next crack. Then he saw a rock sticking out. Ryland swung his body to create upward momentum, enabling him to stick one foot in the first crack and launch himself upward to a ledge. He pulled himself up with ease and then stood on the ledge. Challenge complete.

When he got to the top, he found what he was looking for.

"What are you doing here?" he asked the man with matte-black skin. Ryland had used the few satellites that remained after the war to track his target. There used to be thousands of satellites in orbit, but now only two dozen or so remained.

Now that he was closer to the man, Ryland saw that he was naked. His muscles were well defined, though not overly large, and his skin was a bit lighter on his torso, legs, and arms. His hands, wrists, feet, calves, and groin were dark black, and on the outside and inside of his biceps and quadriceps was a deep neon red, which looked like a massive cut. When the man turned to face Ryland, he saw another red stripe on the man's cheeks. His face was sleek and smooth with no eyes, mouth, or ears.

The place where they were standing was mainly dirt with a few stone monoliths surrounding them. The man—or rather, the alien—was standing in the middle of a circle of monoliths. Ryland felt the alien searching his mind, small vibrations creating pictures and feelings.

This world is better than my world, the alien replied using telekinetic abilities. *Similar gravity and cleaner, clearer air.* The thoughts were coming to Ryland as his own, similar to when he was trying to sleep but his brain continued to think of everything he should have thought of during the day.

"What does cleaner air mean for you, who has no nose?"

The molecules around me here are less aggressive. They move less and are easier to control. And the sun actually comes through the clouds, it's more relaxing.

"Maybe so, but you're used to your world—"

Venus is engaged in a world war!

Ryland felt anger rise within him, but somehow he knew it wasn't his own emotions.

I have already had a taste of your planet, and I'm not going to leave, I need to leave Venus, the alien said. Ryland felt sorrow. He thought of all those people during the World War who would have left earth if they had the option. *A group of your kind already tried to kick me off.* The alien drew a picture in Ryland's mind of the fight that he, Keira, and her uncle had witnessed.

"Yes, I saw, but those men weren't trained, which is why there were ten of them," Ryland replied, standing firm. "I'm trained."

The group of humans the alien killed thought the Venusian was an augmented human, like the augmented animals, the same as the forest dweller. Luckily, most civilians thought the same.

The only reason you want me to leave is because you think the people of this world aren't ready and will create chaos, correct? The alien manipulated Ryland's mind. Controversy erupted in him, this time including some of his own feelings.

"Yes, but it isn't my choice," Ryland replied. "I have my orders."

Your government is too secretive. This planet does not trust itself.

Ryland couldn't tell if that was the alien's voice in his head or his own thoughts. Such a sentiment felt so familiar, having had such conversations so many times before.

The Venusian hovered off the ground. Ryland got into a fighting stance just in case he had to make a fast move.

"Says the alien from the planet with a world war," Ryland shot back.

Do you think you can kill me just with that hidden blade you have? The alien was referring to the blade on Ryland's right wrist.

"If you don't leave, I'll have to try," Ryland replied, hiding his surprise that the alien knew about the blade. *Did he read my mind or see the blade?*

The alien floated down to the ground again. *I like a challenge,* it said.

"So you're not going to leave?" Ryland asked.

Never!

The alien charged, but Ryland spun to his right, leaving a half-circle skid mark in the dirt from his foot. When the alien landed, it threw a punch. Ryland bent over backwards, put his left hand on the ground, and did a backwards cartwheel, kicking the alien in the process.

When Ryland landed on his feet the alien tackled him to the ground, then continued past doing a front handspring. Ryland made it to his hands and knees before he got a shin to the face. A surge of pain shot through his cheekbone, but he used the momentum of the blow to spring to his feet.

The alien swung at him again, but Ryland ducked and stabbed the alien in the rib cage with his right hidden blade. Blood spilled onto the ground and ran down Ryland's blade. It was such a deep red that it almost looked black.

Ryland was pushed away, not by the alien's hands or feet but by some sort of invisible force. It felt weird being pushed by nothing. He skidded across the ground, his shoulders grinding up small rocks that were hidden under the surface.

The alien held his side as he stood, dark blood oozing between its fingers. The alien took his hand off the wound, and the blood stopped flowing out. *They can heal that quickly?* Ryland thought. *I need to end this now.*

Apparently, the alien had the same thought, for he jumped straight for Ryland. Ryland responded in kind, but he was pushed back by the same force as before, harder this time. Seizing the advantage, the alien body slammed him, blasting the air out of Ryland's lungs.

They both hit a rock. Ryland gasped, struggling to breathe. The Venusian grabbed him and pulled him to his feet. He held Ryland by the shoulders while the force that had pushed him earlier held his legs.

You lose, Ryland heard in his mind, although he wasn't sure if it was the alien or his own thoughts. Ryland's panicked mind slowed as he felt a slight pressure under his legs. Was the alien holding him up with a push under his feet? *That could be a reference to the ground.*

Ryland jumped, causing the alien to panic. Taking advantage of the creature's confusion, Ryland thrust his arms up and sliced the alien across the chest. The alien backed up, but Ryland bounded past, got behind him, and stabbed his wrist blade into the alien's rib cage.

As the alien fell, Ryland straightened his back. He turned to face the alien, who tried to elbow Ryland, but he stabbed his wrist blade into the back of the alien's neck, causing the creature to stumble forward as he struggled to stay on his hands and knees. His other hand was holding the back of his neck, blood oozing between his fingers. He looked at his opponent with compassion. He usually felt this once he won, as if losing would help them understand they didn't have to fight. All they wanted was a place away from their war. The alien turned and faced Ryland,

How could you have beaten me?

"I told you, I'm trained," Ryland replied. "The other men you fought were basically civilians with sticks and karate training. Now, you have two options. I can kill you and dispose of you here, or I can let you go."

Please. I want to live. I don't want to go back to Venus. Ryland felt grief and anxiety from the alien's thoughts. Life blossomed in his mind. He assumed that was the alien's voice, but it could have been his own thoughts of letting this alien live.

"You have to go back to Venus," he stepped back in reply and waited for the alien to seal its wounds again. It wasn't healing, it was holding it with telepathy.

The more I wound them, the more focus goes into healing the wound, Ryland thought. *I'll have to remember that.*

He walked away as the alien did the same. Ryland pulled out a benzalkonium chloride wipe for his cheek. It was bleeding from when the alien kicked his face when he was down.

Ryland sat on the mountaintop and absorbed the view as he analyzed what had just happened. The sun was still shining brightly. Only a few clouds blocked its warmth periodically. He closed his eyes and focused on his breathing. Then he emptied his mind and began to pray. His decision to let the alien go was not normal; the alien's choices were out of his hands now.

Feeling cold despite the sunlight, Ryland shivered. His eyes still closed, he focused on the pains from the fight. His cheek stung, his shoulder was scraped, and his chest ached. He concentrated on his tense muscles and the adrenaline pumping through his body, forcing his body to relax. He also slowed his racing mind by focusing on one thing: the alien and his anger. He recalled the alien's replies: Venus being in a world war, the alien's arrogance, and its knowledge of human secrecy and lack of trust, not to mention Ryland's hidden blade.

Then his thoughts drifted to Keira. She was trusting when she met Ryland and was comfortable with him. Why? How could she trust a stranger, a hunter, a traveller with no family?

Ryland opened his eyes and looked out at the forest and the small town below. Feeling the cool breeze and the warm sunlight on his skin, he relaxed. Out of his many pants pockets, he pulled out a notebook. He had discovered it a few weeks back and found the contents intriguing.

FIVE
Five years earlier

"NATHANIEL FINCH," his mother called. He rounded the corner of the house, finding her on an unfinished porch. "Remember, you need to help your father with this porch before going to your friend's house." She was young for having a teenage son. Her cheeks were soft and round, and she had golden blonde hair down to her shoulders. She was wearing an apron, having started to prepare supper.

"I know," he replied. His voice was monotone. She had told him the same thing multiple times over the last few days.

His father came around the far corner of the house, holding his construction tools. "Ready, kid?"

The porch had been rotting and had animals living underneath. Nathaniel's father was a big man with thick fingers and muscles. He stood a foot taller than his wife. He had already renovated parts of the house that his family had lived in for two generations. Selected by his grandfather, the house needed repairs back then, but his grandfather was too busy to get the supplies because he was on town council and was always doing something else.

"Sure," Nathaniel replied. Walking to his dad, he picked up a cedar log and struggled to drag it over to where it was needed. Thankfully, the wind was cool and the sun, sat in the second half of the sky, was covered with white clouds. The logs were cut in half lengthwise to create a flat side. Nathaniel looked at the wood they were replacing and wondered how they got such thin pieces of wood and so smooth. He and his father had sandpaper to smooth their porch, but it was never as smooth as his friend's house, which looked like it had been untouched by the war. He didn't understand how they used to get a log into two inches by four inches. His father told him they have machines for it, but they could not afford one.

Nathaniel slid his log into place on top of cedar joists where they would nail the logs in place. Only a few more logs were needed, but they were heavy, and driving a nine-inch nail through them was difficult. Nathaniel had misaligned one of the nails with the joist, and it took three times as long to get the nail out. Now he knew to pay attention to where the joist was when he could see it beside the log or line it up with the previous nails.

His father grabbed the sledgehammer to ensure the log was as tight against the neighbouring log as possible. Switching to the mallet, he started the nail and then Nathaniel handed him the sledgehammer again. His father worked the hammer like it was nothing, pounding the nail with precision. They did the same thing at the second joist and then moved on to the next log. Nathaniel's father let him use the sledgehammer to drive the nails in. He remembered the first time he tried; it didn't go well.

"Remember, let the hammer fall to the nail," his father said.

Nathaniel placed the hammer on top of the nail, which sat loosely in the centre of the log, the woodgrain flowing around it. Nathaniel lifted the hammer with some strain and then dropped it, his hands guiding it. The hammer slammed into the head of the nail, but it was off balance and fell to the side before transferring its momentum into the nail.

"Good. Keep going. You'll get the balance," his father encouraged.

Nathaniel lifted the hammer again, and this time he held it tighter to stop it from turning on impact, but when he swung, he missed the nail. "Void!" he exclaimed.

"No need to swear," his father said. "Just pick it up and try again. Don't muscle it too much."

Nathaniel lifted the hammer, hands tight around the handle, and let it fall again. This time the nail disappeared halfway into the wood.

"Nice hit!" his father said.

They continued to switch jobs and finished the porch as the sun sank farther in the sky.

Nathaniel's mother, Kandyce, brought out two glasses of water. "Here you are, Richard, my husband." She handed him the glasses with a kiss on the cheek.

"Here, kid," he said warmly, handing one glass to Nathaniel. They sat on the new porch, sweat on their foreheads as they drank their water and looked out at their property. "I want you to know how to do things yourself," his father continued. "Sometimes people won't do things when it's their responsibility, so you may have to take initiative to do it yourself." Nathaniel listened but didn't know what to apply it to. Did his father expect someone else to do the porch?

"Okay," Nathaniel replied.

"If you know how to do many things or are willing to learn, later you can lead people in those things." Nathaniel's father turned to look at him. "That's why I get you to help with repairs around the house."

Richard took another gulp of water, looking out to the property. The grass was green and cut, the trees were scattered far apart, a wind was blowing through the leaves.

"We have to keep humanity at the top of the food chain," he said. Nathaniel had heard his father say those words many times before. "More than that, we need to make humanity better," his father added. "You may think changes are needed, but make sure they're truly needed by testing the ideas with others and working to make that change."

"Okay," Nathaniel replied.

"Alright, you two," Kandyce said. "Supper's ready." She came out and looked at the porch. "This looks amazing. Great work!" Nathaniel nodded in agreement. The porch looked amazing, and it was sturdy. It would last much longer than the previous one.

After supper, Nathaniel went out with his friend, Joash. Down the street was a forest that grew amidst a small gathering of houses and what used to be greenhouses. The tarp-like material from the greenhouses was almost gone, and all that was left was the frame and plants that had once grown there. Nathaniel and Joash met two girls who lived on the other side of the property.

"Hey, you finish that porch yet?" asked Emilee, one of the girls. Her hair was blonde and reached the small of her back when down. At the moment she had it in a neat ponytail, which hung down over her short yellow flowered dress. She had been wearing a ponytail more often after Nathaniel said he liked it.

"Just finished it before supper," he said.

"Awesome. I want to see it," Emilee said, smiling.

"And what about you, Joash?" Rachel, the brunette, asked. "You do any hard labour recently?"

"My dad and I built a fence to keep the predators from eating our farm animals two days ago." His shirt was wrinkled, and Rachel smoothed it out as she came in close. She was wearing a low-cut top to show off her breasts and a wavy skirt. Joash blushed as her hand ran down his shirt. It could have been from her touch or embarrassment at the wrinkles in his shirt.

They all went to a tree fort that someone had built. It was old but sturdy. The girls had furnished it inside. Nathaniel admitted it was childish to be in a tree fort, but he joined them gladly every time.

They played a game that involved cards and dice. The cards were old and weathered, and one die was cracked. Sometimes they could tell which card their opponent was holding due to certain markings or missing corners. When someone lost, the punishment was to do what the other three told them to. When Nathaniel lost a game, Rachel got him to kiss Emilee.

"Since you two won't do it on your own," she said.

Emilee looked down in embarrassment, more modest than Rachel. Rachel turned to Joash and whispered something in his ear. After that, Joash tried to convince them to kiss as well.

Emilee looked at Nathaniel and knew he wanted to do it, so she finally gave in.

As she drew close to Nathaniel, his heart raced. *Is she really going to do this?* he wondered. She continued to lean in, closing her eyes as she did. Just before their lips touched, they heard a stick break on the forest floor. They all hid against the walls of the fort.

"It's Luke," Joash whispered, peering out the window. Nathaniel's heart was still pounding, his mind caught up in the previous moment.

"What's up, Luke?" Joash asked once he got closer.

"Nathaniel! You need to come home. It's your parents." That got Nathaniel's attention.

"What about them?" he said, sticking his head out the window.

"Just come. Please."

Concerned, they all went back to Nathaniel's house, where they found the railing broken on the porch he had just helped his father build and a window smashed on the front of his house. Nathaniel ran for the open door but was stopped by a soldier.

"This is my house," Nathaniel said.

"It's not safe," the man replied. The Circle of Generals had men all over the world. They were a response unit, usually a pair of them for each handful of cities, and each city had local law enforcers. The man was not a local, which meant the situation was serious.

A body bag came out next, carried by the local enforcers. Rachel put a hand over her mouth, thinking the worst, and it was. It was followed by another body bag.

"Are those—"

"I'm sorry, son," the soldier said. "The Blood's Shadow."

The Blood's Shadow was a group of augmented humans who weren't supposed to exist. They had been augmenting animals before the war and then continued doing it after humans came out from hiding, but things went wrong, so the operation was shut down. No one thought they had augmented humans.

The procedure wasn't done properly, and they all became something else. Augmented animals now roamed free, their skin matte black. They grew differently and preferred different terrain than their previous animal kind.

Emilee looked at Nathaniel, tears in her eyes. A few minutes earlier, she had been about to kiss him. Now she was going to mourn with him.

SIX
Five years ago

■

THE HUMAN CONTINUED to search for him. The alien floated among the treetops, watching as the human sought to find the one who had killed its parents. It was always weird to hold himself in the air, like a boat or a car with a sail and a fan pointed at its sail. Because it was all attached to itself, it couldn't push itself. The humans called it inertia. To use the powers given by the Day Star to hold oneself in place seemed like it would operate according to the same concept, but it worked.

The human continued to search the forest after interviewing another human who seemed to think it had seen what it called a Blood's Shadow member in the woods. That was where he followed the human to search for evidence of the creature with the matte-black skin.

It has no idea what it's searching for, the alien thought. Few humans knew what the Blood's Shadow were.

The human searched for a long time, circling and analyzing grass, leaves, and tree trunks for any marks. *Committed and diligent,* the alien thought.

After hours of searching, the human went home. It was staying at a companion's house, though mainly at night.

"Any luck today?" the female asked. Her hair was blonde like the sun and flowed like a river down her back. The male shook his head.

For the first few days, she had protested against him in seeking the culprit who had killed his parents. But then she only asked how to help. She was a good companion, but the male didn't see it or want to see it. Ruined by grief and sorrow, he sought only revenge. Humans could be so easily blinded. They had plans and goals, and it was all too easy to destroy them and, in doing so, ruin the human in the process. This human loved its birth humans.

I had no knowledge of the Blood's Shadow being a wild force running around when I killed the human's parents, the alien thought as he watched the humans enter the house to go to sleep. *I only had to act like a rage-driven beast.* He said to himself, watching the humans enter the house to get sleep.

The day star was gone, leaving only the faint night stars and the larger light in the sky. The moon, as the humans called it. The humans worshiped the day star and the moon, really anything that produced light in the sky. The alien had learned that the last time he was there. He stayed for half a solar cycle and then left. Back home, the next solar cycle was awful, ravaging the planet. Coming to Earth was an escape, as it was for others who made the journey.

When the humans finally fell asleep, the alien got closer, the darkness providing it with cover. It didn't matter if the humans were asleep or not. If he did this right, it would work either way, but the effect was greater if they were asleep.

He got close enough to feel the human in his bubble of telepathy and then whispered into his brain. Sometimes the aliens could manipulate them if they weren't strong enough or if they were sleeping, but it had to be done softly.

■

Nathaniel saw an image of his mother standing at the front door of his family's house. She was smiling. A figure walked past the window; it had to be his father. They had built the house themselves with the help of friends and family around the city. Most people in the world now, after the war, built their own houses or occupied abandoned houses that were still standing. The world seemed a lot bigger, with only small cities or groups of people and little to no travel. Therefore, there were more wonders and dangers. The war brought new and undiscovered things: weird creatures, mystic lands, and strange phenomena.

Nathaniel had heard of people encountering creatures unknown to the pre-war world. He had also once seen a rock shaped like a tree. Its solid stone branches reached into the sky, covered in stone leaves.

The memory faded, replaced by a silhouette and then his mother and father screaming as their house erupted with flames. Nathaniel ran toward it, but there was nothing he could do. The heat slammed into his face like a wave of water curling over his body and drowning him.

As the heat wave enveloped him, so did an overwhelming feeling of helplessness. He watched his parents burn, their bodies falling to the ground and melting. The house itself also burned, the flames consuming everything and everyone he had once held dear. The screams were too much, and by the time he realized they were coming from him, he sprang awake.

As his sweat cooled, he shivered, even though he had felt like he was on fire a few seconds earlier. Unaware of the Venusian just outside his window, hidden in the dark, Nathaniel pulled the covers tighter to warm himself. The feeling of fear from his dream was still boiling within him, stronger than any other emotion he could feel. Finally, he threw the covers off and got up.

In the kitchen, he got a glass of water. Tilting the bottom of the glass toward the ceiling, he was halfway through it when he heard a noise behind him. Emilee.

"You okay?" she asked. He barely looked at her anymore as he once had. He was distracted with finding the Blood's Shadow.

"Fine," he said, returning his attention to his drink.

"I heard you," she admitted, even if he wasn't going to.

"It was just a dream," he replied.

"Of what, Nathaniel?"

He sighed, his grip tightening on the glass. "Of my family."

"How long are you going to look?"

"Until the murderer and the rest of those things are dead," he replied, gritting his teeth.

"No one but the COG agents have ever managed to kill those things," Emilee reminded him. "You should leave it to them."

"Look at what happened when they came. Nothing!" he whispered. He wanted to yell, but he knew others were sleeping, and he was a guest.

"But you can't fight them," she insisted. It wasn't something he wanted to hear. No one in his position would.

"Maybe you're right," he replied, surprising her. "But this city didn't do anything. Not the local security or the COG, and there are no suspects." He stood there, glass in hand, staring out the window, which showed nothing but the blackness of night.

"That isn't your fault," she said.

He turned to glare at her. "The leadership needs to change."

"And who's going to do that? There are no candidates." The leadership had been similar for decades, and the people like the mayor.

"I will," Nathaniel replied.

"But you're too young." Emilee wanted to support her friend, but he was looking at this with a narrow mind. "That's not how the process goes."

"You want me to wait for someone else and then wait for the vote to conclude? What do we do when tradition fails?"

"I'm saying you can start somewhere else. Gather people around you, then make a change. Go to the security forces. See what they say and then show them possible changes." She was grasping at straws, and she knew it.

He shook his head. "They won't listen. We need a change in leadership." He set his glass by the sink.

"And you're going to do it?"

"I have a motive, ideas, and people. I'm doing it for the safety of this city and the world. I'm going to rid this place of the Blood's Shadow for good."

"Many others have said they do it for safety. You're doing it for revenge."

"You know, Emilee, no one else protects us but our parents and ourselves, and I no longer have parents." He turned to walk away.

"Nathaniel, we opened our home to you for protection," her voice quaked, as if something was in her throat, but he neither stopped nor replied. They both went back to bed, though Emilee was not sure if she would get much sleep.

SEVEN

Present day

It always amazes me how we build these structures so tall and strong. We design them in such creative ways. The city glimmers in the rising and falling sun.

Some people think the sun is god. I'm not sure what to think of that. It leaves with the moon at times, and they say the stars are their angels. But that means the sun and moon can't see everything at all times.

Shouldn't god be outside the world? Is there a team that makes up the idea of god? Or is it one?

There are some soldiers in my city now. I'm curious about their presence. Why are they here? To protect us? If so, from what, something outside the city or something that's already here?

This world isn't very trusting. I guess I'm a prime example. Should I be more trusting? Is that beneficial? It would increase the possibility of betrayal. Would it be worth it?

▃

THERE WERE NO dates to indicate when the journal was written, but with the amount of wear and tear, Ryland guessed it dated from before the war. He yearned to know what happened before the war but not from textbooks or novels. When he found the journal, it ignited a new yearning to know from the author's perspective.

He finally got up and started his journey down the mountain. The trip took less time than he thought.

When Ryland got back to town, he saw a man and his son, who was a bit younger than Ryland, putting away some gear for the day. It included jugs that held gallons of water and a purifier, all of it heavy.

"Sir," Ryland said as he jogged to the man and his son. "May I help you with those?" When the man accepted. Ryland grabbed two water jugs and carried them into the man's shed. It was a cold room, like a fridge, but it was the size of a garage. The back of the shed had a bigger purifier. The man hooked multiple jugs to it and would run the water through the purifier overnight, separating the water from any impurities, including radiation.

"Thanks for the help, young man," the man said. "Where are you from? I haven't seen you around before." He was in his fifties, with a grey beard and thinning hair but still well-muscled.

"I'm from the east," Ryland replied. "Past Lakewood."

"What brings you here to little old Mount Horizon?"

"Just travel. My family is scattered, and I'm pretty much on my own now."

"Not many families split up anymore," the man remarked. "Not since the war."

"What do you mean, Dad?" his son asked.

"My father told me that before the war, everyone would leave their parents to live their own lives. Now we mainly stay together and share a house, especially in this town."

"Yeah, my family travelled quite a bit and then separated," Ryland said. "In other towns I've been in, families don't stay together either. Even a baby isn't enough to keep the parents together."

"Ah, I see. That's a shame."

"Do you find much radiation in the water?" Ryland asked.

"Not much. Some days there's more than others," the man replied. "Not enough to make anyone sick or mutated," he added with a laugh.

Perfect, Ryland thought. "Speaking of mutations, you hear much about the Blood's Shadow here?" he asked.

"Ah, not too much. Every so often people bring it up. More so the people who travel to other towns come back with stories."

"That makes sense. I heard about them quite often out east," Ryland said, which was a lie.

"It's a big rumour though," the son said. "It seems to be all over the world."

"We still hear stories of the many gods and that they survived even the war," the father said. "I don't think they're augmented humans though. They did trials on animals, and then the program was shut down. There's no way they could have done it on humans. Not enough funding or support. No one would volunteer for that after the animals failed."

"But the animals are stronger now," the son pointed out. "Not many flaws in them."

"They're too bulky, though. They can't move that well, which would suck as a human," the father said. Ryland had a different opinion due to hunting them.

"True," the son replied.

Once the water and equipment were all put away, the father closed the shed door.

"What's your name, son?" the man asked.

"Ryland, sir."

"Thank you for your help, Ryland." The father offered his hand and Ryland shook it. The man's grip was strong. *Probably from all the work.* Ryland thought.

On his way to his hotel, Ryland passed Keira's house and thought about stopping by, then pushed the thought out of his head.

Once in his room, he grabbed a glass of water. As the cool, fresh water slid down his throat, he felt instantly refreshed. Cold water always reminded Ryland of when he was in training. He and the rest of the trainees had to go out on missions with no water for three days. When they returned, they got a day off, and they sipped water the whole day to get rehydrated. Then they had to go back out on another mission for another three days without water. They did that a lot during their training. As a result, Ryland learned to appreciate every opportunity to get hydrated, but his body was now used to going without water for days.

EIGHT

Two years earlier

∎

BEING IN THE principal's office again was flustering. Anton Rauz didn't know if he was really in trouble or if he was able to look his principal, Mr. Morozov, in the eye because his parents and his Uncle Alek were there to back him up. He was only eleven years old, and skipping school as much as he had was bad, but his parents knew he was learning on his own, and he was learning more than the school could teach him, at least about the subjects he wanted to learn about.

"Your son continues to skip," Mr. Morozov said. "How do you expect him to grow without proper education?"

"I get that, but my son isn't a bad kid. He researches, obeys, and learns on his own and with us. He's striving to be better," Anton's father said.

"None of these kids are *bad* kids, sir, but he doesn't get the same learning environment at home as he would here," Mr. Morozov argued. School was often mandatory, depending on the city in which one lived. Smaller cities usually didn't have schools due to the amount of work that needed to be done. Older kids would teach younger ones individually. Bigger cities had enough resources. Either way, the COG made it mandatory to teach the history of the pre-war world so people could avoid what happened to cause the war.

"And what makes you think your environment is better?" Alek asked. His nephew was a smart kid and social too. "He has friends and a social life. They research and study together. I believe he even hangs out with the regular students after school."

Anton nodded in agreement, though he was unsure if he should.

Hearing his parents and uncle argue with Mr. Morozov made Anton upset. He didn't want to disappoint them, but being in trouble with the principal didn't help. It wasn't that he was coming home with bad grades; he wasn't coming home with any grades. He was skipping out and doing his own thing, which involved learning on his own. He always told his parents and uncle what he was learning. At the moment he was researching computer engineering and artificial intelligence, and that involved everything from math and coding to philosophy to building a personality for the AI. He would try to learn other subjects to challenge himself and make it seem like he was trying new things. And his uncle, who was an engineer for the COG, taught about pre-war history.

"Mr. Morozov, we understand you seek his attendance so he can succeed," Anton's father said. "We want him to succeed too. But your classes don't teach the subjects he excels at to his level."

"Do you think your son will succeed without the school program?" Mr. Morozov asked.

Should I be here for this? Anton wondered as he looked at his father.

Mr. Rauz nodded. "I believe he can, yes."

"And do you wish to keep him in the school system?"

"Yes," Mrs. Rauz replied. She and her husband had agreed several times already that they wanted Anton in school. Since the human race had returned from hiding underground, they had taught and analyzed history and why the war started. Even while underground they passed on the stories and teachings of the pre-war world. But another reason to keep Anton in school was to give him knowledge on other subjects that weren't as easily accessible. It may have been the easy way out for his parents, getting the school to deal with him instead of trying to force him to learn certain subjects themselves or trying to learn about what he was interested in, which they didn't understand.

"Then he needs to participate and learn," Mr. Morozov said. Anton's parents looked at Anton, and he nodded. He would do anything they asked.

∎

The next day, Anton walked to school with his friend, Luka, who was in the same grade and the same situation. When they got to class, they sat close to the back. Anton sat against the wall to the right. The desks were set up in pairs, with three rows. Anton's friend sat on the left side of the room.

Mr. Morozov welcomed the two of them as the other students, who were shocked to see them, made jokes about them showing up for their monthly class. Anton and Luka just smiled and laughed along.

The day had five subjects: history, science, math, English, and computers. They started with math, which Anton and Luka were good at, especially sixth-grade math. They both ended up on their computers, only half listening. Anton would watch for any other way of looking at math. Revisiting the fundamentals was good, just boring. Every so often Mr. Morozov would call on Anton to make sure he was participating. Either he was, or it didn't take long for him to figure out what they were talking about and provide an answer.

"What are you doing?" Anton's desk buddy, Tanya, whispered.

"I'm programming artificial intelligence to have humour," he said, putting it in terms that she could understand.

"How do you do that?"

"First, I have to find an algorithm that works for humour. Then I add it to the base module of my AI to make it part of the personality," Anton whispered as he did just that. Tanya watched as things moved on Anton's computer, showing the AI's programming. Digital code buzzed like an army of ants walking back and forth on Anton's screen.

"Anton, are you paying attention?" Mr. Morozov asked, tilting his head forward.

"Enough to understand," Anton replied.

"And are you allowing Tanya to pay attention?"

The class watched the interaction with curiosity. Anton looked at Tanya. She seemed unconcerned.

"Yes, sir. I'm paying attention," Tanya said.

Mr. Morozov continued his lesson, and everyone shifted back to listen. Anton glanced at the board every so often to see what Mr. Morozov was doing as he pieced together personality traits into his AI program.

■

After school Anton and Luka met with a group of friends at the east city park.

"Why were you guys back in class?" Yuri, a smaller boy, asked.

"My parents and Mr. Morozov agreed to have me stay in school as long as I participate," Anton replied.

"We get to go through this again then, eh? You'll last a few weeks and then stop coming again," Ivan said. He was the biggest in the group.

"Not true. I'm gonna stay," Anton said.

"Hey, we going to play or not?" Luka asked.

"Yeah, we are!" the first boy said. The group of them ran off, forgetting the accusation, and started a game of hybrid tag.

"Who's it?" Anton asked. When no one replied, the group lined up, knowing the rules.

"Last one to the top of the playground is it!" The small boy yelled. They all ran, finding their own ways to the top of the wooden playground structure. Thick wooden beams held metal bars, plastic slides, and ropes, but one platform stood above all the other obstacles.

Anton ran for the ladder. Halfway up, he jumped to the railing of the bridge. Vaulting over it, he ran for the rock wall, which he enjoyed climbing. Once he reached the third level, he ran for the twisted enclosed slide, climbing it on the outside. When he finally reached the highest point of the playground, two others had beaten him, Luka and Aleka. But he wasn't the last. Yuri and Ivan were still making their way up.

Once Yuri beat Ivan, they started the game. Ivan already had the ball on a string, so he counted to ten as the others ran. Once he reached ten, Ivan started running as well. He jumped to the slide and made his way to the playground's third level. Finding Luka, Ivan sprinted toward him. Luka leaped out from cover and jumped over the railing. Ivan jumped to his left and got to the lower level at the same time as Luka, cutting off his escape. Ivan threw the ball and hit Luka, freezing him. Then Ivan ran toward Luka to tag him, but Anton came from the side and tagged Luka first, allowing Luka to move again. They split up, and when Ivan threw the ball, he missed both of them.

The game continued until Anton was it, and Yuri deflected the ball and kept running.

"Hey, I hit you. You're supposed to freeze."

"I deflected it," Yuri said.

"With your hand!" Anton yelled.

"Ah, grow up," Yuri said, still keeping his distance.

"Play fair, Yuri," Luka said from above.

"Shut up, Luka!" Yuri shouted, looking up at him.

"You're it now, Yuri," Anton said.

"You didn't tag me."

"I hit you with the ball, and you kept going. You cheated!" Everyone stopped playing to watch the dispute.

"I saw the ball hit you, Yuri," Ivan said.

"You're all a bunch of losers!" Yuri spat.

"You cheated!" Anton said.

"Give me the ball, Anton. I'll be it," Aleka said, approaching him. Tears were in Anton's eyes as he quieted down, but he wanted Yuri to be fair.

"Forget it. I'm out," Yuri waved his hand and walked away.

"Maybe that's enough for today," Luka said, jumping down from the second level.

"Yeah, my supper might be ready soon anyway," Ivan said. "Yuri ruins everything."

"Yeah, okay," Aleka said with disappointment in her voice. They all went their own ways, heading home for supper.

NINE

KEIRA LIKED TO wake up just before the sun. She enjoyed the silence of the world before the day began. After she took a shower and got dressed, she walked to the store to buy some meat for supper. She always liked visiting the store. It was the only one, and the owner was a nice middle-aged man who knew how to sell. His name was Roger, and he would always get to know his customers and find out what they needed, then find it for them.

"Hey, Roger," she said as she entered.

"Keira. How's the hunting?" he asked, looking up from his work.

"Going hunting in two weeks. Need some meat for supper," she replied, heading to the back of the store where the frozen meats were located.

"Which meat for today?" Roger asked.

"Just steaks."

"That new fella around is interesting," Roger said, returning to his work.

Keira looked up. "Why do you say that?"

"No real reason. Just seems to keep his distance. I saw him the other day walking on the edge of town."

Keira thought about Ryland's surveillance, but she had never thought about it the way Roger did. She had found Ryland on the edge of the city. Was he just entering, or was he staying out there? He had his things in the forest. It wasn't far from town. Why not stay at the hotel, like he was now? Maybe she was overthinking it.

"Yeah, I guess that's true," Keira said. She put the meat she had selected, ribeye, on the counter.

"Nice choice." Roger gave her a wink; there weren't many kinds to choose from.

"We'll see if that new fella keeps his distance," Keira said. "Goodbye!" She took her change and walked out.

The sky was still red as the sun burned it like someone's skin on a hot summer day. After dropping the meat at home, Keira walked to the local hotel and asked if the manager had seen Ryland. He said he had seen him about thirty minutes ago.

Keira went to where they had seen the mysterious man take on the group of ten men. Dew still clung to the ground and the warm air. The sun was just breaking past the horizon, turning the sky blue, a few clouds hanging in the expanse.

Keira didn't see Ryland, so she walked deeper into the forest. The trees were so close to each other that they blocked the view. Keira finally spotted Ryland off to her left.

When she got closer, she saw that he was using a bow and arrow to shoot at a tree. When he saw her, he smiled. "Good morning."

"This your surveying?" she asked with a smile.

"Ha, no. Just practising with my bow."

As he prepared to shoot another arrow, Keira looked at the tree. Several arrows were sticking out of it, all bunched together. Ryland pulled another arrow out of his quiver and handed it to Keira.

"You always start the morning with training?" she asked.

"Usually, I start the day with calming, controlled action."

"I see. I don't have that dedication."

"You could," he said, then fired another arrow. It hit within centimetres of the previous arrow.

"Hmm..." she said in response to his comment. "What's that on your leg?"

He looked down and realized what she was talking about. "Ah, just some stuff I've collected over the years. Wood, metal, bone, glass, and rock. Things that make up the world that I'm interested in." His hand went to the chain and caressed the bone. Something about his tone seemed off, but she decided not to press the issue.

"Whose bone?" she asked.

"Part of a scrapper's vertebrae," he replied.

Keira's eyes twitched with curiosity. Scrappers were small but ferocious augmented badgers. Badgers were tough on their own, never mind with the augmentation. Keira didn't understand why the organization had augmented so many animals at once. They showed no caution. Sure, it worked, but now they were breeding and more dangerous than ever.

"You hunt a lot," she observed.

"Some of the hunting is part of the job. Would you like to try?" Ryland held out an arrow to her. She hesitated, then took it. Ryland stepped aside and handed her the bow. He also showed her how to hold it and where to place the arrow.

Clenching the bow with her fist, the arrow placed between two fingers and three fingers pulling the string back, her arm shook. Ryland told her to breathe and focus on the target. She inhaled, held her breath for a moment, then exhaled slowly. Ryland told her to hit the tree just to the right of his target tree. It was about twenty-five feet away. Right before she fired, she lowered the bow and loosened the bowstring.

"I have a bow at home, but rarely use it," she said. "We've scavenged quite a few guns and ammo. Why do you have one?"

Before he could answer, she raised the bow again and aimed at the tree. When she pulled back on the string, her arms shook from the tension.

"I feel that a bow is purer than a gun," Ryland said. "It may sound weird, but—"

"No, I think I get it," she said, then she shot. The arrow skimmed the left side of the tree.

"Nice try. You were close. First try and you shoot it like that. Nice!" Ryland handed her another arrow. It reminded him of training with Nat.

She was always open to trying new things. Her specialty was biology and intelligence, learning about living things and their thoughts and the hierarchy of species. *Why does she have to remind me of her?* he wondered.

"Ha-ha! Wow, that was cool," she said. "It does feel a little more pure."

They continued to practice and talk. Then they walked through the forest until the sun was almost at its peak. Feeling hungry, they collected the arrows and then headed back to the hotel where Ryland was staying and put the bow and arrows away.

"Someday we can make a bow for you," he said as they emerged from the hotel.

They went to one of the two small restaurants in town. Ryland ordered a fresh chicken burger. Keira ordered a wrap with a salad. After they ate, Ryland told Keira he had to go somewhere for the rest of the day, but he would be back after supper.

After they parted, Keira travelled to where she should have gone that morning: One of the last houses on the east side of town. Most houses in town were one story and small, but Dylan's house was even smaller, only slightly bigger than a hotel room, and that was only because the hotels put the kitchen in the same room as the bedroom. Dylan had his house more sectioned off, and he had it built so it could easily be added onto, at least on the north and south sides. His neighbour on the east side was only a few steps away.

Keira pulled her hair out of her ponytail and shook it to restore its normal shape. She rarely wore her hair down, but she knew Dylan liked it. She knocked on the door. Seconds later, Dylan opened it.

"Where have you been? We had plans today," he said, not accusing but excited to hang out. His hair was dark, short, and spiked, and his face was muscular like the rest of his body, with a defined jawline and wide shoulders.

"I was making sure the new guy in town felt welcome," she said. She didn't know if that was true or not. Most people in town were nice to newcomers, but why had Keira gone to find him first thing that morning?

"The COG soldier," Dylan said, more of an accusation in his voice this time.

"News travels fast," Keira said, surprised. Only last night they had talked about what Ryland did.

"Sound travels faster," Dylan quipped. Keira didn't know if he was implying he had overheard them or if someone else had been eavesdropping. Keira put the thought aside and let herself in, walking past Dylan and taking a seat in the living room.

"What do you want to do today?" she asked. Dylan ran his fingers through her dark long brown hair and then bent over, his hand holding the back of her head as he pressed his lips against hers. Then he pulled back.

"I still have a few things to do around the house. And I have to build another filter." Dylan had learned how to build the filters for the water containers. He was good at figuring out how things were put together, although sometimes small things were hard for him with his thick farmer's fingers, but there was no shortage of help in town.

"Another one?" Keira asked. Filters weren't made too often considering the little stress they went through filtering water.

"We're making another container to store more water."

"Ah, I see."

"But that can wait for a bit." He grabbed her hand and pulled her to her feet. Then he wrapped his arms around her waist, picking her up. She wrapped her legs around him with a squeak and a smile. He walked down a short hallway to his bedroom and dropped her onto the bed. Then he kissed her neck as she slid his shirt off, and they burrowed under the covers.

TEN

THE COMMUNITY OF Mount Horizon started working the land early in the morning. They had gardens to seed and harvest, farm animals to tend to, and fruit to be picked. Once per month, a group would go to the mountains for fresh spring water. Mount Horizon was far from any commercial centre. The nearest large city was Marshville, also known as Scandal Town. It was too expensive to import what they needed from there, so the citizens of Mount Horizon lived off the land, and they were happy to do so. Working for the food they ate and the materials they used for building and living felt rawer and purer. Keira liked the community. Everyone knew one another and worked together. Some people felt isolated and wished for more community outside the town, though. Back when groups came up from underground, some were more isolated than others or weren't sure who else made it out alive and just assumed they were the only ones in the area.

Keira did her gardening and some lawn work, picking weeds and clearing away a few leaves and sticks. After that, as she travelled through the town she heard no talk about Ryland. Since he was a newcomer, a stranger, an outlander, usually people would have known where he was, at least if he was in town. But no one knew. As Keira investigated, she didn't have to go far. She found a note for her at the hotel:

Got called to work in the next town.
I'll be gone for a few days. Keep training.

Well, I guess I can do some training for now then, she thought.

She went back home to grab her bow and arrows, then went to the forest. It was cooler, fog floating above the ground, but the trees acted like a greenhouse, warming the air under their canopy, where there was little to no breeze. Keira thought if it was her room, it would smell musty the warmer it got. This was nature's room, though, and the air was fresh and clean, even after the war that had caused people to think the surface wouldn't be habitable for centuries.

She warmed up with some dynamic stretches, swinging her arms in slow, wide circles both ways as she picked out a tree to target.

Before she started shooting, she did some pull-ups on a low branch, first slowly and then at normal speed. She hoped the pull-ups would help with similar motions.

When she was finished, she spun in a circle to see if anyone or any animals were watching. Then she grabbed the bow and nocked an arrow, pulling the string back. She could feel the tension of the string in her arm and back muscles. Keira breathed, focusing on the tree, and then released. Out of five arrows, only one hit the tree.

Oh boy, this will be fun, she thought sarcastically as she went to retrieve the projectiles.

As she lined up her next shot, the sun broke through the trees and blinded her. She moved east of the target with the sun behind her. The sun's rays hit the tree and formed a small circle, which made for a perfect target. Keira took a deep breath and pulled the bowstring back, aiming down the shaft. She released the arrow, and it broke bark as it skimmed the tree. Keira lined up another shot. This time she hit the tree with two arrows. After retrieving the missed arrows, she saw a squirrel searching for nuts. Knowing she wasn't good at archery, she wondered if she could hit the critter. She nocked another arrow, lining it up with the squirrel's midsection. She fired but missed by two inches. The squirrel disappeared into the forest.

■

Ryland started his day in the dark of night, the cool, damp air surrounding the agent as he walked out of town. The lights of Mount Horizon faded into a dim glow as the moon shone full and bright and made the distant river—Ryland's first challenge—glisten. He knew the river was wide and had small lakes to the east and west. He would have to cross the river or his journey would be more than doubled. He thought of some different ways he could cross as he felt the loneliness of the dark. He liked it; it was what he was comfortable with now.

Sentry agents were scattered and were rarely assigned apprentices or partners. They did, however, move around to different towns and environments. Some places had safe houses with psychiatrist agents, someone to talk to. Since they were in the Sentry program, and the program was small, it seemed comfortable and easy to trust such agents. The psychiatrists were like Sentry agents for Sentry agents. The town he was heading to had a safe house. Ryland felt it was perfect. He could get local information for his mission and vent to a friend. Most agents knew each other well, especially the originals. New members were constantly recruited, though, which was where the rare apprentices came from.

When Ryland reached the river, it looked wider than he remembered. It was hard to see where the river stopped and the land started at the edge of the sunless sky. The small rapids indicated he couldn't just swim across. Ryland looked around for a bridge, but none were in sight.

Great, Ryland thought.

He turned to see what resources he had on his side of the river, his eyes met by a few trees, smooth hills, and a few rocks, or maybe they were dirt piles. Everything was silhouetted in the dim early morning light. There were some sticks on the ground, but they would not suffice to make a bridge or a raft. He looked at a tree nearest to the river and marked a spot thirty metres high. He took off his backpack and took out his hatchet. Out of all his weapons, he was glad he had brought the hatchet. After putting his backpack on, he started chopping the tree. He swung twice from an upward angle and twice from a lower angle, creating a trapezoid shape.

His backpack made it more work, countering his swinging body, but he needed it on for the next part. As the tree started to crack, Ryland kept swinging: top, bottom, top, bottom. As the tree started to tilt toward the weak side, he ran up it until he reached his spot thirty metres high, and his added weight caused the tree to snap. Right before the falling tree hit the ground, Ryland jumped. He landed on his feet and rolled, his shoulder slamming into the ground. His heart was pounding with nerves. He had to time it just right, and even then the landing was hard. His backpack hindered his roll but gave him some cushion.

He turned and saw the tree was getting pulled by the rough water. Ryland stepped out of the way of the branches as the trunk, so close to the river's edge, fell in, and the entire tree was stolen from Ryland and anyone else who could have used it later. If he hadn't climbed the tree, it would have been a waste of energy.

With the sky turning red as the sun rose above the horizon, Ryland could finally see farther than ten metres. A long, wide field of rolling hills expanded in front of him. It would be the easy part of the trip, walking to the city that awaited his aid even if they didn't know it. He had been given orders, and he was going to obey them. It was so much better to have his orders come from someone he could trust. That was why he appreciated his personal relationships with the other agents. "We're in this together," Nick would say. He was the one who had put safe houses around the world to monitor the agents on a personal level.

The rolling meadows were pleasant to walk through. The air was cool and fresh, and from the top of the hills, Ryland could almost see all the way to the city. He felt like the sun as it spread its light across the land, his sight reaching far and wide and giving him a feeling of strength and freedom.

When Ryland walked in the valleys, he felt close to the land, protected by it, being right beside the green grass and wildflowers. Even a few animals were roaming around. With the cool breeze sweeping over the meadows, the sun was uninterrupted by clouds in its low position in the sky, with nothing obstructing its brilliant warmth.

Ryland had worn dark, warmer clothes, including a tight sweater and thick cargo pants. Walking to the city was going to take two days and two nights. With little to no vehicles around, walking, or riding a horse if a person had one, were the only options. Apart from trade, most cities kept to themselves anyway. Only a few people in bigger cities had cars, more prominent were ATVs, especially in towns like Mount Horizon.

Scandal Town, a.k.a. Marshville, wanted to expand their territory, which was where people started to feel the COG was corrupt. Most people said that Marshville was motivated by a lust for power, which was why the mayor wanted to take over Mount Horizon. That was why they called it Scandal Town. There was a rumour that the original Marshville to the north had been destroyed, with the conquerors taking the town's name. People said they had also killed the entire population of the original town, but no one could prove it.

The mayor is a smart man, but he does want power, Ryland thought. He had met the man a few times before. It wasn't the COG who had helped devise the Marshville scam but the mayor himself.

With such a long distance to travel, Ryland had plenty of time to think. He reflected on other agents around the world, ones he had trained with from the beginning and other new agents whom he had gotten to know through the years. Fred was one agent whom Ryland enjoyed running into while out in the field. He was a good leader, a strong soldier, and was welcoming to everyone. Fred was on the same continent as Ryland, located to the north of him.

I should visit him when I get a chance, Ryland thought.

Alek was another agent who was close to Ryland's heart. Located in the east continent, he was a tech genius. Even his nephew was a prodigy. Ryland didn't know much about his nephew or Alek's new life, but he missed Alek's rebellious attitude and his desire to keep seeking new challenges.

As Ryland thought about more of his comrades, he longed to be alongside them, but at the same time he was content with being alone and not worrying about anyone but himself, as was the mindset of most agents, and if Ryland was paired with one of them, he would not have to worry about them. They would be a single unit. A perfect team.

Before the sun fell back below the west horizon, Ryland saw a group of people walking toward him. Ryland turned to the northeast, pacing himself so he was hidden in a valley as the strangers were on a hill. When Ryland got to the top of the last hill, they were in the valley below him, so he had the high ground.

"Hello, sir," one of the men said. There were eight men and two women.

"Hi, there," Ryland replied. "Where are you headed?" He knew there were only a few places they would dare to walk, and most people wouldn't even dare to walk that.

"Mount Horizon," the man replied, though one of the others scowled at him for sharing that information. "How about you?"

"Marshville."

"Ah, nice. You travelling alone?" the man asked, not revealing that they had come from Marshville, which Ryland assumed. There was a mixture of emotions on his companions' faces as they watched the conversation. It was a long walk, and they didn't want to waste time, though some looked thankful for the break.

"Yeah, I am," Ryland said. "It's nice to be alone in a quiet place, but just as iron sharpens iron, one man sharpens another."

The man's face changed slightly, recognizing the reference.

Interesting, Ryland thought.

"We were going to stop and have a fire and food. Care to join us?" the man asked.

"Sure. I've eaten already, but I could still have a bite. Thank you."

They created a firepit beside a few boulders, then started a fire using some sticks, twigs, and dry grass. As the food was cooked and eaten, multiple conversations rose and then died. Most of the strangers were cautious of Ryland. Scandal Town had a lot of crime, so it made sense they didn't trust anyone outside their group.

Why is the talkative one different? Ryland wondered. *Is he their leader?*

The fire was warm against Ryland's face as he sat against the base of a rock, enjoying the company. It was a nice change from his solitary journey, just like travelling with fellow agents. But how long would the feeling last? Ryland wondered why they were going to Mount Horizon. Just as that thought surfaced in his mind, the spokesperson for the group leaned forward.

"I have a vision to share with you," he whispered.

Ryland was surprised. Why was the man whispering, and why would he share his vision with a stranger? When the man shared his vision, however, Ryland soon understood why. He said he had seen Jupiter, and on Jupiter was a field of rye where a ghost, a thief, and a bowman protected foreigners they had saved. And in the field, they found a relic.

Ryland thought the bowman could have been him, thinking back to practising with his bow with Keira. Was Keira the foreigner? What did Jupiter mean? And the relic? The man couldn't answer any of his questions, but he felt he should tell Ryland about his vision because Ryland knew the "iron sharpens iron" quote. Ryland was skeptical about it, a stranger telling him a vision that made no sense, but maybe that made it more believable. He would keep it in mind. Stories long ago mentioned prophecies.

How do you decipher them? Ryland wondered.

"Why did you whisper it to me?" Ryland asked.

"The people I travel with don't accept my view," the man replied. "They think we make our own destiny. But with all that has gone on, with the world surviving the war, there must be something or someone beyond us who is controlling things."

"I agree," Ryland said, nodding.

"I almost forgot," the man continued. "When the time comes, let the thief go."

As the night grew thicker and the fire died down, some members of the group fell asleep. Ryland pondered the vision as he stared at the starry sky. *Jupiter is up there,* he thought. He liked puzzles that related to him. Was it even about him, though? He came up with no definite answers before he fell asleep.

Ryland woke up with the sun. Two girls and one of the men were gathering their things. The girls were talking in the meadow, giggling about something.

As the others woke up, Ryland said thank you and goodbye and then departed. He felt good and rested, ready for the journey.

A few kilometres out he got lucky with a harras, the horses that raced across the grassy hills. He ran toward them, not wanting to lose the opportunity as they sprinted beside a rock elevated above them. Ryland jumped off the rock and landed on a horse. It broke from the group and tried to buck Ryland off, alternating between jumping off its front and hind legs. Ryland tried his best to ride with the movement. It was like being thrown around by a vicious dog. It took 30 minutes to break the horse. Ryland gave it some food, both breathing heavy. He patted the animal, whispering to it,

"It's okay. That a boy."

The horse was now his. He thought he could show Keira how to tame animals.

Keira? Why is she on my mind? he wondered as he nudged the horse's flanks with his heels to get it moving.

The horse made the trip significantly shorter, and he got to Marshville before nightfall.

ELEVEN

RYLAND APPROACHED THE safe house, which had a nice lawn and a small wooden porch with a few potted plants, revealed in the moonlight. Ryland walked to the side door and knocked. A voice came from a box beside the door,

"Hello?"

"The sentinel watches over the city," Ryland said.

"Who protects the king?" a soothing female voice replied.

"The honour guards." The code words were different for every agent.

"Where did Sentinel and Monk begin?" Ryland knew there would be a personal question like that. If anyone was able to figure out the first question, they still wouldn't get past the second.

"Eleven years ago in June. You came into the program already more calm and collected than most."

The heavy security door clicked, and Ryland pushed it open. The warmth that greeted him was a nice contrast to the cool night air. A dimly lit staircase descended away from Ryland's feet. He shut the door, and it clicked shut behind him. Excitement to rest and see an old friend overtook him as he descended.

There was a fireplace to the left of the stairs with two couches and a chair in front of it. A small kitchen was straight across from the stairs, and in the opposite corner was a hallway, from which Liz emerged.

"Ryland! How are you?" she asked, filled with excitement. She welcomed him with a hug, and Ryland matched her excitement.

"Cold! You made me stand out there for so long," Ryland joked. "It's so great to see you, Liz!"

She invited him to sit with her in front of the gleaming fire. Ryland placed his backpack in the corner and then sat down.

"Do you want anything?" Liz asked.

"Water would be lovely, thank you." Ryland took off his sweater, feeling warmer already. Liz was wearing cargo pants and a fitted T-shirt. Her bare feet made no sound on the dark hardwood floor. Her blue eyes were piercing, and her blonde ponytail shimmered in the dim light. Her face was round but had a defined jawline.

She handed him some cold filtered water, and he took a sip of it. The refreshing liquid slid down his throat, cooling his insides.

"So, how are things?" Liz asked.

"Good, travel has been fun, and missions have been successful."

"Where have you visited?"

"Lakewood recently, and I just came from Mount Horizon. Really nice places. Mount Horizon is a dynamic town. The people take care of their own land and people. Lakewood is beautiful, and their port is so efficient."

Liz could tell Ryland was being genuine. As an agent, it was always good to see a city doing well.

"You were always content wherever you went," she said, remembering him in training and other meetings. "I wish I could travel more."

Ryland felt pity for his friend, wishing he could travel with her. When she enrolled in the Sentry program, she had shown promise since day one. Ryland respected her as soon as she showed her talents and confidence, standing up to anyone who got in her way. She rivalled most of the men.

"Remember when a group of us hid from the officers and wreaked havoc during training?" Ryland asked, thinking of the good old days when they were all together. Liz laughed at the memory,

"Yeah, and Bruce took the blame and fought the guards."

Marcus, an introverted, intimidating agent, got sick of one of the officers and knocked him out. Luckily, Alek and Bruce planned a little getaway after that to save Marcus. The officers soon forgot about Marcus's assault due to six agents running away, then sabotaging the rest of the training exercises.

"Yeah," Ryland said with a laugh, "we got in so much trouble for that. Cleaning the whole facility for a month." Even though Liz had entered the program later, she was quickly accepted. In fact, most agents forgot she came in later.

"And no food every other day," Liz added. "That was awful."

Only looking back on it was it funny. He remembered how bad the cleaning got and how doing it on an empty stomach made him and the other agents sick.

"And John fell out of that tree because of those bad berries he ate," Ryland added.

"We told him not to."

Ryland laughed. "We should do that now. Get you out of this town." He winked at her.

"Sounds like we'd be going on strike. It would turn into a serious manhunt."

"We could get Alek to hijack a bunch of dropships," Ryland said, laughing. They all could hijack, but Alek was the best at it, hijacking the entire system to gain access to all the ships at once. He even made a computer fly the ship to a specific destination. Alek had said he could only get the computers to do so for a short range, but Ryland felt he was underselling things to keep his abilities secret.

Ryland went down the hallway where there were three doors. One led to his bedroom, another to a bathroom, and the third to a panic room at the end of the hall. Liz checked that all the security doors were locked and then crashed on one of the couches, which had a pull-out bed. The fire was low, but it was still warm enough that she didn't need any blankets.

She didn't go to her normal bed, instead staying with her guest. Ryland could relate. He remembered when he was young and on holidays. He would be super excited to wake up early and be as close to loved ones as possible. He assumed Liz was similar. He would wake up and have a close friend right outside his room to get started on their mission.

■

When Ryland woke up the next morning, he found Liz just getting up too. She had probably heard him. They went upstairs and had a breakfast of eggs and toasted sandwiches.

"This city is full of pleasure-seeking, non-accepting, war-hungry fools," Liz said. "I go out to beat on thugs for something more interesting and helpful to do than sitting here and going to work. But the worst part is the child poverty. Kids litter the streets, abandoned by their parents."

Before the war, humanity became focused on entertainment and individual gain and success. It changed the idea of truth and caused people to forget about helping others, working as a team, and having an ultimate purpose to work toward as humanity. That situation had continued alongside the need to repopulate the world. Scandal Town had few families but many babies. Parents would usually stay together until the child was old enough to stay with just one parent, usually when they could go to school. Then the parents would split and go their own way.

"What do you think the pre-war world was like?" Ryland asked.

"That's the thing," Liz replied. "I think it must have been worse."

"I've thought the same," Ryland agreed. "At the height of all their technology." It was weird thinking of the humans before the war as "they," like they were a different species.

"Exactly. From what we know about them, they had so much, were able to go anywhere, do anything. It's like this city just continued where they left off."

"At the same time, there were other groups and organizations that fought selfishness," Ryland added. "Even now in this town."

"I can't imagine what it would have been like before the war if things are this bad in some places," Liz said.

"What if it was different?" Ryland asked. "We live our lives based on how we see our parents and peers live. But with how far our parents, or the first ones back to the surface, are from the pre-war world, how can we know how similar we live?" Ryland hadn't thought of that before; it just came to him when he heard Liz talk about it.

"True," Liz said. "But how far can we be?" She was mainly indulging Ryland but was partly curious herself. Either way, things were bad before or after the war or both.

"I'm not sure," Ryland admitted.

"There are only a few ways to live as a community," Liz said, "especially when, in the long history of humanity, we have the recent pre-war world to go on."

"That's a good point," Ryland replied. Out of all the history of the world, when humanity came back to the surface, the most recent way of living was the easiest thing to copy. With the way people lived before the war, humanity was susceptible to continue, save the thing that sent humanity underground. Hopefully.

"So, what does that mean for this city?" Liz asked.

"Um, continue being the disciplinary obstacle between order and chaos," Ryland said. He had given that part a lot of thought. What difference did it make living now rather than before the war or later in the future? Wherever a person was born, they were there for a reason and could have a purpose no matter what they believed in. Ryland chose to believe in an all-powerful being that gave ultimate purpose and an individual purpose.

"Yeah," Liz agreed. "I'll always have that."

Ryland believed in his God with the same resolve. No matter what Liz did, her duty here and now had a fundamental purpose, trying to make the human race a little safer and unified. That was part of Ryland's purpose as well, even without being an agent. Being an agent, for Ryland and Liz, unified them indefinitely. How else could they lead others to unity if they were not united?

A saying from the ancient book stuck in Ryland's head: "Be an example to the flock." Ryland's father used to tell him that when he was a child. He would tell him that being an example meant not just talking about what needed to be done but also doing it. His father was a leader and would get things done, whether himself or by delegating someone else. Ryland's father was a good example to Ryland, but now he was gone.

"You know the legend of the Venusians?" Liz asked after a few seconds of silence. Sometimes it wasn't good to let Ryland think too deeply.

"Yeah, Blood's Shadow." He perked back up out of whatever he was digging into. "It works so well. Civilians have no idea they're aliens."

The Venusians were seen as an experiment, similar to the augmented animals that were now running free. That's what Keira's family had thought the man with the matte-black skin was. They thought the same experiments had been tried on humans, and the legend worked to the agents' advantage, keeping the aliens' presence on Earth a secret. Ryland often thought if the aliens weren't that colour, it would have been impossible to keep the Venusians a secret.

Just another good miracle Elo performed out of the bad situation, he thought.

"Yeah, that one. Been hearing about that every so often. A couple of months ago, they thought they were all dead. There weren't any reports on the Venusians for a while. But there was a sighting just the other week. It fought well." Liz smiled. "But it didn't seem to have its telepathic powers under control. The civilians keep it interesting enough for me not to have to do anything about it. Some think it's true, and others say the program was shut down before human trials. Neither side can be proven, and the thought of aliens doesn't even cross their minds."

"Good thing too," Ryland said. "Couldn't imagine if it hadn't lined up like that."

"It's quite a lucky coincidence for us."

"Yeah," Ryland agreed, even though he saw it somewhat differently. "What else is going on in this city?"

"More weapons have been shipped lately. There have been explosions that are said to be from gas lines and accidents, but are actually from weapons testing. The type of explosions and the residue don't line up with gas. The mayor has multiple 'hands' that run sections of the city. He also has a book for if one of those hands die or if he dies, so they can take over for him. I know them to be Ryan Zing, Travis Mellow, and Lucy Hunt."

TWELVE

AT MIDDAY, RYLAND and Liz went out to explore the city. The buildings were more numerous than in Mount Horizon and were closer together, but there were still a fair number of gardens and plants among the urban environment. The buildings reflected the sun, their bricks and panelling gleaming orange and yellow, creating a warm feeling. Residents and visitors walked around doing their thing, some people teasing their friends and kids annoying their parents as they shopped. Some people sat on benches watching people pass while others rushed to their time-sensitive jobs. It was different from Mount Horizon where people worked the land and had a tighter community with no set schedule. Such a way of life was easier in a smaller town like Mount Horizon, where the atmosphere was less rushed.

Some parks brought nature into the city, providing picnic and playground areas within the trees. But Ryland also saw many kids and young adults with dirt-stained clothing sitting around the city and the park. Some people never stood a chance once their parents abandoned them, as Liz had mentioned.

Ryland remembered being an orphan after his father died. It was rough enough to deal with the orphanage. He couldn't imagine what these kids were going through. On the playground it looked like there were way more kids than adults, with most kids likely there on their own, playing with friends from the neighbourhood. Only the little kids, under age five or six, had a parent watching.

A group of buskers was performing for those who had time to stop and enjoy it. The music reminded Ryland of a fellow agent named John back in training playing his ukulele in the bunks. After a while it became soothing, a time to escape the hard work and pain.

"Liz!" a voice yelled from the park. They looked up to see a teenager approaching. "You bring a new player?" he asked. He was tall with dark hair and new developing muscles.

"I'm on a different job right now," Liz replied.

"But we're ready for our next lesson," another boy said, joining the first teen. He was shorter and younger with blonde hair and a round face.

"I'm sure you are," Liz replied. The way she said it made Ryland think they were an eager group. But what were they eager for?

"What is this?" Ryland whispered.

"Remember the close-combat training?" she replied. Of course Ryland remembered. Liz had always been a good fighter. She understood her opponents and would use their emotions and motives against them. "I've been training them."

"We have time." Ryland was interested in what she was teaching them and to what end.

The two of them joined the teenagers, five in total. Ryland could tell they had not been training for long.

"Alright," Liz said, "today's lesson is to only fight opponents you know you can defeat." Her students hung onto every word, though some looked confused.

The previous lesson was probably something about fighting no matter what, Ryland thought. "Picking real fights with someone you aren't sure you can beat can result in death or serious injury," Liz said. "Challenge yourself with friends and opponents who know the objective is to grow."

"Liz?" the blonde-haired kid said. "The last lesson was on defending and protecting our allies and loved ones. If we can't beat the opponent, should we not fight?" His round face added to his soft demeanor.

"You must fight to protect loved ones no matter what," she replied. "But if you can help it, still only fight opponents you can beat. If you were all to get in a fight against another group, you would try to judge their fighting abilities and match yourselves accordingly." The confusion on their faces still lingered, so she continued. "For example, if you were to choose one person from your group to fight me, who would that be?"

"Brandon," one kid said.

"Why?" Liz asked.

"Because he's the best fighter."

"That's right. Now, if I split the group with Brandon, Livi, and Nim versus me, Chris, and Aaron, how would you match them?"

"Brandon fights you, Livi fights Aaron, and I fight Chris," Nim, a small boy, stated.

"Good. Because that would be the best match of our abilities. If you had Brandon fight Aaron that would mean Livi would fight me. Brandon would have an easier time with Aaron than with me, and Livi would have a very hard time with me." Liz winked at the young, short, stocky girl. "It's a team effort to decide who fights who. So, fight who you can beat, respect your opponents, and protect your loved ones and those who can't protect themselves. Understand?"

They all nodded, so she arranged them in teams of three to face off against each other.

"Why train them?" Ryland asked.

"I feel I can help them protect those they love and to discern wisely," Liz replied as the teens started sparring.

"Some kids won't learn no matter what," Ryland said, thinking of Brandon. He looked like an angry child and with hidden motives.

"I'm sure some won't, but those who learn will be worth it," Liz replied. "You of all people should understand that." She was referring to his religion and his tendency to spread information about it to whomever would listen.

"I don't spread my knowledge and skills regarding weapons," Ryland pointed out.

"Maybe not, but you spread the knowledge for the greater good." Liz was confused about why Ryland was arguing her point.

"You're right," Ryland said. "I see your point, but I don't accept it, and I don't know why. You're giving these kids something to do and a chance to protect what they love. Through your teaching, they're also learning respect, control, and wisdom." Ryland smiled at his friend.

He zoned out on the way to the mayor's office, thinking about the teens and their training. Those kids could be the future of the Sentry program. Was that what Liz was doing? Had she been told to do that? Should he be doing the same?

The mayor's office was in a two-storey building made of dark brown bricks. Inside, the wood was the same deep rich brown colour, though the floors were slightly brighter. Liz and Ryland walked past a few desks before stopping in front of a receptionist.

"Can I help you?" she asked, smiling.

"We're here to talk to the mayor," Liz said, wondering if the woman knew whom she was working for. Her hair had hundreds of tiny curls and shimmered golden from the light in the dark room.

"Do you have an appointment?" The woman's voice was soft, but she seemed flustered. Liz leaned over to nudge Ryland. "There he is," she whispered, pointing to the mayor walking toward the back of the large room.

"Excuse me, Mayor?" Liz stepped away from Ryland and waved with innocent excitement. Ryland was about to try to stop her but instead he just hung his head.

"Ma'am, you need to make an appointment!" the receptionist called after her. Everyone's eyes were on Liz, including the mayor's.

"My friend and I have a complaint," Liz continued.

The mayor looked past Liz and saw Ryland coming up behind her. He raised his hand to the receptionist and then looked back at Ryland,

"You're not from here. You know nothing about this city." He looked at Liz. "She's your informant, and as you come in here so boldly, I assume you're from the Circle of Generals."

The mayor waved them into the room behind him.

Apparently, the mayor knew they were Sentry agents.

As Ryland shut the door behind him, the mayor, whose name was Ezra, licked his lips. "So, what's your complaint?" he asked, playing their game.

"We don't think it's a good idea for you to start a war," Liz said, getting straight to the point.

"There is no war here, unless you're about to start one," Ezra replied.

"We know what you did to the original Marshville," Ryland said.

"What *I* did?" Ezra asked. "I helped that city in the middle of their crisis. Awful, what happened to it."

"Everyone knows that you're responsible for their demise," Ryland said.

"So the rumours say." Ezra shrugged off the accusation. "There's no proof."

"What do you want with Mount Horizon?" Liz asked.

"What do I want? They're good workers, they have good land, and they're independent. With my town's resources, we could make a superior business. I only want us to help each other out." The plan to unite with Mount Horizon had gotten around by word of mouth.

"You should be careful, Mayor," Ryland warned. "With the rumours against you, proven or not, people will not likely go with your proposals."

"It's a shame that just because the majority of people believe rumours, everyone will take them seriously," Ezra replied.

"And what if Mount Horizon takes it seriously?" Liz asked, not expecting him to answer truthfully.

"I'm not enslaving them or setting up their demise," Ezra said. "It would just be switching mayors and combining resources and townships."

"So, this is about their mayor?" Ryland asked.

Ezra laughed. "You're good. I have nothing against their mayor. I just have my own ideas and plans." He licked his lips with pleasure once again.

"What sort of plans?" Ryland asked.

"You'll have to wait and see. But I have no plan for their demise. The opposite, really."

"Why don't you share with your mayor friend in Mount Horizon?" Liz asked.

"Oh, we aren't friends. He takes the rumours seriously. And that town is too exclusive."

"Maybe you should do something about those rumours," Ryland said, struggling to hide his frustration. "And you'd be surprised about their desires." He knew their welcoming atmosphere and some of their desires to be friendlier with other towns.

"Ah, you're from Mount Horizon," Ezra realized.

Liz had had enough. "I saw your 'right hands' lead an attack on the original Marshville, cover it up by helping the townspeople, and politically destroy their township." She had been holding that in for a long time, witnessing the secrets of the mayor's rule grow. He struggled to keep a straight face, but his silence told the agents enough.

"What do you want?" he asked.

"Like we said, we want you to stop a war," Ryland said.

"There is no war," Ezra said, no longer trying to hide his frustration.

"Not if you make the right choice," Liz said.

"Is that a threat?"

"Not at all, Mayor," Ryland assured him, "but know that a war, for whatever reason, will not end well for you, us, or the people in either city."

"There is something more at play than even those people," Ezra said, trying to regain his authority.

"Be careful, Mayor," Liz said. "We have a bigger plan than what is at play too."

As the two agents left, Ezra pressed his lips together in frustration.

THIRTEEN

"**ALL READY?**" Keira's father, Ronan, asked. They were packing for another hunting trip, having finished the meat from their previous trip two weeks earlier. They were taking the ATVs, which were packed with food and their hunting gear. Luckily, they had rifles they had found while looting.

"Yeah, I just have to finish tying the cooler down," Keira said, pulling a bungee cord across the cooler on the back of her ATV. Her Uncle Connor walked out of the house carrying a half-eaten sandwich. "Why do you get a sandwich?" Keira asked.

"Because I'm the best hunter," he replied, taking another bite.

"Pfft, yeah right," Keira said, smiling.

"Relax." Keira's mother came out with two sandwiches in her hands. "I made sandwiches for you two as well."

"Alright," Ronan said, "time to go." He walked up to his wife and accepted a sandwich. "Thanks, honey," he said, kissing her. Keira took her sandwich and thanked her mother as well, giving her a hug.

The three hunters jumped onto their ATVs and headed southeast out of town toward their hunting grounds. The sun was just coming up, burning the sky with a red fury that made Keira squint. She put on her sunglasses, then looked to the south.

The trip took about three hours. It could have taken just two hours, but they had to go around the forest. The sun kept them warm, fighting the cool breeze. Keira had so many memories of driving the ATVs with her brother Reece and her family.

Once they got to their location, they set up camp, mainly to provide shelter if the weather turned bad, forcing them to stay a night. They had a tent but only set up a lean-to for the day. They also set up a skinning rack, which was composed of two metal bars drilled between two trees with a board on a slant for the blood to run down. They would tie the animal to the top bar to hang it against the board. Then they assembled their weapons. As rusty and old as they were, they worked.

They started their journey into the fields. Long grass and wheat shared the flat land, and forest surrounded them. They would search for birds in the grass and four-legged animals in the forest.

"So, how's Ryland?" Connor asked. Keira glared at him. He chuckled. "You had to know it was coming."

"I didn't think it was going to be this soon," she replied.

"You two have been hanging out a lot," her father said. Keira was surprised he was joining in. But he was her father, after all.

"Yeah," she replied. "He's a good hunter and has been training me and telling me stories about all the places he's been." Her family had always told her she should travel a bit before deciding where to stay for the rest of her life.

"Don't count that toward your travelling," Ronan said as if reading her mind.

"I know, but it could help me decide where to travel to," she said.

"Yeah, because he'll be there," Connor teased, earning himself a smack from Keira.

"Where is he now?" her father asked.

"Out of town for a few days. He was called to a neighbouring town."

Remembering the note, she tried to think of what he would be doing. Surveying the land or the town for military analysis perhaps. Or maybe he had been called to help someone there.

"Don't look too worried, Keira. He's just gone for a few days," her uncle said, seeing the concerned look on her face.

Her father crouched, and they all went quiet, focused on the field.

"Just inside the forest line," he whispered.

Keira squinted and saw a deer grazing. They moved closer, having to go around the forest line to avoid making too much noise in the long grass. When they got close enough, Connor lined up a shot. The deer looked up and then sauntered toward them. Connor held his fire. The deer paused, and Keira felt the same tension in her as she saw something else move. A black-skinned beast pounced out of the dark and tackled the deer. Keira's heart pounded in panic, then sank when she realized they couldn't get the deer. The three hunters backed away, being only thirty feet from the animals.

They travelled to the other side of the meadow and into the forest. The ground rose into a small hill, and over the hill the forest thinned out, letting in more light from the sun, which was nearly at its peak. The hunters found no game for the next kilometre, only a few squirrels and small birds. They stopped and took a lunch break.

"What does Ryland do for a living?" Ronan asked.

"He's with the military. He surveys the land and whatever else the government wants."

"Oh, wow, he's with the government." Ronan was impressed. The Circle of Generals was a small group, and few people worked for them.

"Don't get too attached," Connor said as he took another bite of his sandwich. "He'll have to move on sometime."

"I know. I think what he does is pretty cool. Travelling would be cool too."

"But you can't go with him." Connor winked at Keira.

"Going to the Grand Port or Laketown would be a big change and could show you a lot about the rest of the world," Ronan said. He may have been there once before in his life.

Once they finished their lunch, they found a herd of deer. The deer seemed cautious, as if they had heard stories about the augmented beast roaming around, or the hunters.

Ronan, Connor, and Keira spread out in different directions to ensure success. Ronan was on the north side of them with Keira in the middle and Connor on the south side. Everything stayed silent; the hunters, the deer, and even the wind went still.

Ronan pulled the trigger, but all he heard was a click. His gun had jammed, which wasn't uncommon with the old rifles. He made eye contact with Keira and signalled the trouble. She set her sights on a deer on the north side of the herd and fired. The herd scattered at the sound of the gun. Keira's target ran as well but with a limp. She had shot the deer on the northernmost side to ensure that the herd ran toward Connor.

Ronan unjammed his rifle in time to fire another shot at the deer Keira had hit, which was lagging behind the herd. Another shot rang out from Connor, who was closest to the grassy field. Amongst all the noise, the birds took flight, and Connor shot down two. The hunters collected their rewards and then headed back to their camp.

"Probably shouldn't skin them here with that black beast lurking about," Ronan said.

"Right. Let's pack up," Connor agreed. The sun was in the second half of the sky. It had been a fairly quick hunt for them.

"So, Keira, do you have any idea of where you would like to travel?" Connor asked, continuing their previous conversation.

"I like the idea of Lakewood. It sounds like a cool city. On the lake, big yet efficient like we are. But I like the mountains, and I hear there are cliff ranges to the south."

Connor nodded. "More mountains can be found far to the west as well."

"Or there's a canyon to the northwest," Ronan said.

"Oh, okay."

Keira thought about it all. The mountains made her feel safe. It was like living in nature's version of a house, with the mountains serving as the walls. Climbing them was always a good activity to keep things exciting and to keep fit for hunting. Life could get boring in a small town, knowing exactly what was going on with everyone even when nothing at all was going on.

A sound from the field drew Keira's attention. Something was creeping closer. Keira knew what that meant. A predator was stalking them, likely after their kill.

"Dad," she whispered, pointing to the grass. Ronan and Connor grabbed their rifles. Keira's was across the camp with the ATVs.

The men crept to the edge of their camp, taking up posts on either side of a small opening in the trees. Ronan nodded to Connor and then they both fired. A roar came from the grass, and the movement sped up like a high wind blowing through it. As more shots rang out, the black beast jumped right into their camp, slashing at Connor.

"Void!" Connor just dodged its sharp claws. Ronan backed away as he continued to fire, using the trees as cover. Keira ran toward her rifle, and the beast followed her. She jumped over her ATV, just dodging the beast's claws, which scraped across into the ATV's gas tank and the metal rack on the back.

The beast turned to face Ronan, who kept firing, careful not to hit Keira, and prowled toward him, plotting a route through the trees.

Connor ran toward the ATV, dipped a stick in gasoline, then lit it and tackled the beast, jamming the flaming stick into the forest dweller's paw. Fire burst forth, causing the animal to scream. The flames reached up its powerful leg, burning its chest and shoulder. It fell to its side and kicked Connor off. Another shot rang out, and the beast finally stopped moving. Keira held her rifle at eye level, smoke weaving off the end.

"Is everyone okay?" Ronan asked.

"I... I'm okay," Keira said.

"I have a bit of a scratch," Connor said. He had two gashes on his upper arm and a small burn and a cut on his left thigh.

"Oh my," Keira exclaimed. Ronan ran to his ATV and found the first-aid kit.

As her father patched up Connor, Keira packed up the rest of their camp. Her hands shook as she tied the tarp, adrenaline still flowing through her. Connor didn't seem worried about the cuts. The burn was harder to treat in the wild, but they found some freeze weeds, which would help. Breaking them apart produced a healing oil that also protected the burn from the sun.

"Is he okay to drive home?" Keira asked her father, knowing her uncle would say he could.

"Yeah, he should be fine," Ronan replied.

The ride home took a little longer, including a few stops to check Connor's bandages and to make sure his burn wasn't getting worse.

When they got home, they treated the wounds more thoroughly and made sure he rested.

FOURTEEN

LIZ TOOK RYLAND out of town to some abandoned buildings, which were scattered over a kilometre. Moss grew on every brick and concrete slab. Some mayors don't care about explorers searching for history that was lost in the war along with the people that knew the history. Some had shared their knowledge with their children, but it was only ever their perspective, and over the last few decades, history had been vanishing like the wind.

Ryland didn't care too much. His own history was lost to him for the most part. His father was gone, his sister was lost, and his mother's whereabouts were unknown.

"Nice walk out to Scandal too, eh?" Ryland said as they walked over the hill that showed the majority of the abandoned city.

"Yeah. Must have been nice travelling here," Liz replied. The sun was bright at midday. A breeze swept across the grassy meadows, clawing at their pant legs.

"Yeah, it was. Had some other travellers I ran into," Ryland said.

"Oh, yeah? Where were they going?" she asked as they made their way down the hill to the bulk of the buildings.

"To Mount Horizon. Eight travellers in total. Their leader told me about a vision he had of me." Ryland had almost forgotten about it.

"Huh," Liz replied. "Probably scouts for Scandal Town's mayor. What was the vision?"

"It was of Jupiter with a field of rye with a…" Ryland paused to think as he stepped over a small hole at the bottom of the hill. "A ghost, a bowman, and a thief who possessed a relic that had saved foreigners."

"Wow. That's kinda out there," Liz said. "What do you think it means?"

"I'm not sure. It's kinda random. So was the so-called prophet."

The two agents entered a small house. Stairs off to their right led to a basement, and there was a small kitchen against the back wall and a living room to the left.

"You want to check out the basement?" Liz asked.

"Sure."

Ryland turned on his flashlight and approached the stairs. They were covered in vegetation. It was amazing how much life on Earth regrew after the war. Everything was vibrant again. Some books he found showed marvels of the pre-war world. Other living things grew back faster than humanity.

The circle of light from his flashlight revealed two doors, a TV, a few couches and chairs, a desk, and what Ryland assumed was a laundry room. He moved to the TV lounge part of the basement. The couch and chairs were skeletons of what they used to be, lacking cushions or fabric. The wood was rotten, rusty nails lying on the floor. The couch had a metal frame and a thin, burnt cushion on it. Ryland went to sit, but then a whistle came from across the room. He stood and shone his light toward the sound but saw nothing. Upon closer inspection, he found a small hole that led to the outside.

Must have been the wind, he thought.

He turned back and saw a bookshelf on the far side of the lounge area. Some books were lying open on the floor. Others were burnt.

He flipped through the pages to see if there was anything of interest. Scholars wanted most kinds of books. Even fiction talked about the pre-war world. It was said that a lot of the pre-war world was lazy and based on consuming goods and gaining anything people could. People worked mainly because they had to and to get money to buy the next thing they wanted. Ryland had seen giant signs beside broken roads that had advertisements on them. Most of them had been burned, but some survived. He remembered one that had the face of an old man with a white top hat and stars on the base of it. The old man was pointing and had a serious face. The rest of the sign was destroyed, but Ryland was curious what that sign was for.

Ryland put the books back. The majority of them were unreadable. After searching the rest of the basement and finding nothing, he went back upstairs. Liz had met with similar success. They moved on to explore the rest of the destroyed houses.

Ryland found a computer that was in decent shape apart from the monitor. He pulled the hard drive and decrypted it with his laptop. Most of it was junk.

Hmm... you can see the consumerism in this, Ryland thought as he sifted through emails, Internet searches, and social media platforms by code hacking and few satellites hung in space giving access. All of it was meaningless to him. He would still bring the hard drive back to headquarters for the sifters, though. They could take what they wanted. Ryland longed to have the ability to learn like they did. It was as if they could search anything and find answers.

Then Ryland found something that did interest him: an article on planet Earth. It described science in the pre-war world. Technology was at its height, allowing faster and more detailed scientific analysis. Ryland wanted to understand his world, to gain knowledge of how things worked, the planet and how it hung in space with the sun and other planets, and how it survived the war. It was ironic that the technology they used to understand the planet was also what killed the planet, or at least damaged it.

"Ryland," Liz called from another room. "You find anything?"

"Just this computer. Has some info that's intact," Ryland replied.

"Cool. Hopefully it has some history on there," Liz said as she entered the room.

"Yeah." Ryland didn't care for history at first, but over time, the sifters had convinced him that history was important to humanity's future. Having his own history book, he could understand why.

"You think the ghost, the bowman, and the thief from the vision are all someone who is a jack of all trades?" Liz asked.

Ryland shrugged. "Maybe. Like an agent. We don't exist, we're hunters and... well, we don't steal, so maybe not."

"We steal from the bad guys," Liz said, thinking of the times she had beaten up thugs and stole what they stole or ruined their plans. "But that seems like too much of a stretch."

They continued through the city with little other success. They found a few books that had some readable pages, including a few books on history and geography, which Liz was excited about. They also stopped at an abandoned restaurant, taking a moment to reenact what it might have been like when the restaurant was in service.

"What can I get you today, sir?" Liz asked, jumping behind the counter. Ryland saw a smoothie cup, which was still intact.

"Can I get a smoothie and a burger, please?"

"Sure, coming right up. That'll be five dollars and thirty-two cents, please."

"Here you are." Ryland handed Liz a few rusty metal gears that he swiped from a table. Liz handed Ryland a plate and the smoothie cup. Ryland thanked her and then walked to a booth by the window. Liz grabbed another smoothie cup, jumped over the counter, and joined him, both of them now acting like friends who came to the restaurant all the time.

"So, other than agent stuff, how are you?" Liz asked, slouching in her seat and holding her smoothie cup like it had something in it.

"Good. Training has been good," Ryland replied. Liz raised an eyebrow. "What?" Ryland asked. "That's part of my life. In fact, I don't do anything other than travel and agent stuff."

"I know. You like your training," Liz said. "But what's different? You're in a new town. What's going on there?"

"Ah, there's this girl—"

"Oh, a girl!" Liz sat straight up.

"No, not like that," Ryland said, blushing at what Liz was implying. "I ran into her the day I got to Mount Horizon. She killed a forest dweller."

"Wow. That's impressive," Liz said, winking.

"Stop," Ryland said. "She got the jump on it and was going to help me collect it, but then a Venusian was in the forest. Anyway, she trained with me the next day, doing archery."

"Really. What did she think of the Venusian?"

"She thought it was the Blood's Shadow legend. Her uncle didn't think anything of it. Thought he was just a good fighter. And he wasn't wrong."

Liz smirked at the idea of Ryland killing the Venusian, but she didn't know he let the alien go.

"So, this girl, why did you train her?" Liz asked.

Ryland shrugged. "She was interested." Liz liked teasing him like she was his big sister, even though she was a few years younger than him. It was part of her job, providing a place for agents to hide, rest, and heal as well as provide psychoanalysis. Ryland was also an old friend, not just an agent.

"That's Ryland Ambrose for you, always the first one to help," Liz said, smiling. "But there's always the question of why. You separated yourself from Nat because you felt you were doing her harm. You enjoy working alone and only maintain superficial relationships, and you take responsibility for things that aren't your fault."

Her words cut Ryland to his heart. She was right; he barely had to report to anyone, so he kept to himself but also took all responsibilities onto himself.

"You need someone to talk to," she continued. "Someone to report to as a friend and deeper than a friend."

"You're saying I need a girlfriend?" Ryland asked. His hand clasped the necklace that reminded him of Nat.

"No. A friend who stays around, has fun with you, and maybe pushes you. You need a partner. Someone to shadow you, to be part of every adventure. You live in your mind, Ryland, and your mind can conjure many scenarios that don't align with reality. If you don't go with a partner on every mission, I'll assign one for you." She had the power to do that. As a psychiatrist and the keeper of the safe house, the program would do anything she said for another agent.

As Ryland pondered her words, he played with the necklace, glass, metal, and shards of wood sliding between his fingers. She was right.

After living for so long in his head, he knew things inside his mind weren't the same as reality. He could picture himself flying or being indestructible, but in reality he could never make himself fly.

"Alright," Ryland said. "I'll look into finding a partner." He decided to seize the initiative rather than let her stick him with someone he didn't want.

"It'll do you well, Ryland," Liz said, vowing to keep an eye on him to make sure he honoured his words.

"Yes, ma'am," Ryland said, smiling. He stood up, leaving his smoothie cup on the table. Liz followed suit.

When they got back to the safe house, they connected the drives to a console to download and decrypt their contents. They also sprayed the books with a solution that absorbed the charcoal and kept the pages intact for further observation.

FIFTEEN

"HEY!" KEIRA HUGGED her best friend, Ali, one of the few people her age in Mount Horizon. They were heading to help Mr. and Mrs. Sheer, the town's butcher and seamstress, respectively. The two girls walked down one of the town's two dirt walkways. Once they passed the fountain, they found themselves surrounded by a garden in the centre of the town, which split the walkways.

"I always love looking at this garden," Ali said. The garden had many colourful flowers with stones demarking each section. The fountain had channels that ran throughout the garden, watering the plants.

"It's beautiful," Keira agreed.

"You hear about the Blood's Shadow?" Ali asked as she stopped to admire the garden.

"What about it?" There were always rumours about the Blood's Shadow, augmented humans killing and wreaking havoc in cities around the world.

"Two were spotted together in Europe," Ali said. Usually they worked alone.

"Were they after anything specific?" Keira asked. She had never heard any news about them stealing anything or killing anyone specific.

"Not that I heard. They disappeared after killing a few hunters."

"Hmm. The usual," Keira said, feeling bad for the hunters. Although there were some stories of the Blood's Shadow in cities, most stories came from the outskirts.

"Do you think they have an organization?" Keira asked.

"They are called the Blood's Shadow," Ali pointed out.

"Isn't that just the name the public gave them? They don't sound very organized, usually on the outskirts of cities," Keira replied.

Ali thought about it for a moment. "Huh. You're right. They rarely go into cities. I've actually never looked into it."

"I wish there was something I could do about them," Keira said.

"You won't be able to do anything; they're augmented. Let the Circle of Generals deal with them."

Keira wasn't a fan of doing nothing, just living in a small town where nothing happened. Some people liked that, but Keira didn't.

"There's always something you could do," Keira countered. "Public awareness, for instance. People always have different views and different ideas."

"You always think of different things, looking out to the land and the future." Ali seemed content to stay in Mount Horizon, although Keira suspected she wanted out too.

"You know there was a Blood's Shadow here in the forest?" Keira asked.

"What? How have I not heard of it?" Ali asked.

"I saw it," Keira said. "I assume Ryland took care of it." She wasn't sure how many people knew Ryland was with the COG, but it wasn't hard to figure out.

"That's crazy. I didn't think they were anywhere near here," Ali said. "They really are all across the world."

"Yeah," Keira agreed, her voice tainted by fear. The threat was across the entire world.

"What about you and Dylan?" Ali asked as they continued their walk. Keira wasn't sure if she was asking about Keira wanting to leave town or asking about Ryland and Dylan.

"What about Dylan and me?"

"Well, for one, I want to know how it's going, and two, I'm asking how he feels about Ryland."

"We're fine, but I still think there's more that a relationship could be."

"And you think you can find that with Ryland?"

"I'm not looking at Ryland as a future partner," Keira said.

"I know that. You're with Dylan. I'm just saying that he's a good-looking guy, and you have grown to a liking kinda fast."

"You don't know that it's a liking," Keira replied.

"You're usually in your own world, staring into the distance and the future, whether you're with Dylan or out hunting. But with Ryland you aren't daydreaming."

Keira shook her head. "I don't know." She wasn't sure why she had made such an effort to get to know Ryland. "Maybe he's an opportunity to see something new." Ali lifted an eyebrow. "Not that kind of opportunity," Keira said, blushing. "An opportunity to see something bigger than Mount Horizon."

"Do *you* know how Dylan feels about Ryland?" Keira asked.

"You don't know, do you?" Ali replied.

"Dylan and I do the same things. In this town we all do the same things. Ryland is different and new." Keira could have said a lot more, but she was scared of what it could mean.

"Ladies! How are you?" Mrs. Sheer exclaimed as they came within earshot.

"Good!" Keira replied. "How are you, Mrs. Sheer?"

"I'm good. I just need some more material. Could I get you two to buy a bundle of black cloth and purple silk?" In her sixties with a slightly hunched back, Mrs. Sheer reached into her apron pocket and pulled out a bundle of money, handing it to Ali.

"Of course we can do that," Ali replied, then the girls went on their way.

"I guess you're right," Ali said as they walked. "Ryland is part of the Circle of Generals. He could change something. But it's a slim chance. He has a job to do, and he won't have time to spend with any of us."

Keira nodded in agreement. "Yeah, who knows? I'm probably just dreaming. I still want to see what's out there in the world. People used to travel all the time, apparently." She thought of the different modes of travel that might have been. She knew about helicopters. They were rare to see in Mount Horizon, but a few had passed by in her lifetime.

"Yeah, we don't have many fast ways of travelling. You would have to commit. Can't come back home on a day's notice."

The girls walked to the store, got the fabric they needed, then headed back to Mrs. Sheer to help with anything they could.

■

A warning pinged on both agents' phones. Their screens showed a picture of the dragon, a beast augmented like the rest. It was the most infamous beast with the highest bounty, and it had been spotted near the city. Bounties went out when such animals were creating havoc. The dragon had done more than created havoc; it had created a problem in multiple locations and had proved a problem for even the Sentry program. It had trapped the last agents who had hunted it.

"Let's get this beast," Liz said. She was bored and wanted to get out of the city.

Whenever cities put out bounties, the agents knew about them before anyone else through the Circle of Generals. They were the first response program around the world. Ryland opened his phone for more information. "Location is on the west side of Scandal Town, and it looks like five local hunters are after the bounty." He sighed. "Great. Now we have to deal with them too."

"Yeah. But they're on their own. We'll do what we can," Liz reminded Ryland that the hunters were tracking the dragon at their own risk. She and Ryland would protect them but not at the cost of their own lives. If the hunters wanted to hunt, agents wouldn't stop them.

They met at the edge of a small forest on the outside of the city. The five hunters approached the two agents. Ryland inspected his wrist blade, ensuring it was ready to go. Liz cleaned her rifle, which had no rust on it, unlike the hunters' rifles, which had been recovered in the ruins after the war.

"Who are you?" one of the hunters asked. His beard was long, dark, and well kept.

"They are soldiers from the Circle of Generals," another said. His face was clean-shaven with a scar tucked under his jaw below his ear. "Look at their weapons."

"I don't want to share the bounty with them," the bearded man said.

"Without us, you won't be sharing your life," Ryland replied. He sensed arrogance and ignorance in the man's walk, and his talk proved it.

"We're here to help," Liz said. "We don't need the bounty. We only want to stop this beast."

"Oh, holier than thou, are we?" the bearded man said, which earned him a nudge from his clean-shaven companion.

"What are your names?" Ryland asked, changing the subject.

"I'm Eli," the clean-shaven man said. "This is Rick," he opened his arm toward the man with the beard, who looked unimpressed. "And this is Cory, Brad, and his sister Lucy." Brad and Lucy nodded in greeting.

"Nice to meet you all. My name is Ryland, and this is Liz," Ryland said.

"Have any of you seen the dragon before?" Liz asked.

"Oh, look, the soldiers are seeing what our abilities are," Rick mocked.

"If we're to work as a team, we need to know each other's abilities, Rick," Ryland replied with a glare. This was why he enjoyed working on his own. Rick scowled, but Eli answered before he could reply.

"We have not. We have all hunted throughout our lives, using it to get away from the city. And the bounties on the augmented animals give extra cash." Ryland couldn't tell if his comment was scornful toward the town. "And we will help any way we can."

Rick rolled his eyes at the comment. Several retorts ran through Ryland's head, but he knew such a fool would only run his mouth and never listen.

"Alright, well, let's get out of town," Ryland said.

■

The sun was bright in the latter half of the vibrant blue sky, and wind flowed through the trees and flowers that Liz could smell nearby. Most flowers changed after the war, especially their names. Latin was lost, and the flowers' appearance altered, so those who knew flowers gave them new names. Liz's parents had told her about the yellow flower-looking weeds called dandelions and the famous rose that survived the war. She liked hearing about how things were before the war. Some people said the world looked more vibrant and lively now than it did before. Liz's mom had told her that humans were more connected and advanced in technology back then, but it made them less connected with nature and one another.

It was hard to believe that. Her parents died soon after Liz got into the Sentry program. *How could this world be so much better and we be so connected to nature when nature kills so many?* she wondered, a thought that her mind returned to often. She didn't know anything about biology or nature. How could she be more connected than those of the pre-war age who were at the height of knowledge?

"Okay, we're here," Ryland said. There was a cave on the side of a hill surrounded by trees and a small pond a few metres from the entrance.

He always seems to take the lead, Liz thought. *He's a good leader, though, thank the sun. And yet he strives to be on his own.*

"Take a look at that tree," Liz said, pointing to some claw marks on a thick tree trunk. She felt anger toward their prey. It had killed so many, just like all of nature's diseases and creations. So many had died from sickness, and now the animals were becoming more dangerous.

"That's never a good sign," Brad said. It was high up, so either the dragon was tall or it could jump.

"I think the lack of claw marks in front of the cave is more intimidating," Ryland said, looking back to the cave. "It means the beast is intentional about entering the cave without leaving a mark, probably to keep suspicion away."

"You think it's that smart?" Liz asked. It seemed a bit far-fetched, but the stories seemed to portray a smart beast.

"You guys are way overthinking this," Rick said as he approached the cave mouth. Liz pictured the cave itself coming to life and eating the arrogant hunter, but she didn't want anyone to die.

Eli dropped his backpack and walked past his friend toward the cave, ignoring Rick's comment. The others dropped what they didn't need and followed Eli.

Flashlights scanned the cave as they went deeper inside, circles of light bouncing with each step. The only sound they heard was breathing and footsteps. Soon the cave split off into separate tunnels. If they passed that point and the dragon came from the first tunnels, the hunters would be cut off from the only known exit.

"What are you thinking?" Brad asked, turning to Ryland and Liz. Ryland looked down the tunnels. There were two on both sides with ten metres between them. Their flashlights showed nothing but dark dirt walls.

"I'm thinking we split up and explore each tunnel. One person should stay here in the main tunnel to warn us of any danger. The other option, which could lead to us getting cut off from the only known exit, is going down any single tunnel and attempting to draw the dragon out by poking its nest, assuming it's hungry and wants our food."

"What's wrong with poking the nest?" Rick asked. "It'll get the beast to come out."

"It will know our position and be angry, giving it the advantage," Brad explained.

"I'll stay in this tunnel," Liz said.

"Alright," Ryland replied, nodding. "Eli, you go with Rick in the south tunnel. Brad and Lucy, you take the north tunnel on the left. Cory and I will take the north tunnel on the right. Liz, you can radio me, but yell if you see anything. If any of you hear Liz, get back here as fast as possible. Everyone good with that?" Even though it was posed as a question, he said the last part with authority. Everyone nodded in confirmation. Then the hunters paired up as instructed and went down their designated tunnels.

■

Ryland walked down the second north tunnel, their flashlights shining as far as they could reach. As the tunnel started to slope down, Ryland wondered if the other north tunnel did the same or intertwined with theirs. His question was answered when they reached a large, round opening connecting the two tunnels.

"Ryland, get back here," Liz said over the radio. Ryland didn't hesitate, running back to the main tunnel with Brad and Lucy. They expected something big, only to see a small dragon when they arrived.

Shoot, Ryland thought. *A baby.*

"Which way did it come from?" he asked.

"Main tunnel," Liz replied. The creature was at Liz's knees, sniffing around, not feeling threatened at all. Its tail was half the length of its body, and the scales on its back looked harder than those on its underside. Just then, Eli and Rick came back from their tunnel.

"Whoa," Rick said in amusement. He crouched down to let the creature sniff him, then pulled out his hunting knife.

"What are you doing?" Lucy asked.

"I'm going to kill it," Rick replied. Ryland grabbed Rick by the throat and pushed him away from the baby dragon.

"Back off!" Rick pushed Ryland away from him. "You want another one of those things to grow up and hunt us?"

"If we kill its role model, it may not grow up with the same destructive nature," Ryland said in a low voice, not wanting to make too much noise. If there was a baby around, the adult dragon was probably around as well and would notice its little one missing.

"You want to bet our lives on that?" Rick asked. He had a point. If it was the dragon's nature to be aggressive, there was no stopping it.

Nat would take it back with her and train it, Ryland thought. It would be a cool creature to train, if it could be trained.

They mulled over their options: kill the baby and get rid of a potential threat but potentially aggravate the adult dragon, or let it live and continue to search for the adult dragon, which might find them due to the missing baby.

"We could take it back to the city. Get it to a facility that can study it," Lucy suggested, though she wasn't too sure of the idea. There were hospitals in some towns, but a full research facility? Ryland knew of a place they could take it, but he didn't like the idea of taking the creature out of its natural habitat. Even when Nat and he did such things, they did their best to show the animal how to hunt and survive on its own, whereas the hospital would just study it.

Ryland looked at Liz and realized she was reading his mind.

"There aren't many good facilities, and those that are won't care for this creature," she said, though Ryland knew it was a lie.

"Ah, quit stalling." Brad raised his rifle and shot the baby dragon. It let out a screech and then fell over, dead.

"Brad!" Lucy exclaimed.

"Void sucker!" Eli shouted.

"I'm not letting more of those things grow and kill more people like the dragon," Brad replied. Ryland understood his mindset but was disappointed with his closed mind.

"You—" Eli stepped forward but was interrupted by a sound coming from the main tunnel. Ryland shone his flashlight toward the source of the sound and saw two eyes reflecting the light back at him. Rick and Brad opened fire.

Ryland threw a flash grenade halfway between the beast and the hunters, then they all ducked into one of the side tunnels. After it exploded, they jumped out and fired, a mixture of semi-automatic and fully automatic shots echoing off the cave walls. The dragon dug into the north wall and disappeared. A moment later it appeared with a rock and threw it down the tunnel.

"Get to the exit! Draw it out!" Ryland ordered.

Brad and Lucy made it out first and laid down cover fire. The rest of them emerged into the light.

"Shit!" Rick yelled as a rock tumbled past, barely missing Brad. Ryland shoved Rick into the cave wall.

"I don't care if this is new to you or not. Hold your tongue and pay attention!"

As the dragon stepped fully into the light, the hunters were all dumbfounded. It was three metres tall with shimmering black scales running along its back and tail. Like the baby dragon, its underside was white. Its talons were as long as a man's forearm. Its eyes were pure black, but Ryland could still tell where it was looking as he scanned it for a possible weak point.

The hunters surrounded the beast, their eyes on its 1.5-metre tail, which ended with a single talon. They all fired as they escaped near-death attacks, covering each other by distracting the dragon.

Cory got up close and stabbed and slashed at the beast's feet with his knife. Ryland was impressed with his skills as Cory dodged the creature's swiping tail.

The dragon dropped onto all fours, then swung its tail and swatted Lucy, who went flying into the pond. It swung its claws at Cory, cutting his body in two. Eli and Rick moved together, firing at the beast's face. Liz jumped onto its back, attempting to find a soft spot into which she could stab her knife. The scales allowed movement but had few gaps. Even its head was covered with impenetrable scales.

The beast folded itself into a tight ball and rolled into the pond, then popped back onto its feet. It whipped its tail at Brad, who rolled under it, but the tail curled back, and the talon stabbed through Brad's abdomen. He grunted and then gurgled as blood filled his mouth. The dragon lifted Brad off the ground, still impaled on its talon, then shook him off.

Ryland stepped back to flank the creature as he looked for an opening. When the dragon turned toward Ryland, he opened fire. The bullet struck one of the beast's large black eyes. It screeched like the baby did but with more power and volume. Ryland almost had to cover his ears. The dragon jumped over Lucy, who was still lying in the pond, and then disappeared. The ground near the cave entrance bubbled and then collapsed.

"Lucy!" Liz exclaimed. "Are you okay?" Lucy didn't answer. She just sat in the water, holding her abdomen and staring at the dead. Liz and Ryland knelt next to her, and Liz lifted Lucy's hand so she could inspect the damage. "A few broken ribs, and maybe a ruptured kidney," she said, looking up at Ryland.

"It just killed Brad and Cory like they were nothing," Eli said. He was standing just out of the water looking at the cave entrance.

Ryland stood up and walked over to Eli and Rick. "We should go." His tone was still strong, but inside he felt the loss.

They buried the dead on the edge of a cluster of trees and flowers. There weren't any funeral homes or a care to guide the dead to afterlife. There was plenty of room in the world to bury them anywhere, so that's what people did. Lucy hadn't said a thing since the fight. She just stared at her brother's dead body, and when it was buried, she stared at the ground. She wouldn't have done well if they carried the bodies back with them, constantly seeing her brother's body in two.

The trip home was quiet. The dragon was a tougher animal to hunt than even the agents anticipated. Ryland and Liz got the hunters back to town, and Liz took Lucy home to tend to her wounds. Lucy was in shock. If not cared for and treated, she might never speak again.

SIXTEEN

THE NEXT MORNING, Ryland started back to Mount Horizon. He felt like it was the only place to go. He didn't know why. He had travelled for most of his life, restricted only by the COG ordering his survey schedule or calls to intervene in conflicts. He had been to all the neighbouring cities and compounds in his zone. He did have more work to survey near Mount Horizon, but he also realized he was drawn there by Keira. His mind continually drifted to thoughts of her. Could she be the partner that Liz said he needed? First, he would have to train her as an apprentice. Maybe that would be enough. Someone to talk to, to keep Ryland grounded in reality. It was ridiculous to think he would drag someone into an alien-fighting program just so he had someone to talk to.

The sun was to Ryland's left, just above the horizon. Walking across the meadows and the vibrant rolling hills was relaxing. As the wind blew through the grass, it was as if it was also blowing through Ryland's mind, with thoughts appearing and disappearing at random. He thought about his work, hunting animals and aliens, finding pieces of the old world, and training with fellow agents. He reflected on memories of Liz, Nat, and Marcus and how brutally they had trained, using their training to test their trainers. Most of the agents became like family. Ryland felt like he just left a sister. Memories of his real family, what little he could recall of them, had barely entered his mind over the past few years. Now Ryland kept his friends close but only when they reunited. Other than that, he kept things superficial, as Liz said.

When Ryland was a day away from Mount Horizon, he found a rock formation that offered some cover. Above the rocks was a cliff that hid the sun, creating an early sunset. Ryland pulled his backpack off and pulled out his tarp, setting it up in front of the entrance between the two rocks. He placed the rest of his things inside his shelter. Then he climbed the formation and looked up at the wall of rock. The sun set the sky on fire as the light waves were scattered into the atmosphere.

In less than thirty seconds, he had scaled the rock wall. When he reached the top, the sun blinded him. He shielded his eyes as he scanned the sky. As wind blew through his hair, he recalled the image of the Elo pitching a tent for the sun in the sky. It was like a groom coming from his bridal chamber, rejoicing like an athlete after running a race. Nothing was hidden from its heat.

Until it sets, Ryland thought. *Till the next morning.* But it was only to show that the sun was subordinate to Elo.

■

He awoke to a noise from the meadow. He got up and peeked past the tarp, waiting a moment as his eyes adjusted to the dark. He noticed the stars, bright and uncountable. Then he saw it. They were quick, and they blended into the black canvas of night.

Wolves.

Ryland grabbed his hunting knife. He also had his hidden wrist blade. The wolves could be augmented, but either way, they could probably smell Ryland, and he had to move. He grabbed his pack and then climbed the rocks.

Spotting him, a wolf lunged and snapped at his ankles, but Ryland managed to scramble out of reach. The wolves attempted to climb the rocks too, but in seconds he was on top of the cliff. When they saw him standing there, the wolves hurried to flank him.

He looked down at the site of his former camp and saw more wolves sniffing around. He had put pungent weeds in a semi-circle at the entrance to his camp, but the wolves looked as if they could still pick up his scent.

The wolves were mostly hairless due to augmentation, but they had a bit of hair on the backs of their necks. Their muscles were taut beneath their skin, which was as black as night. Travelling in packs, they were scary creatures to face, even for an agent.

Ryland slid over the edge of the cliff and landed on a small rock jutting out from the cliff face. Then he jumped onto the back of one of the wolves and plunged his knife into its neck. It let out a yelp, then sank to the ground, dead.

Ryland saw a glimmer, then a wolf jumped out of his sleeping area. He raised his arm just in time to prevent his face from being mauled. His knife was still in the dead wolf, so Ryland was now in a wrestling match with an augmented beast with four legs, sharp claws, and vicious teeth. And it was not alone.

He shifted his hand to the side of the wolf's face and pinned it to the ground, but it still kicked him with powerful legs. Ryland got one leg on top of the wolf's back legs, holding them with his knee. He could feel the strength in the beast's front paws as it pushed down on his elbow, pinning its head. Blood oozed out of its mouth, but it was not its own blood. The wolf's teeth had sunk down to the bone in Ryland's arm, and it was holding it like a toy.

Ryland let go of the wolf's head, and it took the bait, releasing his arm as it attempted another bite. Ryland grabbed the wolf's upper and lower jaws and twisted. A loud crack rang out, and the wolf slumped forward, its head loose and cranked at an awkward angle.

As the other wolves advanced toward Ryland, he leaped up and ran into the cave, grabbing more pungent weeds. He had had a small fire before heading to bed, so he threw the weeds into the coals and got out his lighter. As he set fire to the weeds, the smell hit instantly. He fed the fire with more sticks. Then he pulled out the largest stick, which was only as thick as his thumb, and swung open the tarp, rifle in hand.

The smell burst out of the cave, and the wolves recoiled in disgust. Ryland swung the flaming stick in a semicircle to scare them off. They only backed up a step, so Ryland fired his rifle. The lead wolf turned and bounded away, the others following. They glanced back toward their prey but decided against pursuing him any further.

His arm bleeding heavily, Ryland ripped off one of his sweater sleeves to wrap it around the worst part of the wound. He ripped the other sleeve to snake around the rest of his arm to slow the bleeding. He would have to keep moving. Fast. The wolves might return, realizing he was injured. But if he kept travelling now in the dark, they would have the advantage. He decided to grab his things to cover as much ground as possible. Letting the wound get worse would only make the travel, or fending off the wolves, worse. He left his T-shirt he wore in the cave, hoping that if the wolves came back they would smell the shirt. Ryland ran through the hills and into the darker forest. Not being able to see made the feeling of someone chasing him much more potent. But he had to keep going, he had to gain as much ground as he could.

It would make the trip longer, but he ran towards the east hoping to find a narrower part of the river. When he got there he was rewarded with piles of holders at the entrance of the lake that he could jump across. Once across he tried to sleep.

■

When Ryland got back to Mount Horizon, Keira insisted that he go to their small hospital, which was located in someone's garage, the lack of vehicles freeing it to be repurposed for other things. As the doctor inspected his arm, Keira told him that she had been training every day. "It added to my free time," she said. The training had made her stealthier in her hunting and given her more endurance and strength.

She's very dedicated, Ryland thought, contrary to what she had said when they first met. *Her parents and uncle raised her right. I wonder what Reece is like and what he's doing. Does he have the same dedication and motivation?*

The doctor did a good job of cleaning and bandaging Ryland's wounds, stitching a few of them as needed. Once he was all patched up, Ryland went to his hotel and slept until midday. When he woke, he continued to read from the notebook he had found.

Fear. How do you beat fear when there's so much we don't know, and what we don't understand scares us? Maybe knowing everything, knowing everything about yourself, drives out fear. Or does it have to be all knowledge?

There's something to say about love. Love, with trust, drives out fear, right? When you trust your partner, you don't fear when they go without you.

So, does perfect knowledge or perfect love defeat fear?

I tried sneaking into the military ranks today without taking anyone out. It's difficult to get a uniform. I gather they're not protecting us from anything originating from outside the city. I think they're testing something. Odd to have them testing in this city. Why this city?

■

Ryland and Keira continued training over the ensuing weeks.

"Do you have to use your combat much?" Keira asked after Ryland used her own momentum against her once again.

"I use it fairly often, yeah."

Their bodies glistened with sweat. The day was warm and humid, and it was threatening to rain, but they continued to train. Keira came at Ryland again, thrusting her fist at him, but he stepped back, noticing her leg was preparing to stop her momentum once her fist was within reach. When she stopped, Ryland moved to the inside of her arm. Keira stepped back, but Ryland caught her front leg with his, and she lost her balance. She tried to grab Ryland's neck, but he blocked her with his left arm, and she fell to the ground.

Keira got back up, the back of her shirt no longer green but brown, the grass torn up from their training. Her muscles were swollen with blood, but her veins didn't pop out like Ryland's. His muscles were sleek and defined, with river-like veins looking like they were on the outside of his skin.

Ryland held out a hand to help her to her feet, but when she grasped it, he let go, causing her to drop back to the ground.

"Hey!" she exclaimed. He reached out again, an apology on his face, but when he pulled her up, pushed her back to the ground again.

"What was that for?" she asked.

"Sorry," he replied. He reached out once more, but this time she didn't fall for it, and she got up on her own, so Ryland body checked her. She fell to the ground once again. He knelt beside her as if to help her up.

"What are you doing?" she asked. Then he threw her to the side.

"Stop it!" she yelled. He remained over top of her, not letting her get to her feet. She tried crawling away so she could seize the advantage, but he was faster than her. She realized what she needed: a distraction.

She started to crawl, digging her fingers into the ground. As Ryland followed, she threw a handful of dirt and stones at his face, then leaped to her feet. Ryland blocked it and lunged forward, knocking her back down.

"Go away!" she yelled. "Let me up!" She kicked at his feet, but he outmaneuvered her. She rolled backwards, but Ryland tackled her into a tree trunk. She fell to her hands and knees, her chest heaving.

"What are you doing?" she asked between breaths.

"Feel the panic?" he said. "Feel the lack of control?" His voice contained no sympathy.

"Yes. Void!" She slid a foot beneath herself, but Ryland pushed her back. She wanted him to stop, but she felt helpless. She tried everything that she knew and had learned, but he continued to keep her on the ground.

With her back straight and her chest out, one leg behind and one in front, she pushed forward against him, but he threw her down. She rolled, and Ryland pushed from behind. She tucked her head, landed on her shoulders, and absorbed the blow, folding her body in half. Just as she was about to kick, Ryland kicked her feet sideways. She hit the ground again, her feet digging into the dirt.

"Stop!" she screamed, throwing a punch at Ryland. He dodged it, but her fists continued to fly. Finally on her feet, Keira used her momentum to spin and add kicks. Ryland dodged, blocked, and pushed her attacks aside. Keira threw a right hook and then tried to trip Ryland with her left foot. He lifted his leg out of the way, and Keira twisted, slamming her right foot into his raised leg. Ryland lost his balance, enabling Keira to push herself up and into Ryland, slamming her elbow into his face. He stumbled back from the blow but kept his footing. Keira ran at him, but he wrapped his arms around her and tossed her against a tree, trapping her.

"Good," he said. "Breathe, breathe." His voice softer now, he continued to hold her tight, giving her no room to fight back.

"Why?" she asked, tears running down her cheeks.

"You live like control is yours to own, but you're not in control. If you were then I would be too, and you'd still lose control because I'm stronger. You need to flow with everything like it's a danger and will turn on you. Prepare for everything and control nothing but your actions and reactions." His voice was filled with sympathy and care.

He released her, and she turned around, wiping her tears and cleaning herself up, not wanting him to see her showing weakness.

"The universe has such an order, and the universe is so much bigger than us that we can't hope to control anything," Ryland said. "What can we do to make the moon full or the trees blossom? We are only a part of this world; we don't control it."

"But like you said," Keira replied, clearing her throat, "we can control our actions and reactions."

"But when something else comes into our lives that we can't control, where is our anchor?" he asked.

"What do you mean?"

"Something aggravated you, and you snapped due to it being out of your control. If you know you can't control anything, your anchor will not be set in your own control."

"How do I put my anchor in something other than myself when I know myself better than anything?"

"But do you know yourself better than anything?" he asked. "Do you have yourself all figured out? Do you know what you like consistently, what you can and can't do?"

"Well, no."

"Do you know your purpose in this world? All your habits and reactions to everything?" Ryland continued. "There is faith, Keira. Faith in something or someone bigger than you."

"Like the sun?" she asked. She looked to where the sun should be. There was no sign of it, the sky covered with thick layers of dark clouds.

"The sun always looks down on us, and the moon is its counterpart. They watch over us."

"I admit that they protect us, as do the planets," Ryland replied. He had found many pre-war books that contained information about the solar system, including information about Jupiter and Saturn, the guardian planets whose massive gravity and size pulled everything toward them, preventing objects from potentially colliding with Earth. "But I don't believe the sun protects us individually or gives us purpose."

"Maybe not," Keira replied, her eyes still on the sky, "but I look up to them even when they're behind clouds. I know they're still there."

"Yes, they're still there, and you have faith to believe as much. Someone like us made us in his image, gave us purpose, and guides us," Ryland said. "You may say you get answers from the sun, but I would say it's the other guy, the one like us. And there's a book on his character and promises. The sun has power, but the God I'm talking about put the sun in the sky."

"How can either of us know what's true?" Keira asked. Some of what he said hurt, but she could tell he was only sharing what he thought was true, holding back some of his harsher beliefs.

"We seek. Looking for the truth using both perspectives, and see what prevails," Ryland suggested, letting her choose if she wished.

■

Ryland and Keira had just entered Mount Horizon when the sky unleashed the water it had held back all day. The rain was warm, and it felt good as it washed the sweat off their bodies.

Once they reached Keira's house, they stood at the entrance, wanting to get out of the rain but not wanting to go any farther to avoid getting the rest of the house wet. Ronan gave them towels to dry off, then Keira went to her room and changed. Ryland placed his towel on a chair to prevent it from getting wet before he sat down.

Keira came out wearing cotton shorts and a sleeveless shirt. Ryland's eyes were drawn to her skin, much more of it showing than usual. She had defined muscles and long, strong legs. Everyone sat at the table as Keira and her mother set out dishes and cutlery. Keira had to reach for the plates in a cupboard, which made her legs look even longer, and her shorts rode up, revealing the curve of her butt. Ryland forced himself to look away.

The room had a dark wood floor with a lighter colour on the walls, which matched the table. The light sand colour accented the darker colours in the dining room and the living room, and the living room furniture matched the walls. A wall separated the kitchen from the living room, but a doorway allowed passage between the rooms.

The clinking of plates drew Ryland's attention back to the table. Keira sat down and undid her ponytail. Her hair was wet and messy, but it fell onto her shoulders in a majestic way. She must have noticed Ryland staring because she gave him a shy smile. Blushing, Ryland grabbed the corn and started spooning some onto his plate.

"What brings you to Mount Horizon, Ryland?" Connor asked as everyone passed the food around.

"I survey this region of Alithia on behalf of the COG, watching for any elevated conflicts."

"Ah, I see. How come we haven't seen you before?"

"I don't always come into town. I can usually survey a small town like Mount Horizon from afar."

"Where are you from, Ryland?" Heather asked.

"I used to have family south of Laketown."

"Where are they now?"

"They aren't alive anymore," Ryland lied. He didn't know where his sister was, and his mother was mentally ill from losing Ryland's father.

"I'm so sorry," Heather said.

"That's okay. Do you worry about anything that might cause an elevated conflict here?"

"Only that some want Mount Horizon to unite with other cities to do business with while others want us to remain a small town," Ronan said. "I don't think it will ever be an elevated conflict."

"Unless Scandal Town convinces Mount Horizon to act."

So they do know, Ryland thought.

"Do you think Scandal Town would intervene in something like that?" he asked.

"I think the mayor would," Connor replied. "The man is a lightless moon."

"We have to believe he has some good plans," Heather said, attempting to inject some hope into the conversation.

"Well, I think he's a fool and useless for that city he claims to run now," Connor said.

Once they finished eating, Keira, Heather, and Ronan cleared the table.

"Ryland, can I speak to you in private?" Ronan asked.

"Sure." Ryland joined him away from the table as Keira and Heather continued to clean.

"What are your intentions with my daughter?" Ronan asked.

Right to the point, Ryland thought. He had anticipated such a conversation.

"Nothing, sir. I'm only here for a military survey."

"I appreciate your honesty, but I'm not sure it's the full truth." Ronan wasn't calling Ryland a liar, just implying that Ryland may not know his own intentions. Ryland had to take his words into account. He had never noticed Keira before in all the times he had been there. "You're a good guy, and you've been around the world, I'm sure, for your service to humanity. Keira wants to leave to explore and learn, and we support her in that and will help her as we did with her brother, Reece. But I don't want you to give her false hope that she can go with you." His tone was sincere and caring, not wanting to hurt Ryland, but Ryland sensed something hidden behind it. He didn't want to read too much into it, though. These were good people, and he wanted to give them the benefit of the doubt.

"No, sir. The Circle of Generals pick people. She will not be able to come with me, and I will make that plain to her." *And to me,* he added in his mind. Then why was he training her?

"Good man. Thank you." Ronan put a firm hand on Ryland's shoulder.

Keira came out from the bathroom and saw her dad talking to Ryland, away from everyone else.

"Dad, what are you doing?"

"Nothing, sweetie." Ronan smiled as he and Ryland returned to the table.

Keira grimaced and rolled her eyes, knowing full well what had just happened.

■

After cleaning up the dishes, Ryland and Keira went for a walk. Ronan made eye contact with Ryland on the way out, as if Ryland needed a reminder of what they had talked about.

"Hey, about our training session," Ryland said. "I was being tough on you to teach you a lesson. I just... the hard lessons require the person to be *broken*." He looked at Keira to ensure she understood.

"I get it," she replied, a catch in her voice. "I won't forget the lesson." It sounded like she regretted it, which would be his fault.

As they walked in silence, Ryland wondered why he had decided to teach her that lesson. He didn't need to. The Sentry program never did. They taught agents to be in control even when they couldn't control every variable. So why had he taught Keira differently? And why was he training her at all? Furthermore, why was she willing to be trained? She was friendly and welcoming, but did she really want what Ryland was offering, or was she only being nice? Was it he who had misjudged the situation?

"When I leave here, it'll be for a change, and hopefully to make a change," she said, breaking the silence. "The things that are done here aren't meaningful. And the Blood's Shadow is out there with the augmented animals and people who need help. I just want to help, to make a difference." She looked at the sky.

That sounds so much like Nat, he thought.

"Well," Ryland said, "I can train you for that, or at least show you how to train yourself."

"Great!" her voice rose with excitement. By then they had made their way around the town's central fountain and gardens, where they saw some kids bullying another.

"Hey!" Ryland yelled. "Leave that kid alone," he strode up to the kids, "You want to progress in life? Then challenge yourself, bully someone bigger, stronger, smarter than you. Or you can continue to degrade yourselves and this kid will surpass you in success."

"Yeah, whatever," the one kid said, and they all ran off.

"Thank you, sir," the bullied kid said. "You think that's true about me surpassing them?"

"If you stay strong and don't let them get to you, yes. And if you keep challenging yourself, but I don't mean bullying older people," Ryland replied kneeling down beside the kid. He must have been twelve years old. "Now go home, it's a bit late for you." The kid ran off. Ryland stood up as the child ran home.

"How do you do that?" Keira asked.

"Do what?" Ryland asked. They continued to walk in the shadowy street, now heading back to Keira's home.

"Talk like that? With such..." she searched for the right word. "Inspiration."

"I guess I get it from the book I have. It's filled with words of proverbs," Ryland stated.

"What's the book?" Keira asked.

"A collection of books written thousands of years ago, the history of God," Ryland said. "It is missing the cover, so I don't really know the name. It talks a lot about community, and I am not too good at listening to that advice. I sit back and watch people, listening to their situations, thinking of what could be taken from the book. So when there are opportunities to speak, I have worked through it in my head," He had always travelled alone, enjoying it but wishing for community all the same.

"Oh, I see. A collection, eh?" Keira sounded interesting.

"Five thousand years ago a man wrote the first five books. The rest were written in different times after that."

"Wow, that's insane," Keira said. With the war just a century before, where the world almost ended, it was difficult to think of how old the world was.

They were just about to Keira's home when Keira said, "I'm sorry about my dad." Ryland didn't expect it.

"Oh, it's okay. He was just protecting you."

"He's so embarrassing."

"Don't worry about it. It might be awkward, but I respect him for doing it."

"What did he say?" she asked.

"He just doesn't want you to get any false hopes about leaving home just yet," he said. The streetlights were turning on as the sun went down, creating red and orange in the sky like a pumpkin had been splattered on a wall. The air was also getting cooler.

Keira was silent for a moment, thinking. Her dad didn't want her to have false hopes?

"I'll be leaving soon to survey other cities and stuff like that. You won't be able to come."

Was that too much?

"I don't want to leave with you. It's your job. Even though I'm used to people around here helping no matter what the job is, I know I can't help you with yours." She looked away. "I'll leave when I'm ready. Soon."

He nodded. "Your father just wanted to make sure you knew that."

"I don't need reminding of that. They remind me often enough. Void!"

"I'm sorry. I didn't know."

"I'm my own woman, and I'm not in love with you or anything, so just leave it alone. Goodnight."

She stormed to her house, leaving Ryland in a cold breeze that wasn't just from the moving air.

SEVENTEEN

A CHILL CUT through the sweaters of the two hunters as they hid up in the trees, waiting for their prey to appear. The cold air reminded Ryland of when Keira's father talked to him five nights earlier.

They had been perched up there for a while, waiting for the small beast to appear. Ryland always enjoyed waiting for his prey. That stage of the hunt was usually quiet and peaceful, giving Ryland time to think about his travels, the family he had left behind, including Natalie, and the family that he had gained, Keira. She had stuck around longer than anyone else.

Am I just an adventure to her? Even if I am, I have to leave at some point.

"You've never mentioned your family. Where are they?" Keira asked in a projected whisper. They were in separate trees but could still see and hear each other.

"I lost my father when I was eight," Ryland replied, not looking at her. "He fell off a cliff to save me from falling." Ryland had been chasing a lizard on the rocks. When it went to the vertical side of the rock face, Ryland went to follow. "My mother stopped taking care of us after that, and my sister and I got put into foster care." He could tell Keira didn't know what to say in reply. *Am I emotionless because of that?* Ryland wondered. *I'm content wherever I am, but I don't let myself get attached to anything or anyone.* He looked up to Keira in the other tree. *I don't want to get close to her, but she's so strong, so much like Nat. Did I fail you, Nat?*

"I'm so sorry," Keira said.

"Thank you," he replied.

Just then the scrapper walked into the view of Keira, whose tree was closest to the trap. Scrappers used to be badgers, but now they had tough black skin and more strength, just like other animals from the augmentations that went wrong. The animals got loose and reproduced and were now part of nature. The government said they wanted them dead, but they weren't doing anything globally about it. Ryland hunted them as a test of his abilities. He also enjoyed the challenge. Other forest dwellers were once tigers. Through the augmentations, they grew horns, and once they escaped, they took a liking to forested areas.

Ryland had laid an electrical wire between two trees with some food on either side. The scrapper ate the food on its side and then sniffed in search for more. Once it got close to the wire, it stopped and sniffed it. Somehow it had seen the wire, even though it was thin and clear and hard to see at many angles. Ryland had never seen an animal find it before.

The scrapper walked alongside it to the tree where it was attached. Keira shot an arrow, which hit the scrapper in the shoulder. The creature yelped, snapping the arrow in two as it tried to escape. Luckily, Ryland had laid another trap. The scrapper tripped it, triggering a small concussive blast. The animal fell over in a daze, and Ryland threw a knife into its eye. The animal slumped over, dead.

"You were too ambitious," Ryland said as they skinned the animal.

"Did you set a second trap because you knew I would screw up?" Keira asked.

"I set up another trap because these animals are smart and difficult to hunt," Ryland said.

Keira took a deep breath and then nodded. "Right. Okay, I'll be more patient next time."

A beeping sound went off, and Ryland checked his phone.

"What was that?" Keira asked.

"A page from the Circle of Generals. A Blood's Shadow member was reported near here." In truth, it wasn't a Blood's Shadow member. It was a Venusian.

I won't be able to get her away in time, he thought. Ryland's heart started pounding and sweat accumulated on his palms. He couldn't avoid it. He had to respond now. *She might be ready combat wise, but what will her reaction be?* This was why Ryland preferred to work on his own. Nat was a fellow agent, but now he was putting a civilian at risk, risk of harm and of finding out about the aliens' presence on Earth.

He reached into his pocket and squeezed the cross connected to a necklace. The cross had a metal casing but was made of wood. As he felt the grooves, he remembered Nat.

"Do you think it could be the same one we saw when we met?" Keira asked, reminding Ryland of the being who had taken on ten men without breaking a sweat.

"Could be," he replied.

"Wait," she realized something. "You were alerted because the COG wants you to investigate or eliminate it, right?"

"Yes," Ryland said.

"That thing took out ten men easily."

"I knew where those men came from. They weren't fighters." *They were rebels with ambition,* he thought.

"You're not going to fight him alone, are you?" Keira asked.

He hesitated, and he knew she saw it, which meant she would not go home.

"I'll let you know what to do," Ryland said, trying to hide his hesitation. He couldn't waste any more time. The satellite could lose it.

The creature was soon within a hundred metres of them. The forest was thick, providing lots of cover. Ryland ran several scenarios through his mind, trying to think of what to do. Maybe he should have ditched Keira, left her behind, but she was with him now, so he had to keep her from the Venusian but still use her.

She might freeze, he thought. *But if she does, it won't be for long. She's tough and well-trained.*

Thoughts of the Venusian attacking her went through Ryland's head. Every scenario had Ryland between the alien and her so he could stop it from getting to her.

Once they got to a small clearing, they saw the Venusian. Ryland wondered how long it would take Keira to realize it wasn't a Blood's Shadow and that the Blood's Shadow was a lie. He whispered for her to stay behind him.

"What are you doing here?" Ryland asked, wondering if the alien would allow Keira to hear its voice in her mind too.

Oh, just visiting, the alien replied.

"You can't be here. You're trespassing," Ryland replied, knowing the Venusian was already well aware of that fact.

You know you humans are too—

"Secretive? Yeah, the last guy told me that too."

■

Keira frowned in confusion. The creature had no mouth, eyes, or ears. How was Ryland communicating with it? *Blood's Shadow. It's real,* she thought. *Why is Ryland asking why it's here? It lives here, doesn't it?* Her thoughts were all over the place. *Ryland is military. He protects civilians. And this thing is the same as the one we saw in the forest. Or do they all look similar?* Keira had only seen the other one from afar.

"Maybe, but I'm not the one to decide that and disobey my superiors."

How is he talking to it? Keira wondered. *What is it, anyway?*

"Everyone must submit to the governing authorities, for there is no authority except from God," Ryland replied.

Keira looked at him, wondering about what he meant. *The sun? No, Ryland believes in another god.*

"I follow them but know there is one above all that has everything in his control," Ryland said. "Until they do something that goes against my God, I see no problem with keeping you from trespassing and threatening anyone."

Trespassing? How is this thing trespassing? Keira wondered. *Are there certain areas where it's allowed?*

Well, you'll have to kill me to keep me from trespassing.

"So be it. Those are my orders," Ryland replied.

I don't see how you could kill me.

"So you're not going to leave?" Ryland asked, giving the alien one last chance to change his mind.

Um... no.

The alien launched himself at Ryland, but he sidestepped it, dodging a punch. Ryland intertwined his leg with the alien's and threw him backwards, but Ryland was pulled along with him. The two of them exchanged punches and kicks, moving like water. Then the alien lunged at Ryland, striking a tree instead and cracking it.

Keira raised her assault rifle and shot the alien. The bullet struck his shoulder, drawing blood that dripped onto a leaf, the droplets coalescing into a single dark blob.

The Venusian lunged at her, but Ryland tackled him to the ground, then swung his wrist blade, just skimming the alien's neck. As the Venusian threw Ryland off, blood oozed from the alien's neck and down his shoulder. It was much darker than human blood.

Keira shot at the alien again but this time he stopped the bullet with telekinetic power. She looked puzzled at the floating bullet. As Keira kept shooting, Ryland wondered how much the Venusian had to concentrate to stop the bullets. If Keira was shooting and Ryland threw a knife from a different direction, would the alien be able to stop the knife too?

Keira was to the right of Ryland, who was right in front of the alien. He considered rolling to his right, but he wanted to stay close to Keira. Deciding to remove the immediate threat, the Venusian dove at Keira. Ryland leaped in to stop the alien, but he was immobilized by some sort of invisible force.

At the last second, Keira dove behind Ryland, and the Venusian missed her and rolled onto the ground where she had been standing. Ryland shot three bullets from his pistol, but the Venusian stopped all of them. Then Ryland thrust his wrist blade at the Venusian's matte-black face. The alien sidestepped it and pushed Ryland's hand away. Ryland swung his pistol up and fired, but he was blown back by an invisible wall. Though maintaining his balance, he slid back a few feet.

Keira had a clear shot and fired again, not knowing what else to do.

What is this thing? she wondered. *How does it stop bullets?*

Her muscles froze up, and she couldn't move. Was that thing doing it? Was it controlling her? Or was she just paralyzed with fear?

All she could do was watch and wait for an opening when Ryland wasn't in hand-to-hand combat with it, staying behind him the entire time.

How can an augmented human have telekinesis? Augmentation is only for speed and strength, isn't it? Keira could not make sense of what she was seeing. The alien was fast and strong, but Ryland matched it. *Ryland isn't augmented, is he? If they're both augmented, Ryland would have telekinesis, wouldn't he?* She watched as Ryland and his opponent exchanged punches and kicks, pushing each other. Either they were both augmented or neither of them was. *If the Blood's Shadow isn't augmented, then what is it?*

Ryland lunged forward, kneeing the alien in the chest, but he was slowed by the Venusian's hands. Ryland went to punch the alien in the neck but was blocked. The alien thrust his right arm at Ryland's stomach, but he deflected it. Ryland went to throw a punch but then opened his palm at the last second, extending his wrist blade. The blade cut the alien's hand, which he had raised to block the blow. Ryland went to punch its stomach, but the Venusian blocked him with his right hand. Ryland swung his right hand down, cutting the Venusian's hand again, causing him to flinch in pain. Weakness, even if only a little, coursed through the alien's body, allowing Ryland to push its arm back and sink his blade into the Venusian's shoulder. The alien grabbed his arm with both hands, but Ryland spun, sliding his hand out of the alien's grip due to all the blood. Ryland pulled his knife out and tried to slice the Venusian's neck, but the alien dodged.

Keira shot a burst at the alien. The Venusian pushed Ryland away and then stumbled, leaving a skid mark in the dirt. He turned to face Keira, her bullets hanging in midair between them. Seizing on the distraction, Ryland jumped on him.

As the faceless being looked at Keira, she realized it could not be from Earth. *An alien?* Fear spread through her body, not because it was coming after her but because the universe had just gotten much more crowded.

Ryland's killing blow missed, and now it was just Keira and the Venusian. The creature jumped, using a telekinetic push. Ryland tried to tackle the Venusian but was only able to grab its ankle. Keira rolled to her right, and the alien and Ryland slammed into the ground.

Ryland launched forward from a push-up position, and the alien rolled over in time to meet Ryland face-to-face. Ryland swung his fist, just missing the Venusian's head. The alien punched Ryland, who absorbed the blow and caused the Venusian to roll onto its bad shoulder. Ryland stabbed the black-skinned space-traveller once again with his wrist blade. The alien rolled onto his back, clumps of dirt stuck to the blood on his shoulder and blood smeared on the grass as if it were a trade.

"Do you want the same offer I gave the last alien?" Ryland asked. "I left him to go back to his ship."

You might not like that when he comes back, the Venusian replied. Fear entered Ryland's thoughts and then grew, his own emotions adding to it. *If he didn't show you, I did. We have telekinetic powers. If we train enough, we can do anything with it.*

"We've known that since the beginning," Ryland replied. "And you're right." Before the alien could reply, Ryland raised his pistol and fired. With no more energy to stop the bullet, it entered and then exited the Venusian's head. His body went limp, and he fell, blood oozing from his many wounds.

Ryland ordered a pickup and then knelt in front of the alien's body. He closed his eyes and slowed his breathing. *So, the alien chose to come back for revenge.* Now he would need help more than ever. The clearing was silent as Ryland prayed. Then he stood up to wait for the helicopter with Keira.

"The Blood's Shadow are aliens?" she asked.

Ryland exhaled and nodded. "I'm part of a government group that keeps extraterrestrial business a secret. So far there have only been aliens from Venus, creatures whom you know as the Blood's Shadow." He didn't care to keep it a secret anymore. "We started out as a first-response team for the Circle of Generals, but then the Venusians showed up. Luckily because of their skin colour, the people gave them the name and thought they were augmented like the animals. Made it easier for us to conceal the truth."

"Who is 'we'?" she asked.

"Sentry. The program I work for."

"And the aliens?" The word felt odd on her tongue. "What do they want?"

Ryland stared at the dead trespasser. "They come here, usually one at a time, to escape from the world war on Venus. If news of them went public, it would create chaos."

"That's what the government tells you, anyway," Keira replied.

He gave her a look. "That may be true. You certainly handled it well." He pushed his thoughts about how strong she was to the back of his head.

Keira laughed. "Thanks, but I had no idea what was going on, and I could barely move. I just didn't want you to get hurt." She paused, her cheeks reddening at the admission. "So, you knew about the guy we saw in the forest with my uncle?"

"Yes. I went up to the mountain to meet that same alien and defeated him, then let him go, which was a mistake."

"You think it'll be a problem?" she asked. As the conversation continued, Keira's thoughts drifted. The Blood's Shadow wasn't real, but a greater threat was. It was the biggest secret in the world, but now that Keira knew it, she couldn't tell anyone.

"It very well could be," Ryland replied.

"Are you supposed to let them go?"

"No. We're supposed to stop them, to keep them from returning to Earth."

"So, what happens now?" she asked.

Ryland paused to ponder his reply. *She just didn't want me to get hurt? What happens now is a good question. I can't let them confine her or erase her memory. Can they even do that? Void! She has to become an agent. I've already started training her, and now she knows about the Venusians. She can't just return to her normal life. What have I done?*

Ronan's question popped into his head like a Venusian's thought: "What are your intentions with my daughter?" The thought of his lie brought an ache to his chest that made it feel like he was choking. Had he lied? Ryland didn't want another partner. Liz had told him to get a partner, and now he was about to get one.

Did I do this subconsciously to myself? The air got even colder at the thought, and now that he wasn't moving, only thinking, he felt his fingers tingle.

"I think you may be coming with me," he said.

Keira knew things weren't as boring and mundane now. *This could be my chance to make a difference, have an impact.*

"This all makes sense with what I want to do. Make a difference, help people, learn more about the Blood's Shadow and defeat them if they do harm consistently. Now I know they're bad."

"Slow down, Keira. I don't know what is going to happen for sure. I just won't let anything happen to you."

"Ryland, when you first came to Mount Horizon a few weeks ago, I was intrigued because you were an outsider, and I wanted to go... outside."

He didn't like where this was going, and yet at the same time, he did.

"I had been struggling with doing my boring jobs that barely helped anyone in my hometown, never mind the world. My brother left because he didn't agree with my parents. He left for a job that he felt he was made for, and my parents thought they needed him here."

Ryland listened intently. He didn't care where the conversation was going anymore. He wanted to know about her.

"He left anyway, and Mount Horizon is fine without him, except for people missing him. I believe I have a job or a mission or whatever you want to call it outside of Mount Horizon." She spoke like it was the last time she would ever speak again or like it was the first time she could. She believed what she was saying with all her heart. "With your training, I could help you, even if my dad made you say I wouldn't."

"Keira—"

"This is what I want, Ryland."

"Okay, but we shouldn't disobey your parents."

"But I—"

He held up his hand to stop her. "I'm not finished yet. The Sentry program is a secret, so we can't even tell your parents if you become an agent, and there will be a cover job, like my surveying. All I'm saying is we need to honour your parents in your decision."

"Sounds good."

She's strong, Ryland thought with admiration. *And she knows who she is, a combination that's hard to find.*

"Ryland." She met his gaze. "I want this." Her voice was soft, and it was like the words pulled her closer, her brown eyes glossy and her pupils dilated. He leaned in as well. Her lips touched his and pressed closer. His eyes closed, his senses were aflame. He hadn't felt this since Nat.

Nat. He pulled away.

"I can't do this," he said. "I... I know I may seem like the older, more experienced guy who knows about the outside world, and you're the girl who wants to know more and explore." He turned and flattened his facial hair. "But I know my corruption, and I can't live with the potential of hurting you."

"Corruption?" Keira had no idea what he meant.

"We can be partners, but I can't... we can't..." He paused at the sound of a helicopter approaching.

"Ryland, I don't just want this because you're an agent." In truth, now that she knew he was an agent in a program designed to keep humanity safe, it may have been why she was so intrigued by him.

"An agent of change that you want to be," Ryland said. "Sorry, that wasn't what I meant to say. You don't need me to be an agent of change." The helicopter was just above them now, descending, so he had to raise his voice. "I just don't want to change you for the worse, to hurt you." Keira stood there in silence not knowing what to say. "Let's just focus on what is going to happen now with you and the Sentry program, okay?"

"Okay, I'm sorry," Keira replied.

When the helicopter landed, the pilots and soldiers picked up the alien's body and then talked to Ryland alone about Keira. They threatened to hold her in custody.

"She hasn't done anything wrong," Ryland said.

"Doesn't matter," the soldier replied. "She saw the secret you were meant to keep." He turned to Keira. "Ma'am, you need to come with us."

"She's not going anywhere without me." Ryland stepped in between her and the soldier.

"Agent, stand down," a soldier said. "This is above you."

"Then take it up the food chain, soldier," Ryland said.

"Void." The soldier sighed and then called the HQ.

As she waited for them to determine her fate, Keira felt empty, scared, and alone, even though Ryland had stepped in to protect her. With the helicopter roaring, she couldn't hear what Ryland was saying into his headset. She could only see his lips moving.

Ryland called a soldier over and handed him the headset. Then he waved Keira over, and they both climbed into the helicopter.

As it took off, Ryland didn't know what to expect. This wasn't her fault; it was his. He wasn't going to leave her to go up against the agency alone. He had trained her for the last few months, and now she was his responsibility.

■

"Why did you show me the alien?" Keira asked. It felt like she was in huge trouble. This was the most powerful group in the world, and Keira was about to confront them because she had seen a secret that only a handful of people knew, a secret that was dangerous to everyone.

"I... I thought you were ready." He didn't look her in the eye, probably because he was scared too.

"You thought I was ready to fight an alien that I didn't even know existed?" She reminded herself that this was probably a big situation for Ryland too. "You could have told me you had an emergency call from the Circle of Generals. I would have been curious, but I would have listened."

Ryland sat in silence for a minute, looking to the floor as he worked out his thoughts.

"You know how I told you about the book I'm reading and how it talks about community?" Keira nodded. "I'm bad at that part, but the bigger part of the book is about how the world was cursed, but the Creator came and saved it, allowing anyone to choose if they want to be healed from the curse. I'm supposed to tell everyone about the curse and salvation. But that's hard to do without community."

Keira was shocked. Ryland was serious. He believed and yet he struggled with it. Keira had always struggled with the idea of the sun as god. She never felt it was helping or protecting her, even though her life was great—boring, but with no real daily struggles.

"Is the world all saved now?" she asked. She had never heard of anything like this before. If it was true, it didn't seem to be very evident.

"No," Ryland replied. "We're still cursed and getting further from fighting the war."

"The world war?"

"No, that was a physical war. This is a spiritual war."

"Why would someone choose not to be saved?" Keira asked.

"The curse is in our nature," Ryland replied. "We choose otherwise every time we go against God."

"Landing in two minutes," the pilot said, causing Ryland and Keira to shift their thoughts back to the present.

The helicopter landed on the roof of a one-hundred-storey building. A man in a black suit was waiting for them. He had a thick jaw that was covered by a black five o'clock shadow. His hair was short on top and the sides even shorter. The front was brushed up and to the left.

When Ryland and Keira got within earshot, the man put his arm around Ryland.

"Do you know why we don't let you guys just go around with your own agenda?" he asked.

"Because we would serve ourselves," Ryland replied.

"That's right. Unlike the agents, I get to see the big picture," the man said. "You can't just add people you like to the program. We choose specific candidates."

Ryland remained silent, his mind stuck on Keira. It had all happened so fast after not being with anyone except while on missions. He told himself he wouldn't be able to settle down like that. A married man was divided, focused on his wife, and a man with feelings for a woman was a man with marriage intentions. *Crap,* he thought, staring at his feet.

"That being said, I have watched her training and done some research on her." The man stroked his rough jaw. "And you may have found the right applicant. Like Natalie."

The man pivoted to face Ryland, gave a look that indicated he might be able to pull some strings, then called Keira over. She approached with a shy but confident posture.

"Keira, my name is Nick. I'm one of the program leaders." Keira shook his hand.

"What program is that?"

"The Sentry program. We train extraordinary candidates to keep watch across the world. At first it was for them to be first responders to human conflict, but then the aliens came."

So, they would let Keira become his partner. Ryland wasn't sure what to think of that. Could he keep his mind on his mission with Keira at his side?

Nick is right. It's like Nat, Ryland thought as he fingered the necklace in his pocket.

Ryland and Natalie had studied the animals, augmented and normal. Then, if needed, they had hunted them to see how the animals reacted to a threat as a group or alone. Now Ryland would do that with Keira.

Natalie always wanted to know more about the radiated animals. They started out as rumours, but as the radiated animals reproduced, the rumours were proving to be true.

Natalie had also taught Ryland how to tame animals, a skill that had come in handy more than once.

Oh, how I miss you, Ryland thought. *I'm so sorry.*

EIGHTEEN

"CRAZY, ISN'T IT?" Ryland said as he and Keira looked out the window of the tallest building in the world. The view was incredible. They could see all the way to the mountains of Mount Horizon to the northeast. "We need to figure out what job will be your cover." He leaned against the doorframe, his arms crossed. She continued to stare out the window, only half paying attention.

"My cover?" she asked.

"We need to tell your family and close friends you have a job in another town so you have no ties and can leave whenever needed. This doesn't mean you can't visit your family, but Mount Horizon doesn't have any jobs that require you to leave town for extended periods of time."

"Right." She pulled her gaze away from the mountains. Excitement fluttered in her stomach, but it was stifled by her fears about leaving her family.

"What are some things you're known for, personality wise?"

She looked at Ryland, giving him her full attention. It didn't look as though he was doing the same. So many things were changing so quickly. *I guess this is what I wanted*, she thought.

"Um, I like helping. I wanted to help with the fight against the Blood's Shadow."

"And you'll be doing that. The Blood's Shadow is the Venusians. We need something legitimate. I have military surveying, which allows me to move around. Fred, another agent, is part of the city council. We don't know how he does that, but he liked to be fully involved and help that way. Dom doesn't have a job because he had no ties to break." That surprised Keira.

"I want to see the world, but I also love my family. I know that isn't much help."

"No, it is," he said. "We'll find something that you will enjoy at least somewhat. I suggest a part-time job in a city to the east. Your brother is to the west, correct?"

"Yeah, last we heard." Keira would love to see him. Maybe she could now.

"That's why I want you to go to the east. I don't want you running into him."

Keira's heart stopped.

"That said, you can now go out and find him whenever you have the chance as long as you're prepared to leave on a call. We rarely know when Venusians are coming."

Keira let out the breath she had been holding.

"How will I travel?" she asked.

"You will get new equipment. We don't get paid to do what we do. The Circle of Generals just gives us what we need. Although you will get a small amount when needed so it looks like you have money."

"So everything is handed to me now?" It felt good but strange. Keira had grown up with good parents showing her how to work and to find those who needed help. She would continue doing that, of course, but now she didn't have to worry about the necessities of life.

"Everything you need will be given to you because you will be doing the hardest job in the world: protecting humanity from invaders that you don't know are coming and keeping it a secret from everyone you know."

Keira thought about the weight of it all. The secrecy and the responsibility of seeking and killing Venusians was overwhelming.

"I think I know just the job for you," Ryland said. "Don't worry about the Venusians yet. As my apprentice, you'll gain the knowledge and skills to deal with them."

Keira felt the weight of her new responsibilities lift somewhat. "What's the job?"

"In Laketown they ship a lot of materials and food, along with messages for specific people. They always need fast, young runners. You'll get to see the world."

"That will be cool. And Laketown sounds really cool." She had heard about Laketown and its different environments.

"Do you like boats?"

"I'm not sure. Never been on one." The only water near Mount Horizon was the spring at the base of the mountains and the river that led to the lake on the northwest side of the mountains. She had never floated on any of them.

"My guess is you'll enjoy the new experience." Ryland seemed excited about the situation as well.

I wonder why he's excited about this, she thought. *The boats, Laketown, a new experience, or having me as his apprentice?*

∎

This was going to be the hardest thing Keira had ever done. She didn't have much to pack, but she was leaving a lot behind. Thankfully, the day was warm and bright, but the mood was a mix of clouds and sun. Keira packed her few things on her new ATV in preparation for her first trip to Laketown as part of her messenger job, which would also see her travelling with cargo ships and trucks or on her own to various townships and countries.

"This job is perfect for you," her mom said, tears threatening her eyes. "I'm so proud of you, honey." She pulled Keira in and hugged her.

"Thanks, Mom," Keira said. "I'll miss you. You've taught me so much, and I will never forget it." Keira remembered the day Reece left, although she didn't remember as much crying back then. She has always looked forward to him visiting, and now she might be able to find him.

She moved to her dad, who was standing beside her mom. They were all outside the house after helping pack Keira's ATV.

"Thanks for taking me hunting, Dad. It was the adventure I needed."

He smiled. "You're welcome. I'm glad you came. I needed someone else to keep your uncle occupied." He winked. "If you end up in the west, find your brother and say hi for us."

"Of course." Keira smiled and embraced him.

It was probably good that her uncle was in the middle of the goodbyes. He was a joker and would lighten the mood.

"Don't get lost out there, kid."

Perfect, she thought. *He always makes me laugh.*

"I won't. And you don't screw up the hunting trips." Keira smiled, a lump in her throat. She was going to miss their bickering and their deep conversations. She walked over to her best friend, Ali.

"I told you you'd leave," Ali said. She had already been crying. Keira let out a laugh that was choked by the lump in her throat. They embraced each other and continued to cry.

"Take good care of Mrs. Sheer," Keira said.

"I will. You go save the world."

Keira smiled, then hugged her friend again. *You have no idea,* she thought.

Keira turned and saw one more person standing apart from the group.

"I didn't think you would actually leave," Dylan said as she approached him.

"Then you don't really know me," Keira said, wiping her eyes. She wasn't sure she even believed that statement. The rest of her family and Ali gave them some space.

"So, you chose Ryland," he said.

"I didn't choose anyone. I'm going because there's more out there and I want to experience it. Ryland found a starting point for me."

"Keira, I just thought you... that you'd stay with me. Here." He looked at the ground.

"I'm sorry, Dylan. Your thing is here, to fix things in Mount Horizon. I want to help on a bigger scale. Maybe this messenger job will let me find ways to do that in more than one place."

"What about us?" Dylan asked, looking up at her.

"We'll have to move on. I think there's more to a relationship than what we had. And now we both can find that." Keira stepped back, choosing not to hug him. "Goodbye, Dylan."

Keira went to her ATV, then looked back at everyone and waved. *I can't believe I'm an agent fighting secret aliens.* The idea made her head spin. She was driving out to another town to cut ties so she could go anywhere at any time to fight aliens and keep the rest of the world from learning about them. *This is insane.* Even with her current training she didn't think she could do it. After all, she had only had a few interactions with the Venusians. She wasn't ready. A memory of hunting the scrapper with Ryland returned to her. She had been too ambitious and shot too early. She had to do things differently this time. She needed to be patient and allow Ryland to train her. She took a deep breath and then relaxed.

NINETEEN

"KEIRA, THERE IS a series of faces in front of you. You're to order them from least to greatest threat," Nick said as he walked the back of the room. It was empty except the two of them, a table in the centre, and some chairs beside a window overlooking another massive empty room. Keira faced the pictures of five faces. One was neutral and bland with no expression. The next had flexed muscles, teeth showing, and fire in the eyes. The third was timid, eyes wide open, eyebrows raised, and full of fear. The fourth face had its lips pressed into a thin line, its eyebrows angled down, and its eyes squinted. The last face was smiling.

Keira ordered them from smiling to timid, neutral, to the thin-lined mouth to clenched teeth anger.

"Good, but the timid face should be after the neutral face. Even if someone is scared, they can still be a threat. Think of a scared animal that's been cornered; it could lash out at any moment. You have to give them space."

They conducted other tests regarding threat analysis and mental capability, memory, spatial awareness, and spatial memory, which Keira assumed was for any combat situation and any time she walked into a new location. Knowing her surroundings could be the difference between escape or capture.

"Alright, this is the physical aspect of the testing," Nick said as he stood with Keira in front of a set of double doors. "We call these two levels the warehouse. There will be four men in the warehouse dressed in red robes. One is dressed in a robe that's slightly different from the others. You need to find and capture him."

The doors opened, and Nick motioned her forward.

The first floor had multiple rooms on either side. Keira walked down the middle, peeking into each room as she passed. Most of the rooms were white. The rooms to her left had light seeping in through windows. Keira was amazed that the entire setup was inside headquarters. She entered a larger room that extended the width of the entire floor. A few people were walking around in white lab coats, seemingly hard at work. Some of them were working at computers, others walking back and forth to desks. One of them was talking about the Venusians and human biology as he sat at a computer with a coworker. The one talking pointed at the screen with two diagrams on it.

When Keira got to the end of the room, she saw red through the window of a small door. She opened the door, feeling the urge to run after the man, then realized that might cause chaos.

The man in the red robe was heading up a set of stairs at the end of the floor. She followed, then realized there were four men in red, and more could be down there. She turned to look at the rooms she already passed. People milled about as if doing everyday work, which might have been true.

When she got upstairs, the floor was dark hardwood, and a wooden desk sat in the middle of the floor. More people were walking around, but none of them were wearing lab coats. More rooms were on either side of the room. It reminded Keira of a bank in a major city, but with fewer windows and more walls.

Where did the man in red go?

Keira stopped and looked around, then continued to walk through the dark section.

As people's voices rang off the walls and high ceilings, she thought she heard someone say Ryland's name. She looked toward the voice but didn't see anything out of the ordinary.

When Keira reached the end of the room, she walked through a set of double doors. That section had light brown walls with dark tile floors. Keira saw two men in red. Her heart jumped, but she stayed still since the shades of their robes matched. They weren't the ones she was looking for. She scanned the section and saw a glimpse of red going down the stairs. Not wanting to lose him, she looked around and saw a staircase to her right. The staircase was metal, like those staircases on the outside of tall buildings in the pre-war world.

She descended one section and then stopped to scan the first floor. The walls didn't touch the ceiling, so she could see into parts of every room. She looked toward the far wall and saw the man in red walk out. His robe was the same shade as the others upstairs. Where was the odd man out?

Keira scanned the rest of the rooms. Then she spotted him; he was in one of the rooms far to her left.

As soon as she realized who her target was, the men in red from upstairs dropped to the platform on which she was standing. She turned and looked at them. Were they going to try to stop her now?

She went to continue down the stairs when a hand dropped onto her shoulder and pulled her back.

Nope!

Keira smacked the hand off her shoulder and jumped over the stair railing. She landed on the wall dividing two of the rooms. Her balance wasn't perfect, and the wall wasn't strong enough for her weight. It wobbled, and her legs collapsed under her. She fell to the floor with a thud. The two men followed, and the man to her right ran toward her. She stood up, then made sure the workers in white lab coats in the room were unharmed.

She ran out of the room into the main hallway. There was one more room between her and the room where her target was. A man in red was running with her on the window side above the short walls. How was he maintaining his balance? One man was behind her, and the last was to her right on the floor. She looked at her target and found he was looking back at her. With two more strides, she was in her target's room. He had to run to the far side to escape.

Her target was just exiting the room when Keira heard thuds behind her that signified the men in red landing in the room. Her target stepped back into the room and then ran for the stairs. She gave chase, though she knew the man in the hallway would be at the door soon. She hit the doorframe with her left hand and foot, causing her to spin. Then she stuck her left foot out to kick the third man in red. He was right where she thought he would be, but he dodged the kick. Fast reflexes.

Keira ran in the opposite direction of her target, racing down the hallway and dodging a few people walking across it. She leaped up and ran across the top of the walls, using only load-bearing corners, then climbed over the stair railing. She entered the upper sections, which had brown walls and dark tiles. She peered into the bank-like section, looking toward the stairs for her target. He would have gotten up the stairs before she did. Did he go back downstairs? She didn't have time to think; she had the other men chasing her.

She walked into the bank-like section and then went toward the stairs. Her target, if he was there, would be in one of the farthest rooms. When she got halfway there, she climbed the walls again and found her target in the far corner of the room closest to the stairs.

The men in red reached the top of the stairs, so Keira jumped into the room. While she was in the air, her target saw her. She landed, cutting off his escape.

Then a thought occurred to her: what did capture mean? Touching him? Knocking him out? Escorting him?

Deciding to go with the first, she lunged forward, extending her arm at the last second to grab him while waiting for a twist or a punch. Instead, there was nothing, and the men in red stopped in their tracks.

"Well done, Keira," Nick said over the public address system. "Come back to the start."

"I can tell Ryland trained you," Nick said once they were back in the room where she had done her first tests. "Now, what colour was the first room where you found your target?"

"Um..." Keira thought back to seeing her target. She was up on the staircase on the first floor. Most of the rooms were white, but some were different.

"Tan?"

"Are you asking or telling?"

"Telling," she replied. "I'm just not sure. It all happened fast."

"Correct."

Keira hadn't even known that she noticed.

"The mental tests and this physical test correlate. You use your brain while fighting and chasing. It's not just physical. You will train to focus more on multiple things. Did you hear any conversations that you can recall?"

Keira thought back through the test. "Someone was talking about Venusian biology compared to a human," she said. "Something about Sentinel and Ryland."

"Close. Sentinel is Agent Ryland's code name."

Keira nodded in understanding.

"Since you're now a full-fledged agent, I will tell you a bit more about the program. There is, of course, a protocol for if a civilian saw a Venusian. Why Ryland didn't follow it, I don't know."

"What's the protocol?" Keira asked.

"We'll get to that. First, the purpose of this program is to serve and protect. We watch over civilians and monitor threats. The Circle of Generals is our governing body, and we work for them. The Circle of Generals is everywhere. The cities have mayors, but the overall rulers are the Circle of Generals. Most people don't know who they are, what they're like, or what they look like. Only major cities may have some direct contact with them. Some people complain about them, but they have no reason to. They complain about the idea of having five people ruling the world together."

The idea of them all being military generals scared Keira. They knew war, and they had the equipment and the power to do it.

"The main goal is to keep chaos away and to prevent people from trying to rule or from harming others. The world war happened because there were governments that wielded great power, and they wanted more. The bigger the punch, the bigger the shock wave."

"With great power comes great responsibility," Keira said, nodding in understanding.

"Oh, that's good," Nick said. "Where did you hear that?"

She shrugged. "It's something my family told me. My whole city says it."

"Cool," he said, then returned to his point. "Obviously, the Venusians are a form of chaos. They show up and threaten civilians in order to get away from the issues on their planet. They come here and create aggression within the human race. So we find them and eliminate them as fast as we can."

TWENTY

"DAD, I THINK I need to leave school," Anton said as he walked into his house from the cold outdoors. They had been talking about Anton's schooling for years, but over the last few months, the conversation had become more frequent. He was too smart for the subjects taught at school. His parents didn't understand where he got it from. Anton was more like his uncle than either of his parents.

"Why are you bringing this up now?" his father asked. His parents were very respectful about his arguments and his interests, even if they didn't understand them. "You're about to go into secondary school, where the classes will be more informative." His father was cleaning up after cutting firewood, which he used himself and sold to their neighbours.

"I know," Anton said. "But I want to get to the next part of life." His father raised his eyebrow at that. "I want to move on. Make changes to the world."

"You can make changes in your community," his father said. "You rarely work around town because you're too busy with your computing."

"But I can do more than just in my town."

"Sometimes you have to start in the small places before going to the bigger changes," his father said.

"But if I'm meant for bigger things…"

"Then you can start by helping your community and then later you'll get to the bigger goal. You haven't had a job, and it's time you get one."

"I don't want a job." This was not going how Anton thought it would.

"You need a job, Anton. You've barely made a change in your own town because of school and your computing. You spend most days in your room. You can quit school, but you will get a job."

"I—uh, what? I can quit?" Anton didn't think the conversation would end like that.

■

The next day Anton's step was light as he went out looking for a job, the weight of school lifted off him. As he rounded a corner that he had walked hundreds of times, the grass flattened by all those who had walked that path, he saw the playground where he had always gone with his friends.

I remember playing all sorts of games on that playground, he thought. *All those games with all those friends. Aleka, Luka, Yuri, Ivan. I don't see them much anymore. And I won't if I quit school now.*

They kept me active. They were the friends to go out with, but I don't go out anymore, with anyone. I want to. They are my friends, and I want to play sports and explore, but I'm so close to finishing my AI.

"Hey, buddy," Luka said from behind him.

"Hey," Anton said as he turned toward him, his surprise showing.

"Where you going?"

"I'm looking for a job," Anton said, holding his fist out so Luka would bump knuckles with him. "My dad is letting me quit school." He could barely hold in his excitement.

"Really?" Luka exclaimed. "I wonder if I can get out of it too."

"Probably." Luka didn't seem to be as tied down as Anton, although Anton didn't see being tied down as such a bad thing. He respected his parents. "Where are you going right now?"

"I'm heading to my grandparents to help around the house," Luka said. "Is getting a job part of you quitting school?" Luka asked as he walked alongside his friend.

Anton wondered if they would have been friends if one of them wasn't as smart as they were. "It is," he replied. He wasn't sure how he felt about getting a job. All he knew was that he was free from school.

"Maybe I can use that as a reason to leave as well," Luka said.

"Maybe we can get a job at the same place," Anton said, and they both laughed.

After walking in silence for a while, Anton looked at his friend. "Hey, I had some ideas I need to go over with you."

"About what?"

"My AI." Anton always went to Luka since he was the only one, other than Anton's uncle, who could talk on his level about his AI. Luka was researching his own projects.

"But of course," Luka said with a smirk.

"Can you put a biological chip into my AI?"

"What? What does that mean?"

"Computers break on their own," Anton said. "If we could put a biological component into a computer, my AI could grow and live longer. Adapt, even."

"Okay. But I don't see how that's possible," Luka replied. This was all new to each of them. They weren't sure if the pre-war world had even done it. They weren't sure if it could be done at all. "I'm also not sure you would want an AI adapting."

■

Once Anton got back home from talking to people around town, he went straight to his father. "Dad, can I talk to you?"

"Of course, son."

"I don't know what to do."

"About what?"

"I miss my friends. I want to go out with them to play and explore, but I'm so close to finishing my AI."

"You're growing up so fast, and this is part of life. Work, priorities, they all change your friend group, and your friends will go through the same thing. But right now you have to choose. Not that it's one or the other, but you can still decide to go out with them sometimes or stay home and study and build your AI. And when you get a job, you will face other decisions. As you grow older, you will need to make even more decisions."

Anton felt a weight increase on his heart. He had hoped for an answer, but it was only something everyone had to deal with. That meant Anton was going to suffer through this simple aggravation that everyone went through for the rest of his life. He went to his room to process it all.

■

Why isn't it working? Anton had just attempted to amalgamate a hacking code into his AI. His room was dark, as usual. His computer, which he had convinced his parents to buy after years of asking, was on his desk, and his room was lit by a single lamp, which helped him focus. With the light only illuminating his work, it forced him to focus on the task at hand. The code was, in a sense, an argumentative algorithm to fight against other computer programming. It seemed like a basic piece of an AI, designed to manipulate the codes and rules of computing to beat other computers. It wasn't working, though, as if it was missing a wire to complete a connection.

"Why won't it work?" he yelled, slamming his fist on the desk. He got up and headed over to Luka's.

"I, uh, I need to hack into the COG," Anton said, not wasting any time. They had gone for a walk so they had some privacy.

"What?" Luka asked.

"I can't figure this algorithm out. My AI can't figure out how to hack. I need to see if they have any clues."

"We would get in so much trouble," Luka said. "Not just with our parents but also with the generals."

"I know. I could use your help to do it without getting caught." His desperation was palpable.

"Can't you just ask your uncle?" Anton's uncle was an agent with the COG.

"He would never allow me to do it."

"So you'll hack in and get in so much trouble with your parents, uncle, and the COG? They'll kill you, Anton."

They both stopped walking, focusing on the conversation.

"I need to get into their computers!" Anton insisted.

"Anton, you need to be careful. You can do it on your own."

Anton turned away, not wanting to accept it. "I need to show my father that I meant what I said."

"What do you mean?" Luka asked.

"I told him I'm ready to move on to the next part of life."

"What does that mean?"

"I wanted out of school so I can help with the world's progression."

Luka finally understood what he was talking about. Schools always talked about the COG's goal of helping humanity to flourish, but not like in the pre-war world, which nearly ended in total destruction.

"I know how you feel," Luka said as the two young men continued their walk.

TWENTY-ONE

"HEAD TO THE east, and flank him from the northeast," Ryland said through the comms to his new partner/apprentice, Keira.

"No, he's heading to the west. If you drift to the west now, you might be able to cut him off at the forest exit," Keira said, her eyes focused on the alien trespasser.

"Then we can push him toward the mountain," Ryland replied, thinking of the environment around them.

The two continued to run in their assigned directions, closing in on their target. The forest ended and the mountain began, causing the alien to stop before a giant rock wall. The agents came out of the forest soon after, and the alien turned to face its pursuers.

Ryland made sure he was a few steps closer to the alien than Keira was. In the event their foe attacked, Ryland wanted to make sure Keira was the farthest away from danger.

The air was fresh and warm. With no breeze, it was easier to run, but it was also hot. The sun, which was now in the latter half of the sky, had barely been obscured by clouds throughout the day. They stood in the giant shadow cast by the mountain.

"I think you know the drill," Ryland said, assuming that, like the last alien he had encountered, it knew about the Venusian that Ryland had let go.

Keira hung back and watched. The protocols she had learned were pretty relaxed. As long as they got rid of the threat, they could kill it or capture it. Ryland got to know his opponent by engaging in communication. It helped in battle, but it seemed to get him in trouble. The alien relaxed its posture.

Yeah, I'm here to give a message. The alien you fought and let go is coming back in seven days with two others. They will—

"Why are you doing all this?" Keira asked, not hearing the trespasser's thoughts. Ryland had told Keira about the Venusians' ways of communication, how it could feel like their own thoughts, but there was a way to tell the difference; namely, a sudden change in their own thoughts and emotions. Most thoughts were unrelated to what was in a person's head, more random than their own brain could be. Sometimes when thinking, a person's thoughts could feel random, but they could always be traced back to the original thought process. The Venusians' communications were sudden and felt different and stronger, like the difference between a gas and a liquid.

We like your planet. It's much comfier, the alien said, communicating to both agents this time. *And the majority of those on Venus don't care how nice this planet is. They only care about the war. We can't convince them to wage war on Earth, and you won't tell people about us because you think people will panic.*

The shadow-skinned alien painted a picture in their minds. Keira saw Venus, explosions, and meetings discussing war on their planet and on Earth, then panic on earthlings' faces. Keira still hadn't gotten the translations down since she couldn't practice with Ryland or any human.

"There are millions of people on this planet," Ryland replied. "You never know how they'll react. But you don't care about that. And in regard to your message, sorry, but you won't get the 'ride home' option."

He stepped to his right to obscure the alien's view of Keira. Ryland motioned with his hand, and Keira stepped back into the forest. The shadows engulfed her, and she was gone.

The alien launched at Ryland, but he stepped back, leaning back to throw his fist into the alien's chest, lift it up, and slamming it into the ground. The alien brought its matte-black knee straight up into Ryland's head, causing him to stumble back.

The alien turned and flew at Ryland. Ryland landed on his back with his opponent on top of him. The grass was ripped from the two of them skidding across the ground, revealing dark brown dirt.

The Venusian recovered faster than Ryland did. It launched into the air and then landed on his feet, ready for another strike. His head twisted, followed by the rest of his body, from the kick that disappeared as fast as it came. To Ryland, the alien's skin felt thick and leathery.

The Venusian kicked Ryland in the stomach, doubling him over. He grabbed the alien's leg and twisted it. Then Ryland stabbed his hidden knife into the back of the alien's knee. Dark red blood oozed out.

With its knee on the ground as a pivot point, the Venusian wrapped its other leg around Ryland's head, tossing him to the ground.

They both got up, with space between them. Ryland's neck ached, and his head wound was pounding. He took a deep breath to concentrate and was about to make the first move when he was knocked over by a rock the size of his head.

The alien didn't move. Ryland didn't know where Keira was, but he hoped she was ready. He got up, but the alien grabbed his wrists. Its grip was so strong, Ryland could barely move. He attempted to reverse the technique but was met with too much resistance. He kicked the alien's wounded knee, which caused it to stumble. The Venusian released Ryland's left wrist and brought its arm under Ryland's right leg, lifting and tripping him before he could react.

Ryland tried to dropkick the alien, but his foot struck only air. Then the alien rolled on top of him, folding his body in half and picking him up, just to slam him to the ground again. Ryland had seen that move in training, and he wondered where the Venusian had learned it.

With the air knocked from his lungs, the alien used telekinesis to pick him up. Ryland realized the alien was putting Ryland between him and Keira, using Ryland as a shield.

Void sucker!

A shot rang out, and a bullet appeared next to Ryland's left hip. The alien had seen it and stopped it with little effort.

The Venusian dropped Ryland and launched himself at Keira, who was concealed in a cluster of trees. Ryland grabbed the alien's foot just in time, slowing him down. The alien kicked Ryland's upper thigh, causing him to fall face first, but he landed on his hands and knees. Then the alien picked him up by the throat and slammed him against the mountainside.

Feeling his throat closing, Ryland lifted his knees to his chest and extended them both over his assailant's arm. Then, thrusting them down, he freed himself. He landed on his feet, only to be met with a swift elbow to his head.

Another shot rang out, but Ryland didn't hear it as well as the first because his head was still regaining its blood flow. When nothing happened, Ryland thrust his wrist blade at the alien's torso, but the Venusian caught it and punched the inside of Ryland's elbow, then twisted and threw Ryland over his shoulder.

The Venusian picked Ryland off the ground by the neck. Ryland reached for his pistol, hoping to get a shot off before the alien could stop it at such close range. His fingers grazed the pistol's grip, but he couldn't move any further, the Venusian holding his entire body in place.

Ryland's face became hot and his mouth dry as the alien cut off the flow of air and blood to his head. His head wound pulsed harder, and his vision narrowed. He tried to stay calm, but he felt panic building. He swung his legs in a vain attempt at escape, but he was too weak.

A faint explosion went off, and his body swung toward it. Ryland heard the cracking of branches and a loud thud from a tree. He tried to focus on escaping, but the Venusian tightened his grip.

Keira came from behind, attacking the Venusian in hand-to-hand combat. The alien dropped Ryland, and he gasped for air. He couldn't think straight, but he knew there was something he had to do other than breathe. Then he realized Keira was attacking his opponent on her own.

He reached for his pistol and fell onto his back, trying to find his target. Keira was moving fast and fluidly considering how little training she had had. Hoping it was enough, he pulled the trigger.

The bullet struck the alien's head, creating a small entrance wound. It slumped to the ground, lifeless.

Keira and Ryland let out a breath, and Ryland dropped his head to the ground and looked toward the sky, finally about to relax.

"That... was not... fun," Ryland said between breaths.

"Are you okay?" Keira asked as she stood over him, her face full of concern.

"Ish," Ryland replied, wobbling his hand back and forth. "I'll recover. We need to tell Nick about what it said." He wished he didn't have to, but he had screwed up, and now the first alien was coming back to kill him.

As Ryland sat up, he put his hand to his forehead, his wound pulsing with pain. Keira stared at him with concern, not knowing what to say.

"Where did you go?" Ryland asked, having been unable to concentrate in the heat of the fight.

"He kept you between us," Keira said, confirming Ryland's observation. "I almost ran in to help, but then I took a second to think."

Her training is working, he thought.

"I remembered the aliens having a telekinesis field around them, so I set up an explosive to knock a tree down, then walked farther away, hoping I was out of its sensory field, and flanked it. When I was behind the alien, I felled the tree as a distraction and then rushed in."

"I'm impressed," Ryland said. "Good thinking. Now help me up."

■

Ryland signalled the helicopter as he covered the alien's body, then prayed for the Venusian's soul, if he had one, and for the coming catastrophe that he had caused.

He walked over to a small ledge on the side of the mountain and sat down. Keira joined him, still full of adrenaline from the battle. She experienced more now that she had to confront the Venusian. Leading up to the encounter, she had thought through all the scenarios that could happen, which didn't amount to much since even most agents didn't know much about the aliens. At least she had Ryland training her. He didn't know much about the Venusians' biology, but he did know how to fight them.

"You know this is going to get worse, right?" Ryland said.

"No!" Keira replied, realizing where Ryland was going. "You're training me. I'll get stronger."

"Keira, these aliens are warriors. The Venusian we just faced almost killed me, and the alien that's coming back has been training. This is all my fault."

Why is he doubting now? she wondered. *Is it because he almost died?* It wasn't like he could just take it all back. She'd been trained as his apprentice and as an agent.

Keira looked Ryland in the eye. "I was there to help. I'm not leaving. We can clean it up together." Keira's eyes glistened with tears. Ryland didn't want her to get hurt, and she didn't want him to get hurt either. It was either they both fight or they both run. She was an agent now too. This was her job now. But she was just an apprentice, *his* apprentice. She would stay by his side unless instructed otherwise. Ryland had to finish her training soon so she could be ready for upcoming Sentry work. But in a week?

That's when Ryland saw a creature in the corner of his eye, an augmented lion. He leaned over to Keira,

"Look at that," he whispered.

"Is that..." She fell silent when she realized the lion had a companion: a lamb that walked beside it. As the two creatures disappeared around a corner, they decided to check it out while they waited for the helicopter.

When they rounded the corner of the mountain, they saw an old, massive castle. They looked at each other,

"Did you know this was here?" Ryland asked.

"No, I didn't," she replied, shaking her head.

As they made their way toward the castle, the lion and the lamb were nowhere to be seen, which made the agents cautious.

As they entered the castle, they had their rifles out. The halls were wide and tall with pillars too wide to hug. They spotted the lamb at the end of the corridor that led to the foyer. Once they entered the opening, Ryland turned to look for the lion, but it was too dark, and their flashlights revealed nothing but cracked walls, corners, and pillars.

Ryland and Keira followed the lamb, which led them down a set of stairs and then vanished.

The basement was smaller, the ceiling only ten feet high and the hallways only five feet wide. It was much cooler and darker. There was a faint light at the end of the stairway.

Once they got to the bottom of the stairs, they realized the light came from a computer. How was a computer still working there? Were people living down there?

"Keep your eyes and ears open," Ryland whispered. As he looked at the computer, Keira watched his back. She saw a dark hallway to her right. On her left was the one through which they had entered. The hallways were perpendicular from each other.

The computer was in sleep mode but still running minimum functions. Words were scrolling across the screen, talking about augmentation trials and "a potential successful trial available." It was followed by a command, "Open vault to obtain altered serum."

Ryland looked to his left and saw a locker-size vault door. He wondered how he could get into the vault. Keira looked over his shoulder at the screen,

"Serum?" she said. "I thought that was terminated years ago."

"It was five years ago." Ryland took a closer look at the screen. "The date on this message is from three years ago."

"So, either someone is still here…"

"Or this is an active AI."

"What does that mean?" she asked. "Just like a computer?"

"A computer only holds the info and waits for someone to search for what they desire. An active AI can search on its own."

"So, this AI is still working on its objective?" Keira said.

"Could be," Ryland replied. Then he saw another message: "Consult General Ambrose."

His cell phone beeped, indicating that the helicopter had arrived. Ryland said nothing about his last name or the fact that his father had been a general. Was the message actually referring to his father, or was it just a coincidence?

The two left everything as they found it, walked back to their rendezvous location, and helped the soldier load the Venusian's body into the chopper.

"We'll take things from here, agent," one of the soldiers said.

"We need a ride back to HQ," Ryland replied. "We have information that needs attention." The soldier nodded, then the four of them got into the chopper.

The flight didn't take long, with headquarters located a few kilometres southwest beyond the mountains.

Keira nudged Ryland. "Remember when you told the last alien about submitting to the authorities?"

"Yeah."

"What did you mean?"

"Any authorities that are in place are put there by God, the one who is the authority over all."

"So, you just do what they ask?"

"God put them in power for a reason and uses them in their power position. If their rules don't interfere with any of God's rules, we should listen."

"But if God put them in power, why would they go against God?"

"They are still human and do evil," Ryland replied.

"Huh. Okay."

Keira admired Ryland's integrity, but it didn't all make sense to her.

As she stared out the window, Ryland analyzed the alien's body. He saw how the bullet had entered its body. The Venusian's skin was thicker than human skin. Blood had clotted around the wound, thick and dark red, almost black. The bright red parts of its skin looked like glass. Ryland leaned forward and ran his finger over the red skin. It was hard, like a glass-and-metal alloy.

"We don't know what kind of material it is," the soldier sitting beside him said. "But it's not from Earth."

Ryland leaned back in his chair, nodding in understanding.

Then the helicopter began circling the one-hundred-storey HQ building. It looked metallic and had balconies on every third floor. The two floors between looked like one solid opaque window. The building was surrounded by forest and swamp on the north side and a small city on the east side.

When they landed, the soldiers rushed Ryland and Keira out. Then the pilot took off, another helicopter already making its approach.

Must be from another agent, Ryland thought. *Are there really that many aliens sneaking onto the planet now?*

The soldiers led the two agents into an elevator, which took them down to the seventieth floor. Once they got out, they walked down a walkway that turned three times before coming to a split.

"You two are going that way." The soldier pointed to the door to the right. Ryland looked at the giant wooden double doors, then turned back toward the soldier, but he and his companion had already gone through the left doors. Ryland and Keira looked at each other, then at the doors, and started walking.

The doors opened automatically to a large room with a black carpet that covered the entire floor. The ceiling was pure white, like the hallway. The room had to have been twenty metres wide by fifteen metres from the door to the window straight ahead, which looked out into the city below. Beyond the city was forest, and in the far distance, mountains.

The room had a large hexagonal table in the centre with chairs around it. A wooden desk sat to the far right. Beside the desk was a fireplace. It reminded Keira of her home, not the one with her parents but the one she had bought to help provide cover for her "new job." She was gone a lot more, and she couldn't tell her family, so she decided to find a place to move out. The house was close to the city's west border. Her living room had a small fireplace, which she loved. This fireplace was huge compared to hers and had a white mantel. There was a couch and two chairs in a square formation next to the fire. To the left was a small kitchen, and beyond that was an elevator. The elevator dinged, the door opened, and Nick stepped out,

"Sentinel! I hear you have some information for me," Nick said. Ryland stood straighter and saluted. Nick walked over and stuck his hand out for a handshake, not acknowledging the salute. Ryland lowered his hand and reciprocated the gesture.

"So, what's so important that it demands my attention?" Nick asked, motioning the two of them to the seats by the fire. Keira and Ryland sat on the couch while Nick took the chair across from them. Ryland leaned forward so his back didn't touch the couch.

"The alien we brought in today gave us a message. He said the first alien has been training and is coming back with two comrades. This will be out of my hands if they come. We will need the others."

"How will I know where to send reinforcements?" Nick asked. "They've obviously gotten past security."

"Can we tighten security somehow? Find some way to see their ships?"

"Not that I'm aware of," Nick replied.

"Other than that, I know they'll be coming for me," Ryland said, "though whether they come to the same location or search for me specifically, I don't know."

"You know I need more than that," Nick said, standing up and beginning to pace.

"I know, sir, which is why I came for help."

"How long do we have?" Nick asked, turning back to Ryland.

"One week, sir."

"*One week?*" Nick exclaimed.

"That's what the alien told us a few hours ago," Keira said.

Nick rubbed his hand through his stubble of a beard, then exhaled. He walked over to the table and waved to the others to join him. Nick swiped his finger across it like it was a touchscreen. It turned out the table was a computer. Nick pulled up three files with the code names Hunter, Banshee, and Jovian.

"I can bring them here and have every vehicle ready to fly. Once we know where your friends are, we can ship you all out."

The agents were all overlapped, so they had support, but now they would be spread thin. Ryland scanned through the files. He knew all three of the agents and was glad they would be coming to help.

"As for you," Nick said, looking at Keira, "you need more training."

Returning his focus to the computer table, Nick took the three files and entered some commands, and just like that, the plan was in effect.

■

Minutes later, Nick pulled Ryland aside. "I have to ask. Why did you give this alien a free ride home?"

"Once I beat him, I gave him a chance to learn from his mistakes."

"And you thought that was a good idea?" Nick asked in wonder. "It's dangerous, but I trust you, and if you saw something good in this alien, I'll stand by you. But no more decisions like that unless you clear them with me first. Got it?"

"Got it. Thank you, sir." Nick was Ryland's superior, but they were good friends and respected each other as such.

"Nick, can I ask you a question?"

"Of course."

"What do you know about the serum?"

"The serum made to augment animals?"

"Yes."

"The program was shut down five years ago when the agency broke apart. Why?"

"On our last mission, we found a deserted base. There wasn't much there, but we found plans from three years ago, not five."

"That is weird," Nick replied. "I can look into it, but right now we have bigger problems."

TWENTY-TWO

▄

THE SETTING SUN created a reddish-pink sky as cool air settled over the land. The forest on Dom's property was large and had two trails, one from his house to the nearest town, Hillside, and one that circled his house. He went for a run on the latter path.

The cool air kept Dom, code name Banshee, from overheating as he ran through the forest. He had built many obstacles and scattered them throughout the forest where he ran. Some were tall walls, and some were simple wood pallets nailed to trees, adding more exercise to his run.

He ended his run just outside of his back door. Sweat dripped down his shirtless torso. He grabbed the high bar he had made and lifted himself up, raising his chest to the bar and then lowering himself down. He added weight after a warmup, his muscles twisting and pulling against the extra burden.

The routine was second nature to Dom. He did it every morning and night except on Sundays or if he had a late night or early morning involving Venusians. He never let himself lose his fitness level or his edge in battle. The agents knew him as Banshee, and he lived up to his code name. He took pleasure in intimidating others and making his opponents lose their cool. Setting traps was part of his expertise.

After a shower Dom sat in a tree overlooking the city. The sun was closing in on the horizon, beaming the city buildings and streets from the east to Dom's right. A few cars were coming into town from the later work. They looked like ants returning to their hill.

It had been a few days since a Venusian had entered Dom's zone. *Maybe they're scared of me,* he thought, smiling. *But they wouldn't be scared of me. Most Venusians die at the hands of agents. They can't tell other Venusians to avoid a specific location. Or can they? Do they have communication with the other aliens on Venus? Maybe I'll ask that next time I get the chance.* The aliens were a tough opponent, with telekinetic powers. Dom liked it. It was one reason why he loved being an agent of the Sentry program.

Other people, civilians, just work the same job every day, never pushing their abilities, Dom thought as he watched the cars filter into the city, full of people returning from their jobs. *It's too bad they need money to live. Work is good; it keeps you busy, but it's so hard to get a job that you can enjoy.*

Apparently, things were similar before the war. There were many more jobs, but there was a surplus of humans to work, approximately eight billion. Often, even those with education could not get a job in their field of study. Now they just did the bare minimum jobs that the cities needed. The job was there because it needed to be done. *I guess it's purer this way,* he thought. *So, when am I going to get to work?*

He looked at his phone. It was military grade. Those who had phones would have called it life proof, but it wasn't a commercial product; it was a military Sentry program promise, and it could take an indirect hit from a bullet.

His phone rang. *What a coincidence!* It was from the Sentry program, but it wasn't a warning about Venusians entering Earth's atmosphere. The call came straight from headquarters.

"Hello?"

"Banshee, we need you at HQ for backup," the caller said.

"Backup?" Dom asked. They rarely called for backup. Aliens showed up without notice, and agents had to act fast, so there was rarely time to call for backup.

"We have a threat warning, and we're sending in Jovian and Hunter. We will pick you up in a few hours after Hunter."

Jovian and Hunter? Not just me? This is serious. I wonder what happened.

"Roger that. I'll be at the rendezvous."

He hung up and started to pack. He didn't need much—HQ had everything—but Dom packed his weapons and what he needed for hunting and battle.

■

Dom had been waiting at the rendezvous for twenty minutes before he heard a helicopter approaching. He guessed it would arrive in about five minutes. As the helicopter flew over the city, everyone would be watching its path. Only the COG used aircraft, and people who lived in a small town like his would wonder where the helicopter was going.

The helicopter landed five hundred metres south of the hill on which Dom lived. If it landed on his property, the townspeople would become suspicious and ask questions. Dom was already an oddity in the town: quiet, often disappearing, living outside of town. Even the mayor didn't know much about Dom. He was a strange man living on the hill, and no one really knew about him. But they did know that Dom would be there if they needed help.

As Dom approached the helicopter, it was like the air from the propellers was attempting to push him away. He liked making long trips and travelling on his own to HQ, but that would have taken seven days. There was no time for that. This was an emergency, enough to gather three agents within hours of the call.

He entered the craft and saw a fellow agent sitting in the far seat. They nodded to each other in recognition.

"You know what this is all about?" Dom asked once he got his headset on.

"Nothing yet. Told we will be briefed at HQ." The other agent, Marcus, code name Hunter, was wearing dark brown pants and a tight green shirt. His hair was short like Dom's but black, matching his beard. His eyes were a rich brown colour and full of confidence.

"What's your fastest time?" Hunter asked. He was referring to the time it took to kill a Venusian. Hunter was a lone wolf type, just like Dom.

"One minute and thirty-four seconds," Dom replied. "You?"

"One fifty-seven."

Ever since the other agents had labelled them as similar back in their training days, they had had an ongoing competition for who was the best agent.

"Hmm..." Dom said with a winning tone.

"I killed two within an hour," Hunter countered.

"Two?" Dom said. Venusians rarely travelled together.

"Would have been faster, but the second one ran."

"You're lying," Dom said.

"You'll see." Hunter turned to look out the window.

■

The helicopter took two hours to travel what would have taken Dom seven days over land. He would have preferred the seven-day journey over the helicopter ride, a long trip on the open land alone. The view from the air was spectacular, though. Looking down on the great canyon, then over the two lakes merged by a waterfall. Nightfall made the lakes look like space, shimmering in the dim light.

One time when crossing the shallow waters of the waterfall in the dry season, Dom lost his vehicle to the current. There was a small bridge-like feature that, in the dry season, as it was now, would be covered by three feet of water instead of the six feet that flowed over it during the rainy season. But the water still had a lot of power, and Dom had to jump out of his vehicle and let it go over the waterfall. He managed to get the vehicle out, and he only had to bang out a few dents. The jeep was military grade, the same as their phones, and it could take a beating, diving included. His trip was only delayed by a few hours after that, and now he used a cable to keep the jeep on track whenever he had to cross the water.

His job was all about learning. The Sentry agents had to improvise and figure out how to kill the Venusians when they showed up even though they knew nothing about them. A lot of agents died in the process, and the Sentry program was thinned out. Agents used to be paired up and closer together. Now they were scattered across the globe, often with only one per every five hundred kilometres.

So many agents dead because of those selfish aliens, Dom thought, reminded of his hatred for them.

Hunter and Dom landed on top of the one-hundred-storey HQ building and then found their way to the seventieth floor where Nick worked. Hunter agreed with Dom that the huge building attracted too much attention. It was the tallest building in the world, and they had a secret government headquarters operating out of it where aliens were being studied. Sure, the first two floors were a cover, as was the small town at its base, but it was still way too close for comfort.

The building, mainly the room where they met with Nick, had become like a second home, like the home of a distant relative whom they visited for the holidays as kids. Hunter remembered his grandmother's place when she hosted Christmas. Even though they lived in the same town, Hunter never visited her except during the holidays. It was like a small vacation in another house instead of another country.

When they opened the door, another agent was sitting in the room, code name Jovian. He stood and walked over to greet Dom and Hunter, shaking their hands and hugging them. He was a friendly, big brother type.

"How are you guys?" Jovian asked.

"Apart from the fact that I'm here on an emergency call? Pretty good," Hunter replied.

"Yeah, who needs help?" Dom asked.

"We all do," Nick replied as he exited the elevator. "A trio of Venusians are coming to wreak havoc and seek revenge. We need to stop them and hopefully without any civilians knowing."

"How do we know they're coming?" Hunter asked. They never knew when the Venusians would show up.

"Sentinel got the message after letting an alien go," Nick replied.

"So, it's Sentinel," Dom said. "He let one escape?"

"He fought the alien and then gave him a chance to live."

Dom was about to speak but Jovian stepped in. "It's just like Sentinel to show mercy."

"As a weakness," Dom said.

"Back off, Dom, he's a good agent," Hunter said. Dom was the "kill first, ask questions later" type. No mercy, no forgiveness. *Way too harsh,* Hunter thought. *Sentinel—Ryland—might be too soft but that's always been a likable trait of his. It's also why he and Nat worked so well together. Sentinel is just too hard on himself, though. He understands others and has too high standards for himself.*

"So, what's the plan?" Jovian asked.

"First," Nick said, "we have a new agent, Keira. She's currently being trained and will be on this mission alongside you. She's Sentinel's apprentice. They're downstairs right now. Let's go get them."

TWENTY-THREE
Six days before the Venusians return

RYLAND ATTACKED KEIRA, who diverted his punch, twisted, and hauled him over her shoulder. He hit the ground with a thud.

"Are you sure that isn't going to leave a bruise or anything?" Keira asked. They had been doing this for a while. Ryland wanted Keira's mind to be sharp in the art of combat. The day before, he had trained her in how to read her opponent. Then they had woken up early to practice it firsthand. The training area was a few levels down from the floor where they met Nick. It was the equivalent of two floors, with a high ceiling.

"It's fine," Ryland replied. "Okay, now the second counter."

He punched, and she dodged, intertwining her legs with his. With her hand on his chest, she slammed him to the ground again, hearing the air burst out of his lungs.

"Good," he said, gasping. "Now, there's a counter to the counter."

Of course there is, she thought.

"So, let's try it again, and I'll demonstrate."

Sure, so you can get back at me, she thought, though she knew Ryland would never do that.

This time he punched, and she dodged, but when she tried to slam him to the ground, he brought her down with him. They both got back up, and she wiped the dirt off her knees.

"As you bring me down, I can grab the back of your neck, using your energy against you," he explained. She had felt the hold on her neck, and her neck was even a bit sore from it. She knew if they continued to do it, her neck would be aching for days, like her muscles. "Let's try," Ryland said.

This time he stepped forward, she punched, and he dodged, then went to slam her to the ground. Her hands slipped from his neck, though it slowed her fall.

"Again." Something seemed off in Ryland. He was more aggressive as they sparred and yet still in control. This time she executed the move flawlessly. Maybe a little too well, as Ryland scraped his head on the ground.

"I'm so sorry," Keira said as Ryland walked away, rubbing his neck and then his forehead. Her instincts had told her to hold on as she fell. She still needed to gain better control over them.

"It's fine."

"Are you okay?" she asked. She wasn't talking about his head and neck. She was more concerned about his mood.

"I'm fine. We need to prepare you for the enemy." That was true, but that wasn't why he was so closed off. He had been training her for a while now. Keira thought back to the archery practice, the fighting in the forest, the hunting, even the control scenario where he wouldn't let her up. Even then Ryland was not as cold as he was now. Was it the kiss?

"Sentinel, Keira, come meet your team," Nick's voice said, interrupting the moment.

Keira and Ryland walked over to the side of the room, sweat glistening on their skin. The other three men were all wearing baggy clothes with knives and guns strapped to their holsters. They had come from the nearest cities, which was still a long journey, a week over land at least, to help with the situation.

The first agent was wearing dark brown pants with multiple pockets and a tight, dark green shirt. He was holding a beige hooded sweater. His hair, which was short and black, continued down the side of his face into a neatly trimmed dark beard. Around his neck was a necklace with teeth and claws hanging from it, intertwined with metal. He was the shortest of the three, and his face was defined and sculpted. His dark beard hid his jawline, and he had a soft, wide nose. He rolled his wrists like he was stretching them.

The second agent was wearing black and baggy grey jeans with a black cargo jacket. He was also wearing black-and-white gloves. His hair was blonde and buzzed to a few millimetres. He had facial hair around his mouth, which was hard to see because it was blonde on light skin. He had a strong jawline, and his nose had a rigid crease, the bridge of his nose sticking out like his cheekbones. His lips were sharp lines, and his eyebrows were darker than his hair. He looked displeased, and it intimidated Keira. He was carrying a backpack with a gun holstered on the side and a black-and-white mask.

The third agent was wearing brown pants with a golden-brown long-sleeve shirt. His hair was a little longer than the others, extending down to his shoulders in the back. It was light brown, and he had dark brown eyebrows, beneath which were piercing green eyes. He stood an inch or two taller than the second agent, who stood three or four inches taller than the first agent. The first agent had a mesomorph body type, and the other two looked like ectomorphs. All of them were built from their training, but the first was stockier than the other two.

The green-eyed man was the first to step forward and offer his hand. "Hello, my code name is Jovian, but since we're all on the same team, my real name is Fred."

"Keira," she replied, shaking his hand. Jovian stepped over to Ryland and extended his arm for a hug. Ryland was distracted, rubbing dirt off his hand. Though he accepted the hug, he appeared frustrated.

"Code name, Banshee, real name, Dominic." The code name suited him, His demeanour unsettled Keira. He took Keira's hand firmly and then did the same to Ryland, also grabbing his forearm with a firm grip. Ryland nodded in reply.

"Marcus, code name Hunter," the first agent said. He shook Keira's hand and then Ryland's hand then pulled him into a hug.

Nick led the agents to a door that led to a staircase. They went up two flights of stairs and into a room with leather couches set in a square around a table. A TV was off to the side of the couches. On the opposite side of the room was a billiards table and a small bar.

They all took a seat on the couches, and Nick opened the conversation, "so, we've all been briefed about the situation?"

"Ryland, what were you thinking, letting him go?" Dom asked.

"I gave him a second chance. I didn't think he would come back to fight," Ryland replied.

"Void, Ryland. Have you done this with all your targets?" Dom asked.

"No."

"Then why this one?"

Maybe this is why Ryland is so frustrated, Keira thought. He knew he was going to be accused because of what he had done.

"It... it was a moment of a new perspective," Ryland replied. "These things deserve to live too."

"No, they don't!" Dom said.

"If it was a human wreaking such havoc, we would put them behind bars, not kill them."

"But they aren't just wreaking havoc," Marcus said. "They're killing."

"Some, yes," Ryland said, "but they are living, conscious beings. Who are we to judge?"

"They're aliens trespassing on our planet," Dom said, his annoyance growing, "killing and destroying what we have rebuilt."

"Our orders are to stop and kill them at all costs," Ryland said. He looked at Nick, who was watching the conversation unfold. "But we barely know their story. We give them no chance to tell it, and we offer no help."

Dom threw his arms up and turned away in disgust.

"Alright, that's enough," Nick said. "Let's focus on the situation. Our first problem is locating the aliens' descent into our atmosphere."

"I may have an idea about that," Ryland said. "If we place our satellites in a way that makes it look like we're trying to detect them, we can force the aliens into the location where we want them as they try to take advantage of this 'hole' in the security."

"That might work," Fred agreed. "If they think we're looking for them, they'll avoid any chance of being detected."

"Anyone else have any other ideas?" Nick asked, surveying the group.

"So we can't detect the aliens at all?" Dom asked.

"No," Nick replied, shaking his head. "They just appear on the planet."

"Do we even know if they come in ships?" Dom asked.

"Now that I think about it, I have no idea," Fred replied, reflecting on all his encounters. The rest of the agents shook their heads, none of them having seen any extraterrestrial ships either.

"Don't we have an alien in custody?" Dom asked.

Nick checked a tablet that was sitting on the table in the middle of the couches. His finger swiped and poked a few times. "Yeah, we do. Let's go see if he can help." He stood up, as did the agents, and they all followed him out.

They took an elevator up three floors, all of them silent until Dom turned to Keira. "So, how did you get sucked into the program?" he asked. Marcus chuckled at his mention of being "sucked in."

"Ryland started training me for fun, then we both ran into an alien."

"So he couldn't take on the alien alone, eh?" Marcus asked, grinning. Ryland just gave him a look, then smirked.

"You remember who saved your butt on that north training exercise?" Ryland reminded Marcus.

"And do you remember who taught you the art of stealth?" Marcus replied.

The elevator door opened to a floor that Ryland and Keira had been on when she first met Nick. Now they went through the door that the soldiers went through. It led to a long hallway with room after room filled with medical beds and supplies. It reminded Keira of a hospital. *This building has everything,* she thought, *and we haven't even explored more than five floors.*

"Fred, you still on your city's council?" Ryland asked.

"Yeah. It's the best way to know what the city is doing."

"And they don't mind your random disappearances?" Marcus asked.

"They know I'm involved," Fred replied with a smirk.

"I can't believe you're directly a part of the city," Marcus said as they walked past dozens of doors.

Nick stopped in front of a door labelled "Interrogation Room One." He opened the door, and there in front of a table sat an alien with odd looking handcuffs that were forcing its arms to the table. It didn't even look up at him, though it couldn't really look at anything seeing as it didn't have eyes. Keira tensed when she saw it. Nick invited everyone inside and then he sat down,

"We have a few questions for you," he began. "But first, what's your name? What do they call you on your planet?" The alien didn't reply. After a few seconds Nick tried again. "Come on, we don't have to be enemies here. We're just trying to set some ground rules, species to species."

Your species is weak, the alien replied, fast and sharp, its voice in the minds of everyone in the room. Even Keira "heard" it. She almost jumped. It was odd, as if someone was yelling in her head.

"Well, we can still respect each other," Nick said. "Come on, what's your name?"

My name is Zhelm.

"Alright, Zhelm. Did I say that right?" Nick received an affirmation in his mind, so he continued. "So, Zhelm, when you come to our planet, do you travel in ships?"

As Nick waited for an answer, Keira found the silence intimidating. Was that the alien's doing, or was it just because she wasn't comfortable in the scenario?

You still don't know how we get here? Zhelm said in a mocking tone. *Yes, we use ships.*

"Do you use cloaking?" Nick asked.

No. We warp right into your atmosphere.

"Alright, that's impressive. Okay, so you warp right to us. We've been working on warp drives too."

Nick got up and walked around to Zhelm's side of the table. Ryland and the others knew that Nick was a good interrogator. The subject would think he was on their side and then he would turn. The agents wouldn't want to be under his thumb in an interrogation.

You humans are so pathet—

Zhelm was interrupted when Nick pulled out his knife and slammed it into Zhelm's thigh, right on the red part of his skin. The skin was so hard that the knife only penetrated half an inch. Everyone in the room heard Zhelm screaming in their mind. It was odd that the *scream* was only in our minds, and it was silent to the agents' ears. It was more like a pain within the brain rather than hearing.

"We have plenty of bodies we've been examining," Nick said. "You probably know what happens when I twist. It's similar to glass. It absorbs light, and if I break it, energy will be released and could start burning. But the worst part for you is the shifting of your skin. So why don't you play nice and tell me what I want? Respectfully." Nick paused for a moment, his eyes fixed on where Zhelm's eyes would have been, if he had any. "So, how exactly do you get into our atmosphere?"

We warp right into your atmosphere, about one kilometre above the planet's surface.

"And how can we detect your ships?"

You don't have the tech. But I can show you how we detect them.

They agreed not to harm Zhelm if he showed them the detection process. It turned out to be complicated and could only detect the ships after they entered normal space. Nick sent the algorithm to Sentry's scientists and mechanics to see if they could create some sort of detector. He still had more questions for Zhelm.

"How do we stop them?"

They are coming here for refuge. There are three sides in the war, the two warring sides and those who just want to get away from it. They won't stop just because you ask them to.

"And this is one of the aliens I let go, so he isn't just gonna walk away again," Ryland said.

After thanking Zhelm for his cooperation, Nick and the agents exited the interrogation room.

"Okay, we have six days to figure out how to stop the aliens or hide their existence," Nick said. "Let's talk locations. Ryland, where did you fight the alien?"

"It was on the mountains in Mount Horizon," he replied.

Keira thought back to when he said he was out the second day they met. That was probably what he was doing.

"Okay. Where could the possible landing locations be?"

"You have Mount Horizon, Scandal Town, anywhere in the grasslands, the cliffs..." Ryland counted off the places on his fingers as he listed them.

"How were you informed of the Venusian?" Fred asked.

"Headquarters. They saw him in the grasslands heading toward Mount Horizon. Liz was occupied, and I was on my way already." The Sentry program, along with the COG, had access to all the surviving satellites from the pre-war world.

"Okay, so maybe it landed in the grasslands," Nick said. "I'll get all the satellites programmed for warp detection as soon as possible. What about taking these things down?"

"Distractions," Ryland said. "They can't stop multiple things at once, especially if they're big or heavy objects."

"Getting up close and personal too," Dom added. "Just like humans, they need more time to react."

"I eliminated one without it knowing I was there," Marcus said. "I snuck up to it during a concert in the town he was approaching and stabbed it in the neck."

"Liar," Dom said.

"This is no time for legends or myths," Marcus said. "I'm not lying."

"So, they can hear?" Ryland asked. "The sound of your approach was masked by the concert?"

"No, Ryland, he's lying," Dom said. "He's just trying to one up-me."

"Not everything is about you, Dom," Fred replied. "Grenade explosions close to them seem to disorient them too."

"Whatever," Dom said, shrugging.

"So, up close and personal and distractions, fast or big," Nick said, recapping. "We have three of them coming this time. We'll need to contain them and execute them quickly. Got it?" The others nodded in agreement. They were agents, and they were prepared to improvise with every Venusian they encountered.

"Also, we have something for each of you, including Keira," Nick said.

He led them down one floor to a room with caged lockers full of weapons and armour. Nick opened four of the lockers.

"Diamond-titanium Kevlar-bonded suits," Nick said.

"How did you get them to bond?" Hunter asked.

"Melted them together and added water and xenon, which filled in the blanks as they cooled. And don't think that was the only issue. The mobile underlayer is carbon fibre reinforced with iridium. The iridium makes it rough to the touch, but it's still flexible and can take a direct slice from a carbon-fibre sword."

"Impressive," Fred said.

Dom walked up to one of the suits for a closer look. It was black with sharp edges. The carbon fibre with iridium felt like fine gravel, and the light reflected off the iridium, adding a sparkle to the fibre.

"The armour can be worn under all your clothes and can stop a bullet with minimum damage to you."

"They've been tested?" Fred asked.

Nick nodded. "We had Alek help engineer them and test them." Alek owned his own electronics and engineering shop. He made, repaired, and improved his town's mechanical devices during his down time. "He said he was pondering the same idea, and you know him." The agents knew that meant Alek was probably making his own as a side project.

Nick dismissed them to get some sleep, saying they would try the suits the following morning.

TWENTY-FOUR

Five days before the Venusians return

▬

THE NEXT DAY, Ryland was sent on an emergency mission south of Scandal Town. Keira was told to stay and train with the others. Ryland left wearing his new armour. Nick set up a tutorial for him on the helicopter ride there as well as a list of recommended actions. The suit fit well, like sliding on a new layer of skin. It hugged every part of Ryland's body, and soon he didn't even notice it. His movements were smooth and unrestricted. His armour also had a wrist blade built into it. The armour gave him a better sense of protection, making him feel more confident and relaxed.

The sun was midway between the horizon and high noon. As the helicopter travelled transversely to the sun, Ryland noticed a storm rising to the east. Ryland wondered what the mission entailed. It was another alien, but why was it such an emergency?

As the chopper flew above the meadows he had travelled before, he could see so much farther in the air. The land was vast, covered in smooth, grassy hills.

When the helicopter landed, Ryland jumped out and ran to the southwest where his coordinates led him. When he reached the top of a small hill, he saw an alien. The Venusian was standing with his hand out toward something that Ryland couldn't see. He pulled out a high-powered rifle and shot two bullets at the alien's head. Both bullets were stopped, which didn't really surprise Ryland, but he thought he'd given it a try since it was an emergency, and the alien appeared to be distracted.

When Ryland got around the boulder he'd been hiding behind, he saw what looked like two dirt walls rising out of the ground. He walked around them and saw Liz stuck between them, keeping them from driving spikes into her. Ryland stayed calm in front of his opponent.

The scars given to Vaul will be repaid in this way, the alien said, referring to Liz. Names were a clear confirmation that the thoughts were not from the hearer. The pronunciation *Vaul* came into Ryland's head. He examined the trap in his peripheral vision. Her foot was already impaled by something akin to a bear trap within the larger trap. Liz's arms started shaking. Ryland used his rifle to prevent the trap from closing further.

"I'm going to get you out, Liz," Ryland whispered when he got close to her. She looked confused at first, not knowing who was inside the suit. Then her face flooded with recognition.

No, you won't. The alien picked Ryland up using his telekinetic powers and held him still. *You have gone against one of our own. Then you let him go to tell the tale and unite more,* the alien said as it walked toward the two trapped agents.

"That won't happen again," Ryland replied.

Oh, I agree, the alien said as it edged closer. Sometimes with weaker aliens, Ryland assumed, a person could slowly budge when they were holding the person's entire body. He guessed it took a lot of concentration to hold every inch of a body still.

The alien was about three steps from Ryland and Liz when Ryland set off a flash-bang. The alien dropped Ryland enough for him to touch the ground and lunge at his opponent. The alien was fast enough to prevent Ryland from sinking his wrist blade into his chest, only getting a scratch on the shoulder instead.

The Venusian threw Ryland high into the air, from which he threw multiple concussion grenades to keep the alien somewhat dazed. As soon as his feet hit the ground, Ryland ran at his enemy and threw his right fist at the Venusian's face. The alien dodged it, then threw a punch at Ryland's ribs. Ryland brought his left elbow up and struck the alien's head. Ryland spun into a crouch and thrust his right hand with the wrist blade into his enemy's thigh. He heard the Venusian's scream in his head as the alien threw Ryland five metres back.

The alien walked toward Ryland, who got up and went to attack but was caught in a chokehold. The Venusian slammed Ryland into the ground, leaving an indent in the soft meadow. Ryland curled into a ball and stuck a grenade on the alien's matte-black skin before kicking himself away. The grenade exploded, sending the Venusian soaring through the air.

Ryland ran over to Liz. "Are you okay?" he asked.

"Just holding on," she replied, attempting to smile. Ryland tried to pry open the trap, but it wouldn't budge. Then he had to jump out of the way as his foe threw a rock. Ryland pulled out his pistol and fired as fast as he could. Bullets stopped in a cluster near the Venusian's chest. Ryland reloaded and holstered his gun, then swung his leg up in a kick, but the alien stopped it. Ryland threw a knife, which stuck in the alien's chest. Ryland dropped onto his back, and he swept the Venusian's legs while simultaneously firing his pistol. The bullet struck right next to the knife wound. The alien fell to his knees, clutching the wound. The Venusian ripped out the knife. Thick, dark blood oozed from the wound. Ryland left the alien to bleed out and went over to Liz.

That's a bad idea, the Venusian said.

"What is?" Ryland asked.

"He put in precautions," Liz said.

Ryland thought for a moment, then scanned the ground and the air around the trap itself. Liz was still holding it back from closing, her arms shaking.

The Venusian coughed up blood, creating a small puddle of dark red slime. Then it dawned on Ryland: the Venusian was the precaution. The alien was taking his last breaths, and he was holding the trap open. There was nothing Ryland could do. The Venusian's life was fading and with it, so was the trap.

"Open it!" Ryland demanded, turning back to the dying Venusian.

No, the alien replied, his voice faint in Ryland's mind.

Ryland ran over to the dying alien, handcuffed it, then opened a pouch on his thigh that contained medical supplies. He pulled out gauze and pressed it on the bullet wound.

What are you doing?

Ryland couldn't tell if that was his own thoughts or the alien's voice, but either way, he ignored it. The alien knocked Ryland over to stop him, but he got back up and continued to apply pressure to the wound. The Venusian fell over, which made things easier for Ryland, but he knew it was only because the alien was dying.

The alien threw Ryland to the ground, then pulled the knife from its chest and stabbed itself in the throat. Ryland turned and saw the hold on the trap vanish like the Venusian's life.

"No!" He slumped to his knees in front of his dead friend. Blood dripped onto the ground as Ryland's heart sank.

The storm in the east cracked with thunder.

■

Back at HQ, Ryland was sitting in the forested area reading more of the journal. He wasn't sure why, but he couldn't think of a reason to stop.

> *The military presence is moving. I need to follow if I want to find out what they've been doing. They are packing up reinforced crates, which indicates they're not leaving what they were doing behind...*
>
> *I snuck onto their watercraft. I had enough time to grab some of my food. I don't know how long this journey will be...*
>
> *We've been on the water for days. A week, I believe. I hear the soldiers talking about some new weapon. It must be what's in the crates...*
>
> *We have arrived on land. Luckily no one has needed inside the closet I've been hiding in. The land we have come to is more natural than urban. There are local generals. This must be a meeting about the new weapon...*

I heard about countries making alliances for the world war, Ryland thought. *So many countries with so many weapons of mass destruction.*

Keira approached. "Whatcha doing?" she asked.

"Needed time in the silence," he replied, not turning to face her. He was sitting cross-legged with the book in his lap. "You know, I didn't think the decision I made would have turned into this."

Keira noticed that the necklace he had when she first met him was lying across his leg. "You never really know what any of your decisions will lead to," she replied.

"I have been trained to analyze threats, but I didn't analyze my decisions. This is what the job is, Keira. Looking out for what's best for Earth and its people. If you can't do that, maybe you should go back to Mount Horizon."

Keira was tempted to leave in a rage. She knew she wasn't ready, but to hear it from Ryland stung. Then she relaxed. She knew he didn't mean it. She could see it in his eyes as she sat next to him.

"Maybe so, but you have a strong team with you to help with the situation. You're not alone, and your team needs you too. You made a mistake, but you have a team to count on and they're counting on you too."

When Ryland stayed silent. Keira turned to walk away, then stopped and looked back at him. "You told me that to me, you seemed like the older, more experienced guy, which was why I was attracted to you, because I want more experience. Well, right now you seem pretty immature, pushing me away."

Ryland stood and turned to face her. "I brought you into this, and these aliens want this planet. As an agent, you're the only thing standing in their way. They don't have morals like us. They may not have morals at all."

"And that's your fault?" she asked.

"I pushed you away so I wouldn't become more attracted to you or you to me. But I'm training you as my partner now." His voice was filled with regret, but he had also said he was attracted to her.

"And you don't want that?" she asked. "You're the one who said I was coming here because you weren't going to let anything else happen to me."

"Liz said I needed a partner," he replied, talking more to himself than to Keira.

"So that's why you chose me?"

"I wasn't sure what would happen. If you weren't good enough, you would have been kept under their watch, probably at a desk job."

"So you don't want anything more from me?" she asked, wanting a straight answer.

"I don't think I deserve you, and I'm the first one who showed you the outside world."

As if that's an excuse, Keira thought, though he did have a point.

"We can train, prepare for the aliens, but I don't want any more agents dying." He wished with all his might that it would all go away with no casualties.

There was a long pause, and if there was a way to read their two minds, the room would have sounded chaotic.

"Why did you let the alien go?" Keira asked. She had heard the question asked before but had never heard the real reason. Ryland looked at her, weighing his reply.

"I struggle with whether I should have mercy on them or not," he said. "I don't know if they can be saved."

Saved? Keira thought. *From their war?*

Before she could ask him, Nick's voice came over the PA. "Keira, your suit is ready. Please come to the armoury."

Keira and Ryland stood in silence for a few seconds. "I don't know much about the Sentry program," she said, "but I know there are many agents that are part of the same team." With that she left for the armoury.

When she got there, Keira found Nick talking to an engineer.

"Keira, your suit is to your right," Nick said.

Sitting inside a locker, it was the same black and grey as the others. It also had a bow and arrows beside it. Ryland must have requested one to be made. Above her armour was the word THIEF. *What was that supposed to mean?* She thought.

"Like it?" Nick asked as he walked over and observed the suit on her.

"I love it. I can't wait to train in it," Keira replied.

"That," Nick saw she was looking at the word above it, "is your code name. We had to see how you trained. We try to make the code names reflect your style."

"I'm a thief?" Keira asked.

"No, you are good at exploiting your enemy's strengths; using them against them," Nick said. "Here are some engineers to help with your armour."

As she put on the armour, she couldn't help but feel that everything was happening so fast. She had some engineers helping her put each piece on. Her armour fit well. It was sleek and rounded with sharp edges. Her visor fit from her mid forehead to her mouth.

She thought of meeting Ryland now as a full-fledged agent with her own armour to become the best of the best, defending Earth from something she had thought was only an augmented human but which she now knew was an alien.

TWENTY-FIVE
Four days before the Venusians return

▬

"LIE ON YOUR back now," Marcus said, dressed in his new shadow armour. The rough underlayer looked like stone but was flexible enough to allow movement while the thin outer layer had sleek edges and covered the bulk of the body. Altogether, the armour was only an inch thick. He had even customized it, with bones hanging from his belt and an animal skull tied to his shoulder. The skull looked identical to an extinct tiger, with long sharp teeth protruding from its mouth. *Was it from an augmented animal?* Keira wondered.

He laid on his back, facing the ceiling, which was obscured by trees and bushes. Keira, his partner for the exercise, copied him. Her armour faded to match the shadows, and Marcus's did the same. The ground was cool, and the dirt was soft beneath them.

Fred, Dom, and Ryland were fifteen metres away, searching for them. Marcus was teaching Keira how to be silent and invisible. Marcus was better than the other agents at blending in and being in the background, even without the camouflaged armour to help.

Dom changed directions and started to walk toward the hidden agents. Did he know? Ryland turned to follow Dom.

"Do as I do," Marcus whispered to Keira over their private comm link.

Dom was almost at Marcus's shoulders when Ryland joined him. The two stood next to each other, probably using their silent team comm as well. Fred was still ten metres away.

When Dom was within arm's length, Marcus grabbed his legs and rolled onto his shoulder, using Dom's legs as anchors. Marcus's feet connected with Dom's chest, knocking him down.

Ryland drew his gun, but Keira grabbed his legs and did the same move as Marcus.

Marcus landed on Dom's chest, then drew his pistol out and shot him with a training bullet that shut down his suit.

As Keira knocked Ryland over, Marcus grabbed Dom's limp body and rolled onto his back, using Dom as a human shield against Fred. Marcus fired three shots, but Fred dodged to his right, taking cover behind a tree. After finishing Ryland, Keira shot Fred.

As they walked out of the arena, Keira was smiling.

"What advantage did you have over me?" Fred asked, testing her.

"You were in the open with no cover to get to fast enough," Keira said, having thought exactly that right before she shot him.

"Exactly. Always know your surroundings, and make sure you know how to get to cover or an exit."

"Ready for my lesson?" Dom asked as he approached. "I get into my opponents' heads. Make them lose their cool. Then I can break them." His voice was calm and confident, making Keira fear him even more. Before he got the code name Banshee, Dom was nicknamed "Pred," which was short for predator.

"You can usually play with your prey a few times before you strike," he continued. "Depending on their skill and experience."

Keira felt he was already analyzing her and figuring out how to mess with her.

"How do you get into their heads?" she asked.

Dom smirked. "I'll show you." He put on his black helmet, which had a white skull on the visor, and walked into the forested arena. Keira followed.

He explained that the objective was to catch and "kill" the opponent. By intimidating Keira, Dom made her feel small and inexperienced. She felt like Dom was breathing down her neck, always watching.

Throughout the thirty minutes they were in there, Dom made noises in every direction, creating tracks for Keira to follow or to make her think she was going in circles. He even trapped her with a spring-loaded leghold trap.

When she escaped from it and continued to look for Dom, the noises got louder and closer. That was when Keira realized how Dom got into his opponents' heads. After she found more of Dom's traps, he appeared behind Keira, holding a knife to her neck. "Kill," he said. He had won and gotten in her head in the process.

"Don't worry; he's on your team, and you'll soon learn to do the same, even to him," Fred said to Keira as she walked back to the small room just off from the forest floor.

Ryland stood to the side, not saying a word, even as Keira looked to him for advice. He started toward the door, and Keira followed.

Fred looked back at Dom as he was reaching the entrance. "Let's go," he said, egging Dom on for a fight. Dom turned to Marcus and nodded, signalling for him to join them. They were all excited to keep testing the new suits.

They took an elevator up to an urban environment, which was located on the floor above. Nick watched the entire thing from an observation area.

"Aren't you going to train with them?" Keira asked Ryland as they entered the observation area. Ryland didn't feel up for training, but there wasn't much else he could do.

"Yes, he is," Nick replied, answering on Ryland's behalf.

■

Ryland entered the training floor. All agents knew the arena by heart from previous training exercises. There were two tall buildings to his left, north, and a school in line with those buildings to the east, in the centre of the arena. There was also a line of residential homes on the northernmost edge. On the south side was a grocery store, a bank, and a two-storey office building. Gardens, abandoned cars and trucks, and trees that have overgrown the concrete were scattered throughout the streets and buildings. Nick had made it appear lifelike.

Ryland assumed Fred might go for a vantage point while the other two would stay hidden, setting up traps and decoys. So Ryland headed south, into a gas station. On the other side of the station was a restaurant. He made his way through the north side, watching out the windows for any sign of movement.

As he made his way east, he kept an eye out for Fred or anyone else who might try to gain a vantage point on top of the first ten-storey building. Ryland felt distracted and unmotivated. Liz was dead, and here they were playing with their new suits. He knew they had to train, to become comfortable with the suits, but Ryland wished he had found the first alien that killed Nat. Now his feelings of guilt were building following Liz's death.

Hearing a window smash, he set his emotions aside and moved. Realizing it was probably meant as a distraction, he crept across the street toward the school, using a transport truck with deflated tires as cover.

Once in the schoolyard, Ryland made his way around the building instead of going inside. There were too many hiding places for someone to use against him. He didn't know exactly where the smashed window was, but he moved toward the sound to gain a perspective on where his opponents were. His muscles and his mind were both relaxed.

When he was almost at the end of the school's north side, a shot ripped through the air. Ryland leaned against the wall, his body tense. Peering around the corner, he saw nothing. There were so many bullet markings on the ground that he couldn't tell which one was from the sniper. He was about to peer more to the west, toward the tall buildings where he thought the shot had come from, when he saw Dom, whose identity was evident from the white marking on his helmet, climb through a window in the house.

Ryland moved east. The school's parking lot and the cars on the street would provide more cover if Fred was in the tall buildings to the west, and if Dom was to retreat, Ryland could flank him. First he had to move south, passing through a building that aligned with a mail truck on the street.

When he heard a flash-bang, he ran across the street behind a truck and the car. He was now at the building that he had seen Dom come out of. As Ryland moved closer to the target building, Fred came soaring through the air straight toward him. At first Ryland didn't believe his eyes, but then he noticed the zip line. *How did I miss that?* he wondered.

Ryland threw himself back into cover, hoping Fred hadn't seen him. Then he heard Fred land, followed by silence.

Ryland peeked out and saw no one, but then he heard a gunshot. He moved alongside the house, hoping to catch one of his opponents when they tried to retreat. He spotted a shattered glass door and peeked through it. He was just in time to see Fred spin-kick Dom into a table in the kitchen on the east side of the house, where Dom and Fred had entered.

Ryland had to act fast, realizing Fred had seen him. Ryland leveled his pistol, but Fred dove out the window, and the bullet struck the windowsill instead. Dom came out from behind a half wall separating the kitchen from the rest of the house and threw a chair. Ryland blocked it, but another came, and by the time Ryland blocked that one too, Dom was out of the window as well.

Ryland checked the rest of the house for threats before moving on. He saw Fred heading back toward the tall buildings while Dom ran toward the school. Ryland decided to follow Dom.

The school was U-shaped with ten classrooms. It was messy and destroyed with many hiding spots. Ryland entered the first classroom and scanned it for movement. Seeing nothing but desks and chairs scattered about, he moved to the room across the hallway to do the same, but before he could, the door to the school opened.

Ryland flattened himself against the wall. Twenty seconds of silence passed and then a pistol appeared in the doorway. Ryland jumped at it and rolled into his opponent, who turned out to be Marcus, and threw him over his shoulder and into the hallway. Ryland continued his motion into a side flip to land on Marcus with one knee. Marcus grunted, but his suit absorbed the majority of the impact.

Marcus punched Ryland, knocking him off balance, but he rolled backwards. Both agents were on their feet in seconds. The hallway was quiet for a few seconds. Marcus went to jump backwards but was hit in the chest with a bullet.

What? Ryland thought. Then he realized someone was behind him, probably Dom.

Ryland jumped for the classroom across the hall, but a bullet hit him in the back, shutting his suit down and rendering him unable to move for five seconds. When he got up, Fred and Dom were in the hallway. He didn't have to ask who won because Dom was slouching while Fred stood tall and proud.

"And you thought you were the scary one," Fred said to Dom.

TWENTY-SIX

AFTER TRAINING, RYLAND snuck down to the ground floor of the HQ building, where a vehicle depot was located. He had left his cell phone in his quarters and deactivated the tracker in his suit.

Ryland crouched beside a vehicle, eyeing a modified ATV across the room. It had extra gas tanks already on it, which was perfect for Ryland's planned journey. He scanned the room, taking in the locations of the security cameras as well as the security guards and drivers. Luckily the vehicles provided good cover.

He moved to his right, out of view of the camera and past a driver, who was facing the opposite direction. Ryland stopped between two armoured SUVs, waiting for the next camera to turn and for a mechanic to pass. Then he ran for the ATV.

Once he reached it, he started it up and took off. The tires had deeper tread, and the body was raised higher than a typical ATV, which was good for extreme terrain.

The journey was rough, which was to be expected, taking him first through a forest. From up high in the HQ building, the forest looked dense with wide treetops; however, the trees were fairly far apart. The exposed roots forced him to slow down somewhat, but soon he sped out of the forest and into an open field, which extended for several kilometres.

Natalie always enjoyed the post-war world, he thought, *although she didn't know the pre-war world.* The open field made him feel like he was the only one alive and that he had no worries, which was not true, and thinking about Natalie was never peaceful. Even when he thought about the positive memories, it still hurt. He also had just stolen an ATV and left without permission to explore something that he hadn't told Nick about. Agents always worked alone, allowed to do what they wanted as long as they answered the call when a Venusian appeared. It was nice to go alone again, but this time he was AWOL. He was the one who started this, but where he was going was for something personal.

Ryland looked back and saw the trail left by the ATV. The long grass was flattened, and the dirt had been turned from the deep treads. There was a storm to the north, dark clouds rolling over each other like waves. The storm was going to intercept Ryland before he made it to the mountains. The south had cliffs that could provide shelter, but Ryland kept northeast.

The farther northeast he went, the wetter the ground became, and with the long grass, Ryland couldn't tell if the land would soon turn into a deep marsh. If that happened, the ATV would likely get stuck.

Nick's voice came onto the radio of his suit. *He is trying to call me back.* He thought. But Nick began a speech for a funeral. *This was about Liz.* Ryland couldn't listen to another one, he flicked off the radio and pushed the throttle on his ATV.

As the storm clouds dominated the sky, the sun disappeared. Ryland had no cover, and the storm was sending down a wall of rain in the distance. Once it hit him, visibility would be reduced to zero. Ryland decided to head south toward the cliffs, hoping they would provide shelter.

Within a kilometre of the cliffs, Ryland came across a massive hole. He couldn't see the bottom until he turned on the ATV's lights, which revealed it wasn't a hole but a tunnel. It went almost straight down. He decided to take a risk and drive down the steep angle. The tunnel was about twenty metres in diameter. Ryland wondered what made the tunnel, which was fairly close to a perfect circle.

As he travelled down, he heard the storm getting closer. Thunder cracked above him, and lightning flashed in the tunnel entrance.

Moments later, water came pouring into the tunnel. The ground started sliding, and so did the ATV. As it slid, he turned the vehicle to shine the headlights around, searching for an escape. To his right he spotted a walkway. Ryland steered and pumped the throttle in an effort to get to it.

Mud and water continued to push the ATV down. The storm made it hard to think. Rain was pounding down, and thunder was cracking, sounding like it was going to break through the ground and come straight after him. The mud got thicker and the water rougher.

As Ryland neared the walkway, he pumped the throttle, and the front tires caught the semi-solid ground and pulled him to safety. Ryland relaxed, then took a breath and sat against the dark wall. Looking at the flow of water and mud, he allowed his eyes to wander and investigate his surroundings, realizing he could see. Either his eyes had adjusted to the dark or his suit's visor provided lighting. Then he realized where the light was coming from. Glowing crystals hung from the ceiling like a chandelier in a massive cave. At the bottom was a broken city, which had been reduced to giant piles of rubble and a few partially standing buildings or walls. Ryland wondered why it all wasn't buried. What kept it safe? He wanted to go down and explore, but he already had a mission: to get to the castle, to see what the serum was, to see what the AI knew about his father, and to make sure there was no activity at the castle.

I also need to rest, Ryland reminded himself.

■

"You guys know where Ryland is?" Keira asked. Fred and Dom were looking at strategies for beating Venusians and the aliens' biological makeup.

"He ran away," Dom replied, then turned back to his papers. Their helmets were off, but they were still wearing their armour. Nick wanted everyone to get used to it, like a second skin.

"Ran away?"

"He stole an ATV and left on a solo mission," Fred explained. Keira thought his code name, Jovian, suited him. It referred to the planet Jupiter, which was known as the solar system's guardian planet, protecting Earth from asteroids with its massive gravitational pull. Fred had a protective personality and a strong pull of likability. "Don't worry," he said. "Nick sent Marcus as a backup."

"Trying to be the hero," Dom said under his breath.

Fred scowled. "You know he beats himself up for this whole thing."

"Well, it is his fault," Dom said. "He should have had more balls and killed the thing."

"At least Ryland is more of a gentleman than you, Dom," Fred said. Dom shrugged, then continued reading.

"Do you really think this could be that bad?" Keira asked. Dom looked up at Fred, who shot him a look that told him to remain silent.

"If we can't shut down the three Venusians quickly, the world will most likely find out about the aliens' presence," Fred replied. "This isn't going to be a regular encounter. They got a second chance and they used it to go home to gather comrades and train."

"At least we outnumber them, even without me," Keira pointed out, trying to look at the bright side.

"Only by one," Dom said.

"And they have the element of surprise," Fred added. "Yes, we know they're coming in a few days, but we don't know exactly when or where."

"She's like Nat," Dom whispered.

"What?" Keira asked, caught off guard. "Who's Nat?"

Fred sighed. "Nat was Ryland's last partner."

"He had a partner?"

"More than that," Dom said.

"Do *you* want to tell the story, instigator?" Fred asked, glaring at Dom.

"Ryland and Natalie loved each other," Dom continued. "Ryland had a problem with loyalty, so he abandoned her."

"You really like screwing with people, don't you?" Fred said to Dom, then turned to Keira. "Yes, Ryland and Nat loved each other. They were both agents, but Ryland kept pushing her away. His family was divided when he was young, and he was used to being alone. He felt she was going to leave him too, and he felt he wasn't worthy of her. So he left her and assigned himself elsewhere."

"What happened to Nat?" Keira asked.

"She went missing," Fred replied. "Then Ryland found her body—mutilated. We assumed a Venusian had tortured her, but we never found out for sure."

"That's awful," Keira said, her hand over her mouth.

"Yeah, it was hard on Ryland, of course," Fred replied, nodding. "That's why he moves around so much and never gets attached to anyone."

"And you think I remind him of Nat?" Keira asked, guilt creeping into her voice.

"I think you give Ryland a bit more life," Fred replied.

"He's just filling a hole," Dom said.

"No, he isn't," Fred protested. "If you love someone and you lose them, then you find someone who is like the first person and you're going to fall in love with them."

"To fill the hole that the first person left."

"He didn't have a hole before Nat. She didn't fill a hole," Fred said.

Keira felt sick. *Does Ryland actually like me?* She wondered if she just reminded him of Nat.

"He might not have known the hole was there."

"He didn't search or need to fill the hole. She just showed up," Fred said. Dom didn't say anything else, and Fred wasn't about to continue the conversation, especially with Keira there. "Sorry, Keira," Fred continued. "None of this is your fault, and you aren't just filling a hole for Ryland. You're giving him hope."

"Do you guys believe what Ryland believes about God?" she asked.

Dom rolled his eyes and sighed.

"Ryland has a specific old belief," Fred replied, "which is a very honourable religion. He has made good points in how religion can last through all ages, since most people believe that after the war, new religions were needed. But if Ryland's god is the true god, he can last through a war of his creation."

Fred respected Ryland, but it seemed he wasn't sure about all this. Keira felt off about Fred not having an answer about something so personal. She had no answer, and she was sick of not having an answer to such a fundamental question.

"And yet, where is his god?" Fred asked.

"He seemed to make good points that made me doubt the sun and moon as god," Keira said.

"There is no god," Dom declared. "If there is, why is there so much war and death?"

"And how do you explain war and death?" Fred asked.

"We're our only authority, and we all think we're above everyone else, which makes it okay for us to kill others."

"Then we're no better off," Fred said. "If there is a god alongside this war and death, maybe something else is at play too."

"Something else that God can't control or get rid of, like war?" Dom asked.

"Maybe God is letting us choose," Fred suggested.

"Ryland did say something about a curse and us choosing God or going against him," Keira said, recalling Ryland talking about it in the helicopter when she first came to the headquarters.

"Pfft. Some god." Dom shrugged off the idea. "It doesn't matter. All humans are mortals and amount to nothing."

Nick entered, interrupting the conversation. "Got a situation," he said.

"What is it?" Fred asked.

"We found Cowen Rache." He had been stealing from the COG for the last decade. He listened to no rules and had his own base of operations, which had been hidden from the COG until now. Some agents had found the base to the southwest in a desert.

"I want you to take him down," Nick said. "You have permission to eliminate him on sight."

"What about Marcus?" Fred asked.

"This mission will have to be done with you three," Nick replied, indicating Fred, Dom, and Keira. "I'm confident you can all handle it. Now go."

■

"The coward," Banshee said, looking at the base. It had massive walls surrounding the vehicles, aircraft, and weapons. It also had sniper towers at each corner, its own power plant, and various buildings for its inhabitants.

Jovian thought Banshee would have had a different opinion of the man, who lived by his own rules, taking advantage of what is available.

"He steals for his own reasons and then destroys the lives of the people he stole from using the very things he stole," Banshee continued. "He's selfish, and I'm glad to have a chance to put him down."

"Let's put him down, then," Jovian said.

"Thief, with me," Jovian ordered. "We'll cover Banshee as he goes in."

Jovian set up his sniper rifle and motioned for Thief to do the same. "Take out the towers first, then the outside patrols near where Banshee enters."

Banshee crept down the sand dune, leaving his comrades behind. Despite his armour's slight camouflage abilities, it had a difficult time blending in. He moved slowly so as not to disturb the sand. The land used to be full of roads and buildings, but the sand had covered them long ago, with nothing to stop the wind.

By the time Banshee made it to the wall, Jovian and Thief had shot six guards as silently as Banshee climbed the wall, his armour protecting him from the barbed wire.

When he landed on the other side, he made his way to the building where they hoped to find Cowen. Men were moving supplies into a shed in the southeast corner of the fort. Seizing on the distraction, Banshee snuck past them toward the building.

■

Jovian and Thief lost sight of Banshee when he hid from the men who were moving supplies. They surveyed the area, swiping from side to side with their scopes, watching for any potential threats or Cowen himself. Helicopters and armoured SUVs were scattered around the base. Cowen could use any of them for escape.

"Look to the northwest," Jovian said. "Target on the walkway."

"Got him." Thief put her crosshairs on his head, then moved to his chest, aiming a few centimetres ahead for a negative lead.

"Now watch when he crosses a few metres away from the watchtower."

Thief had no idea what was going to happen, but when the target moved to where Jovian was talking about, the sun glared and reflected into her scope.

"That's why we wear the sunshade on our scopes," Jovian said. "They still obstruct our view but not as much, and they prevent our enemies from seeing a reflection from our scopes. Okay, take him out when you're ready."

Thief watched as the glare faded and the man continued walking toward the watchtower, which was empty. Thief stopped her breathing and squeezed the trigger. She felt the recoil, the bullet already striking its target, passing through the man's chest and rupturing the cavity and multiple organs. Target eliminated.

They looked back to where Banshee was and saw he had made his way up to the main building. On the catwalk surrounding the observation floor, Banshee assassinated one of Cowen's men and dragged him back around the corner where Thief could see. Banshee moved out of sight again. Seconds later, Banshee was thrown back against the catwalk railing, bending it. As a heavily armed man approached Banshee, a bullet from Jovian's sniper tore through the man's neck, finding an impossibly small gap in his armour.

"There are more," Banshee said as he got up and jumped over the railing onto the stairs below. An alarm sounded, and within seconds mortars were firing, trying to find the snipers. Timed explosions rang out, sometimes hitting the sand and others blowing up in the air.

"They might get lucky," Jovian said, his voice calm. "Let's move."

They crept back down the far side of the dune and then went in opposite directions. Once in a more concealed location, Thief saw a mortar explode a few feet from their primary position. Banshee was still inside the base, having to face who knew how many soldiers by himself. She looked through her scope and saw Banshee outmaneuvering two heavily armoured counterparts, but he wouldn't last long with all the other men converging on him. Thief had to do something but didn't know what. She couldn't pull off the kind of shot that Jovian made on the first armoured man.

"Cowen is in the building, just... watching," Banshee said as he struggled against his opponents. "Jovian, get a clear shot through the front window. I have an idea."

"Roger."

Jovian ran toward the west, aligning himself with the front of the base and keeping his distance. He didn't care who saw him. Thief fired at the men who were tracking Jovian. That drew their attention toward her, but they couldn't pin her down.

As Banshee ran for the mortar, Thief fired on the armoured men to slow them down.

"Jovian, you better be ready," Banshee said. Then he disappeared from view.

"Go," Jovian replied. "Thief, give him a way out. Main entrance."

"Roger that."

An explosion went off, and Thief saw that Banshee had thrown a mortar at the window of the main building, allowing Jovian to shoot Cowen. Thief fired at the armoured men who were in Banshee's way. Then he hijacked a small vehicle to drive out. As he did, Thief loaded explosive rounds into her sniper rifle and fired at the hinges of the main gate, blowing them off just as Banshee zoomed through the opening.

Thief stood up and ran toward their aircraft. Banshee met her partway there, and she hopped into his vehicle. Another mission complete.

TWENTY-SEVEN

Three days before the Venusians return

▄

THE MUD ON Ryland's clothes was heavy and starting to crust over. The abandoned city was made brighter with every flash of lightning. He crouched at the edge and looked out over the city. His suit activated night vision, with every flash of lightning it would turn off and back on again. There stood the remains of six buildings with three streets running from north to south and two streets from east to west. There was also a flat area that was free of rubble. For some reason, it reminded him of the land of rye in the prophecy he had been told a while ago: on Jupiter in a field of rye stood a bowman, a thief, and a ghost using a relic to save foreigners.

What does it mean? Ryland wondered as he cleaned his ATV. *Rye on Jupiter? That's impossible. And what or who are the bowman, the thief, and the ghost? The foreigners are the humans saved from the Venusians, but the relic?* Ryland paused. *Could that be the serum? But I don't know how to use it, or is it even supposed to be used?*

As he thought through the prophecy, he was distracted when things got stuck or he couldn't get the dirt out of an important part of the ATV.

Could the bowman, the thief, and the ghost mean unusual people coming together? But how are the dead involved? he wondered as he cleaned the rear axle. The mud had covered the wheels almost completely. *And who are the unlikely allies? Scandal Town. Are they going to team up with Mount Horizon against the Venusians? Shoot, how bad did I screw up? What are these Venusians going to do?*

Ryland felt nervous and anxious, as if he was about to do a presentation in high school with little preparation. Trying to push the anxiety to the back of his mind, he pulled out the stranger's journal and read another excerpt from it.

> It's amazing the hierarchy we implement through history, church as the state, dictatorship, democracy, that is still easily corrupted, and now most cities are on their own, run how they want, and yet we conspire and think there is an overruling power, and they departmentalize.
>
> A god may help with this, but that would be a dictatorship. No one typically likes dictators. I guess that depends on the person. A good god is needed. Does that mean there's no god due to all the evil?
>
> The generals have talked for a while, as expected, and the soldiers patrolled around. I have had to move and sit still for hours now. Now they are moving toward the one crate they brought out.
>
> I recognize one of the generals. I think it's, yes, it's Damon Ambrose.

What? Ryland thought. *This isn't a journal. It's a—*

He was interrupted by his scanner popping up in his head-up display with a green dot in the direction where he had entered the cave. A name popped up as well: Marcus Lee.

Ryland looked back up the tunnel. "Hunter?"

"Yeah. Radar ruined my stealth," Marcus replied. "Disappointing."

Once he came into view, Ryland saw he was sliding down on his feet, which were covered in mud. When he made his way to the ledge where Ryland was, Ryland had to catch his arm or the mud would have pushed him off.

"What are you doing?" Ryland asked.

"I should ask you the same thing," Hunter replied. "I was told to follow you but not to bring you back. Just so you had support."

"How bad did I screw up, Marcus?"

"I don't know. We defeat the Venusians at a ratio of one to six. You know how boring this job gets with all the politics. Most agents want the fight. They're kinda excited for this new challenge. We got your back, Ryland." Marcus rolled his wrists as if warming up for the fight.

"Right. Thanks, Marcus," Ryland said.

"You knew we would notice your absence. Why'd you leave without telling anyone?"

"It's a personal thing, I found something with Keira on the outskirts of Mount Horizon." Suddenly, his eyes widened. "Keira!"

"She's fine," Marcus said, confused by Ryland's outburst.

"She's the thief!"

"Yeah, that's her code name."

"And then the bowman and the ghost, that's you and Dom," Ryland said, the words of the prophecy finally coming together in his mind.

"What are you talking about?" Marcus asked.

"A prophecy that a man shared with me a few weeks ago," Ryland explained the prophecy and what he thought it meant.

"Doesn't Jovian come from the word 'Jupiter'?" Marcus asked.

"Oh, right. Yeah, it does." Ryland hadn't thought of Fred's code name.

"So, what about the relic? What's it?" Marcus asked.

Ryland shrugged, unsure. As he stared straight ahead, not blinking, memories of training entered his mind, people he had trained with, working together and competing against them. Then his mind drifted to the few memories he had from before training. Thinking about his sister made his stomach lurch with longing to be with her again. He hadn't seen her in twelve years.

He also thought about the day when he and Destiny paired up against their parents. It didn't work, and they got in trouble for it. Afterwards, Ryland's father told him that he respected him for protecting his sister, but he needed to do so for the right things.

As his eyes wandered around the cave, for a split second he thought the person sitting across from him was Natalie.

"Ryland." Marcus's voice brought him back to the present. Ryland didn't know if he would have preferred to stay daydreaming or be brought back to reality. "Whatcha thinking about?"

"Ah, I was thinking back to our training days and before that to my family," Ryland replied, not telling the full truth. It felt like the fire had drained him, and he didn't want to lie.

"You have a sister, right?"

"Yeah."

"I had an older sister and a younger brother," Marcus said. "They passed away from a flu when I was twelve. Guess that's how the Sentry program found me because I didn't get sick."

"Your whole family got sick, didn't they?"

Marcus nodded. "Yeah. Crazy to think back on it, but I guess that happens nowadays."

"Sorry you had to go through that," Ryland said.

"Ah, it happened, and I made it through. Got into this program because of it."

Ryland couldn't tell if he was being genuine or just telling himself that.

"Your god says everything happens for a reason, right?" Marcus always tried to understand people's beliefs and relate to them.

Ryland nodded. "He's in control and has a higher purpose for things. Not that I use that to comfort people. People usually don't see it until something greater happens, like you getting into the Sentry program."

"How do you justify those who died?" Marcus asked.

"When God came to Earth, he was betrayed by one of his closest followers. He knew it would happen all along, but the betrayal had to happen for God to die humanly as a sacrifice. It also shows us our fate. We're not going to live forever. The pre-war world used science to keep people young, but it never worked—or if it did, it didn't last long. It's good for us to realize that we will die, showing us we should do something about it. We shouldn't attempt to stop death. Instead, we should find the life after death and one way to get that."

"Right, okay," Marcus said. "Just seems hard to justify."

"The bottom line is, we're cursed and need saving from evil. Death is only in this world because of that curse."

"Why doesn't God do anything about evil?" Marcus asked.

"He is doing things, He kept you safe from that flu your family had. But he also gave us free will, letting us decide where we go and where the world goes, giving us opportunities to choose him, to follow him, and be a light in the darkened world."

"Well, that's a lot to think about," Marcus replied. "Why would he serve my family up to the flu, just so I can become an agent?"

"I don't have all the answers, Marcus. I don't know the reasons. I just know there are two forces fighting in this world. I'll leave it at that. You're a good friend, Marcus. Thanks for listening and trying to understand."

Realizing the rain had stopped, Ryland looked back down at the city. It seemed different somehow. The border looked like a dry moat surrounding the buildings, and the rubble appeared to have been pressed into the ground. What had been there before?

Then a massive whale-size worm came from the near side of the moat and dug through the wall to the agents' right. The worm was eight metres wide and fifteen metres long. The ground shook, and the agents were filled with fear, never guessing that something so big lived under the ground. It was big enough to eat both of them by accident. Was that what the radiation from the war had done to the animals? Ryland had heard people talking about interesting changes to animals: eagles that glowed, animals with two tails, and frogs that could make their poison evaporate, making it even deadlier.

Ryland realized the worm was making a new tunnel, which would be dry. Ryland packed up his stuff, as did Marcus.

"Did you know such a creature existed?" Marcus asked.

"No, and I'm terrified that it does."

"Me too," Marcus said. "Makes me wonder what else has changed from the radiation."

Marcus got on the ATV, and Ryland pushed the throttle. The ATV dug into the dry ground and launched off the ledge and into the new tunnel. After nearly flipping, they drove up the tunnel's sharp angle until they reached a peak, where there was a small hole that led to the surface. The agents used the tunnel wall as a ramp and rocked back to the surface, emerging in the grasslands. Marcus went and got his ATV and then they continued to the northeast.

TWENTY-EIGHT

ONCE THEY REACHED the mountains neighbouring the castle, they left their ATVs behind and started climbing. Ryland enjoyed climbing mountains. It was a good way to train.

When they caught sight of the castle, they also saw a camp set up at the base of the mountain. Ryland recognized some of the gear. It belonged to the prophet and his companions. What were they doing there?

"Who are they?" Marcus asked.

"I met them a few weeks back when I was on my way to Scandal Town and they were heading to Mount Horizon. Didn't know they were coming here."

The two agents moved closer to get a better view of the prophet and his companions as they walked around the castle and their camp. At one point they brought two boxes out from the castle.

Once things settled down, the agents snuck closer to the castle, taking up a post on either side of the entrance. When they thought it was safe, they crept down the hallway, guns in hand.

They continued until they reached the stairs that led to the basement. The agents crept across the marble floor, guns swiveling back and forth. They didn't use flashlights, their suits equipped with night vision.

When they reached a doorway, they heard what sounded like a fight, including grunts, screams, and bones breaking, as well as a noise that the agents couldn't define.

The fighting noises stopped, and it seemed the whole castle was empty. The light from the computer screens grew brighter at the end of the hallway. As they moved toward it, Ryland saw a body on the ground, followed by eight more. Ryland scanned the bodies and realized that only the prophet was missing. Had he done this? If so, why? And where had he gone?

The agents travelled down the only other hallway. It led to a wide room with cryogenic chambers against the walls. What was going on there? An active AI with a serum and a room of cryogenic chambers?

It took them a little longer to clear the room, but nothing was there but snapped wires and broken glass. There was a door up a few stairs on the far side of the room. It was thick and reinforced but had been blown open.

"This just happened," Marcus said as he examined the fresh scorch marks. They had seen a scorch mark in the computer room as well. If the trap door had stayed intact throughout the war and all the years since, what could have blown it open now? If it was the prophet, he could have gone any direction, and it would be impossible to find him.

The agents returned to the computer room. Upon entering, Ryland saw some handwriting on the wall in a style that he recognized. It said, "Follow the foreigners."

"I know that handwriting," Ryland whispered.

"How?" Marcus asked.

"I have this journal. I thought it was from before the war, but I just found out the author was following my father. And now I know who wrote it." It was as much a shock to hear himself say it out loud. His father was still alive and a COG member, and the journal—which revealed his father's status—was written by a man he had met and who had now committed murder. What was going on?

"Your father?" Marcus asked.

"Exactly. Not only is my family not a part of my life, they're not who I think they are." His voice showed his frustration. The lies were building up. Family, the unit that was supposed to be concrete, the bond that never broke, had been shattered, only to be remade into something else without him.

"What does that mean?" Marcus asked, looking at the writing on the wall.

"I'm not sure." Ryland was becoming more frustrated with this prophet guy. There were few people he could trust in this world. If the prophet did this, he had now murdered seven men and two women. Ryland looked at the dead bodies and the scorch marks on the wall, then stepped closer to see more detail. "These look familiar," he muttered.

"What do you mean?" Marcus asked, joining him. "They're burn marks."

"But look at how symmetrical they are. If it was done by fire, they would be uneven. And these marks that spread from the centre, they look like lightning." Ryland ran his fingers over the marks, feeling the indents.

"How are they familiar?" Marcus asked.

"A while back I investigated a bar fight in Laketown. There were no witnesses, but these scorch marks were on the wall and on the victim's chest," Ryland remembered the smell of booze. "It wasn't from a makeshift Molotov cocktail. The barkeeper only heard one bottle smash, and there were two of these marks."

"What happened with the investigation?"

"Nothing. I couldn't find any clues regarding the murderer," Ryland said as he moved on to search for any clue on the victims. Then he realized the vault door was unlocked. Was that why the prophet and his companions had come? Ryland opened it, and the serum was still there. Why didn't the assailant take it?

Marcus pressed a few keys on the computer console, and words scrolled across the screen: "A potential successful trial available. Take serum."

Ryland picked up the serum, and the computer came to life with an avatar on top of the keys. It looked like a person wearing a hooded parka that extended past its waist. It turned toward Marcus and then Ryland, but inside the hood was nothing,

"I was wondering if anyone was going to come." The avatar's voice was smooth and not too deep.

"Who are you?" Marcus asked.

"They call me NEO, Nano Electronic Organism. I'm an artificial intelligence. Although I like to think of myself as a real intelligence. I know a lot, you know."

"You're an organism?" Marcus asked.

"I don't really think that descriptor is accurate."

"How do you know General Ambrose?" Ryland asked.

"He's one of the Circle of Generals. He progressed the Sentry program, and he perfected the super soldier serum,"

Ryland fell silent for a moment, pondering this revelation as Marcus wondered what was going on.

"Damon Ambrose died twelve years ago!" Ryland said, his voice full of anguish.

"He didn't die," NEO replied. "He joined the Sentry program ten years ago."

Marcus was silent as he watched his friend process the confirmation that his father was still alive. He could only imagine the pain Ryland was feeling.

"I'm part of the Sentry program," Ryland said as if it meant something. NEO pulled up a picture of Damon working with the Circle of Generals. Ryland felt rage build within him. His father had made Ryland think he was dead and that it was Ryland's fault. He had finally come to terms with it, years later. Maybe the whole reason he joined the Sentry program was to help others who were in need like he was.

"Yes, he made a new recruitment program, recruited you as a candidate, and then recruited others to monitor and train them." The news sounded weird coming from NEO, who had such childish speech and mannerisms, yet the avatar looked so mysterious.

"Where is my father now?" Ryland asked. So many emotions were stirring in him. He was happy to know his father was still alive, mad because his father had lied to him, and frustrated that he hadn't known his father was a General and a head over the Sentry program. What else didn't he know? Did Nick know all this? Was Nick constantly talking to his father?

"I don't know, which is why I suggested we consult with him."

"Do you know who these people are?" Marcus asked, gesturing to the bodies.

"They were affiliated with General Ambrose, workers with the augmentation program," NEO replied, his avatar peering around the room.

"From five years ago?" Ryland asked in surprise.

"Yes. It was never fully shut down. They just went underground."

"My father was involved with that?" Ryland exclaimed. What else didn't he know?

"From what I know, yes," NEO replied. "These men are from Marshville, and they came here to collect the serum, I believe."

"What do they want with it?" Marcus asked.

"They're planning a war," Ryland replied. "Liz…" Ryland recalled his friend trapped in the spikes that impaled her, taking her life. "And I confronted the mayor."

"What happened?" Marcus asked.

"We didn't get much out of him. Liz knew all about his assailants." Ryland hung his head.

"Hmm. Who was the assailant here, NEO?" Marcus asked.

"I don't know. They covered their identity," NEO replied.

"My guess is it was the prophet," Ryland said. "He's the only one missing. I don't know why he would have done this, though." Ryland recalled his encounter with him. He was the most open among the group, the person whom Ryland assumed was the leader. "And he left the serum."

"Let's get it back to Nick," Marcus said, preparing to leave.

"Yeah, alright," Ryland agreed.

"Take me with you," NEO pleaded. "There's a microchip and a case I can travel in. In fact, your suits might even suffice." Ryland grabbed the case and NEO's microchip, inserted the chip, then put it in one of his many pockets.

When they got back to their ATVs, a helicopter was waiting for them.

"What's this?" Ryland asked.

"I called it once we found NEO," Marcus replied. Ryland realized it was probably a good call, seeing as the trip back to base would only take a few minutes.

TWENTY-NINE

"THERE AREN'T ENOUGH agents around the world to act fast enough," General Ambrose of the Mesanian country said. There were four main countries that each general watched over, one of which was split by a wide river. There were five generals, and this conversation had come up multiple times since the Venusians were first sighted on Earth.

"The public's reaction to the presence of aliens would be too unpredictable," General Leonid agreed in a strong Karpos accent. He controlled the northeastern region. He shifted in his chair, which was situated around a table in a dimly lit bunker, each general accompanied by their respective political advisers. They weren't needed, but they needed to know everything that the generals talked about, so they knew what their generals were thinking for when they had to speak to the press.

"They need to know. They deserve to know," General Finch of the southern Alithia country protested. He seemed to care for the civilians' free will, but the others sensed another motive behind him and his advisor. Nonetheless, it was still a pressing issue.

"They will request more security," Leonid replied.

"Then we'll make them aware of the Sentry program as well," Finch said.

General Weston from Lithos, who watched over the Centre Islands as well, sat back in his chair as he listened to the conversation, collecting his thoughts, his political advisor beside him.

"They won't trust us to protect all of them with twenty-four agents," he said, his strong jaw contrasted his round muscles.

"That's what's been protecting them for years," General Zane said, speaking slowly and articulating each word due to her heavy accent. She led Lunatia, in the northwestern region. "If they don't know about the aliens, then that shows we've done enough." She was slender and had dark skin with jewelry that accented it.

"The Blood's Shadow legend is really about the aliens," Weston said. "People know about them; they just don't know they're Venusians."

"But it's true we've protected them for this long," Zane said. The agents had covered their tracks using the Blood's Shadow rumour.

"We got lucky," Weston said. "The only reason it works is because their skin is similar to the augmented animals."

"What about weapons?" Leonid asked. "They'll want their own protection."

"We don't have weapons," Ambrose said. "We can barely make weapons with what we have." It was a vulnerable thing to say, being a general and all, but after the war, few weapons were left in the world.

"Our weapons have been ineffective against the Venusians anyway," Zane said, her voice slipping into her deep accent, "so there's no point."

"They will request something other than the agents for protection," Ambrose said. "We will need to offer something."

"But what can we offer them?" Finch asked. Everyone fell silent, deep in thought.

"They may want offensive protection to take things into their own hands, but defence may also be an option," Ambrose said. "How about building a bunker in each town?"

"In each town? That's a huge task," Finch said. Even if they were small bunkers, to build one in every town far and wide would take far too long.

"What about an alarm directed to the Sentry agents?" Weston suggested. "Use the civilians to speed Sentry's aid."

"That could work, but I still think they will want more, something they can use," Zane said.

"If we give them something they can use to attack, they will soon learn that they stand no chance against the aliens," Ambrose protested. "More people will die, and they will just sound the alarm anyway. We should skip the death part and just give them an alarm."

"You're suggesting giving them a button to call the agents and notify where the aliens were seen?" Finch asked. "What about prank calls or false information?"

"He has a point," Weston said.

"How do we stop that?" Zane asked. "We need a way that is convenient to call but also ensures they don't lie about their information." The generals all pondered the question.

"How about proof?" Ambrose suggested. "Demand they have proof before they initiate the call."

"It could work, but then we'd have to ask the civilians to stay in harm's way while they obtain the proof," Zane said.

"How easy can we make the proof process?" Leonid asked, sounding positive about the idea.

"We can contact Nick in the Sentry program to see about a scanning mechanism for confirming a Venusian's appearance," Ambrose said. "General Finch, can you do that?"

"Yes, I can," he replied, nodding.

THIRTY

Two days before the Venusians return

■

WHEN RYLAND AND Marcus returned to base with the ATVs, the mechanics came with a pressure washer to clean the machines. After taking one look at the agents, though, they used the pressure washer on them instead.

Once all the mud was cleaned off, Ryland pulled NEO out of his pocket and looked at it, wondering what all of it meant. *Does the Circle of Generals even know about this?*

"You okay?" Marcus asked.

"Yeah. Let's just get this to Nick." Ryland turned to go, but Marcus stopped him.

"Look, I get that it was big news. But don't think you're above reproach for what you just did. We're a team, and we take care of each other."

Ryland was quiet for a moment, then nodded in response.

When they got to Nick's floor, they saw Fred, Keira, and Dom walking toward them, clad in their body armour, which was required now to get them used to it.

"How was your trip?" Fred asked. His voice was sincere, but it also had a hint of frustration. Keira gave Ryland a questioning look. Then Dom grabbed him and threw him against the wall,

"You think your *holier than thou self* is better than everyone else?"

"Dom, let go of him," Marcus said, placing a hand on his shoulder.

"Back off, Hunter," Dom said. Code names were only used on the battlefield, which made Dom's use of it a serious threat. Ryland swept Dom's arms away, but Dom just stepped closer.

"You think you're better than us?" he asked.

"No," Ryland replied.

"Gentlemen," Nick said from down the hallway. As he approached, he dismissed all the agents except Ryland. Once everyone was gone, Ryland handed him the serum and NEO for analysis. Then the two of them walked to the elevator and headed to the scientists' wing.

NEO was very excited. He was like an extrovert who had been stuck in solitude for years and was now seeing old friends for the first time,

"Whoa, you guys have tons of equipment. Is that an A-one-Delta computer analyzer? You're going to test my abilities. Awesome!" NEO's avatar appeared and then disappeared around the room, as if that was how he was able to see.

"Ryland," Nick said when the door clicked shut, "why did you run off? You even deactivated your tracker."

"I had to check something personal." He nodded toward NEO.

"That," Nick pointed to NEO. "Is not personal. I get that Liz's death was personal. It was a serious loss. She was a good agent and a great friend to all of us. But you have to stop thinking you are totally autonomous. We're a family, Ryland."

That hit Ryland hard. He had just found out that his father was alive and working with the mayor of Scandal Town. Could family even be trusted?

"Right," Ryland replied. "Did you know about my father?"

"What about your father?"

"Don't lie to me, Nick!" Ryland said, glaring at him. "He's had a direct part in the Sentry program and is a general."

"I promise you, Ryland, I had no idea he was the one in charge. I only deal with General Finch." Nick's voice was sympathetic, and his eyes reached out to Ryland in his pain. "Isn't your father dead?"

"NEO just showed me a recent picture of him," Ryland replied.

Just then, an alarm sounded on their phones, indicating an alien presence. The other agents would have received it too.

"Go," Nick said, standing. "I'll find out what NEO knows about your father."

Ryland looked at the coordinates for the alien sighting on his phone. "Liz's students are in Scandal Town. Can you make sure someone checks on them?"

"I may not have the resources," Nick replied, "but I'll see what I can do. Now go."

Ryland hesitated. He had just returned from a long journey after losing Liz. Then again, his journey had been unauthorized. *I don't deserve a break now,* he told himself, but his body protested that he did.

■

"Got him," Hunter said as he spotted a black alien beyond the tree he was leaning against. The rest of the team would be on their way soon with their dirt bikes and four-wheelers. They were spread out by twenty kilometres, searching for the mysterious man in black. The agents knew the aliens' origin and power, but civilians only knew of them as a legend. Civilians had seen the aliens on only a few occasions, but no one believed them. There was never any proof. Even when Keira told her uncle the story of seeing a Venusian with Ryland, her uncle just shrugged it off.

Hunter stayed hidden as he watched his target. The Venusian walked through the forest alone, then stopped in a clearing. What did the Venusians do when they weren't being hunted? The black-skinned alien crouched down and felt the grass. He seemed peaceful. Was he happy? The Venusian stood back up and looked at the sky between the trees.

As he watched, Hunter felt the slight breeze disappear. The suits had microcavities to let air in, but they could be closed in dangerous environments.

The Venusian threw his arm back, and a rock followed, slamming into the tree that Hunter was hiding behind. The Venusian had thrown the rock with such force that the tree exploded, sending bark flying in every direction. Hunter hit the ground, the cold dirt digging into his armour. He did a backwards somersault, landing on his feet. Leaves drifted down from the sudden impact.

"I've been engaged," he said into his comm. With a crack, the tree tipped over, adding insult to injury, but it was caught on neighbouring trees, so it didn't hit the ground.

"What? How?" Banshee asked, his question hurt, and Hunter had no answer.

"I don't know." He rolled out of sight from the alien. "Just get here."

Hunter took another step, only to land in a trap. It exploded, throwing him ten feet into the air.

When Hunter recovered, he saw the alien standing in the clearing, watching him. It was probably a funny sight for the alien. Perhaps he wasn't attacking because he had traps everywhere. Hunter decided he would have to be more cautious.

Raising his gun, he shot at the alien, but the Venusian stopped the bullets with a tree that it moved with its telekinetic powers. Hunter ran to the right to get a better view of the alien, only to discover the Venusian was gone. The tree fell, and Hunter set off in search of his foe, keeping an eye out for traps.

■

Keira loved riding four-wheelers. It reminded her of when she and her brother would go out and explore the forest and mountains. Reece would always make it a race home. Gripping the throttle reminded her of her struggle to keep up with Reece, who knew all the shortcuts. They were west of Mount Horizon, and now Keira was racing toward her teammate instead of home, a race against the alien threatening Hunter instead of her brother.

The first person who arrived at Hunter's aid was Banshee. By then Hunter had the alien pinned to the ground. As Banshee slowed his approach, preparing to join in, Hunter was swept off his feet and thrown into a nearby tree.

Banshee twisted his throttle, then sped his ATV straight toward the alien. At the last second, he cranked the handlebars and then leaped off, sending the bike flying toward the Venusian. But then it stopped in midair. The alien was holding his hand up, stopping the bike without actually touching it.

Meanwhile, Banshee continued to walk toward his target with confidence. His black-and-white armour with the skull on the helmet still frightened Keira, especially knowing who he was under that helmet.

Hunter and Banshee always had stealth competitions, but Banshee was confident in how much fear he struck into his opponents—or victims, as he liked to call them. This alien was now Banshee's victim, although he seemed confident enough not to fear the armoured ghost heading toward him.

An explosion went off from the bike, a grenade placed by Banshee, sending the surprised alien flying backward. In response, the alien lifted the ground below Banshee and threw him as well.

Just then, Sentinel arrived on the opposite side of the clearing. He got off his ATV and crept forward.

"Thief, stay hidden for now," Ryland ordered over the comm.

"I'm not a rookie anymore," she protested. "I'm ready."

"It's not that. Just hang back."

He remained behind cover, as did Keira, even though she didn't understand the reason for his command. They watched as Hunter and Banshee circled the alien, trading blows.

Even though she wasn't thrilled about it, Keira took advantage of being on the sidelines to analyze the alien and the agents' movements and techniques.

The alien got the upper hand only a few times, but it took advantage of every opportunity. The agents knew how to handle themselves against such trespassers, though, and it was two against one now. Gunshots went off every so often, but the bullets never actually reached their target. Guns were nullified in such battles. The three observers didn't interfere because Banshee and Hunter had the upper hand for the majority of the fight. Sentinel didn't know what was going on with the alien, but he didn't like that there was something different.

The air felt cooler to Thief as she watched the artful dance of combat in the clearing. It was as if three shadows had come off their surfaces and started fighting. Finally, Hunter and Banshee got the alien to the ground in a vicious hold, but the alien broke free and slammed his fist into Hunter, sending him flying into the tree line. Hunter pulled a knife and attempted several times to stab his opponent. During his next attempt, the alien twisted Hunter's knife around and thrust it into Hunter's lower ribs. He doubled over, clutching the knife.

"Shoot!" Ryland exclaimed from his hiding spot in the tree line, ready to jump out.

Banshee shot a barrage of bullets and then charged the Venusian. The alien stopped the bullets, then launched himself into the air. He stopped above the trees and flew over Thief. She and Sentinel jumped out and ran toward Hunter while Jovian and Banshee pursued the alien. They didn't get far before they saw the Venusian warp into space.

■

When the agents returned to headquarters, Hunter was rushed to the med bay. Luckily, the knife stayed in place, and he didn't bleed much due to his armour. It took half an hour to remove the knife and stitch Hunter up. The other agents were all relieved. They had all gone through worse injuries, but a stab wound that deep and near vital organs could be severe.

"How you feeling?" Ryland asked.

"I'll be fine. Missed the good stuff," Marcus replied.

"Why did we stay back?" Keira asked, not bothering to hide her irritation. If they hadn't, she was sure the injury could have been avoided.

"That alien was a scout," Ryland said. "Setting traps is not the norm. The whole thing was a trap to see how many of us there are."

"Ryland is right," Marcus said. "It wasn't causing mayhem. It was enjoying nature or waiting. It knew I was there."

"You aren't as stealthy as you think, Hunter," Dom said with a friendly smirk, which Keira had not seen before. Marcus smiled back.

"Why would it want to know how many of us there are?" Keira asked.

"My guess is to give that info to the crew that will be coming in two days," Ryland replied. "If they know how many enemies they're going to face, they'll have a huge advantage. They could bring more reinforcements and set more traps."

"Also, coming here to see the number of agents they will encounter, we may have given them enough info just by letting two agents fight," Fred said.

"How so?" Keira asked.

"The usual number of agents encountered is one. Then, suddenly, another agent came to Marcus's aid. That might tell the alien we have increased security, specifically in this area," Fred replied.

"Shoot. That could mean they might attack somewhere else," Ryland said.

"You did well keeping our numbers hidden," Nick said, joining the group. "So, they're scouting us," he continued, pondering. "Interesting that they're doing this two days before the original alien is scheduled to return."

"Not many Venusians get away to inform that the usual number of agents is one. This encounter of two agents may not have been that odd," Dom said.

"Unless they've been scouting us for a while now without us knowing it," Marcus said from his hospital bed.

"A scary thought, indeed," Nick replied. "We'll just have to continue training and figuring out how to detect their arrival. Rest easy, Marcus. Ryland, can we speak for a moment?"

∎

"I learned more about your father, General Ambrose," Nick said to Ryland once they were alone.

"What did you find?" Ryland asked. He felt so exhausted, he almost didn't care anymore.

"He was the one who made the augmentation program. When it was shut down, he abandoned the castle, but someone stole NEO and brought him back to the castle to continue the augmentation without your father's permission."

"NEO thought they worked with my father, though."

"Yes. He didn't know he was being stolen. The thief overrode his protocols and told him it was a mission assigned to them," Nick said. "The thief left a hole in the overridden system, though, so we were able to bring the original code back and even trace the thief."

Nick held up a file. It was for a man named Erin. "Now, back to your father, He made the Sentry program, then moved on to the augmentation. When that failed, he disappeared. But I looked into your whole family. Your sister went missing two years ago. Your mother is still receiving money and support through a private, secure account."

That woke up Ryland up.

"Here's the thing: if a civilian tries to search for Ryland Ambrose, they get a missing file and a dead-end trail, just like what I found with your sister."

"So what does that mean? How is Destiny part of a higher clearance than the Sentry program?"

"I'm not sure. I don't know about any other programs. There were no files, no trails. Nothing."

"What does NEO know about it?"

"He didn't have anything after he was brought back to the castle. Sorry, there isn't more."

Ryland stayed quiet for a few seconds staring at the floor, thinking. "Thanks," he said finally. *Destiny has a higher clearance than me? Or was she taken or killed by someone with a higher clearance?* The thought made Ryland sick. He had left her alone when he became a Sentry agent. *Why did I do that? Because I was selfish.* He couldn't do a thing. He couldn't find out, and he likely wouldn't be able to find her. He struggled with the idea of finding her no matter what and staying with the current mission, which he had screwed up. The Venusians were coming, however, so his sister would have to wait.

THIRTY-ONE

One day before the Venusians return

■

THE LAND WAS vast, flat, and yellow with wheat. Ryland and Fred seemed like ants in a field of giant fans as the wind turbines scattered the gold flatlands. They had left headquarters to find pre-war materials. Ever since the agents arrived at headquarters, looting had stopped because the agents had been training and planning to face the Venusians. Ryland wondered if this was Nick's way of giving them a break. It didn't seem like it would do much. Ryland was more interested in finding out about his family, going out and finding his father, or relaxing on his own as he figured out what he wanted to do.

The agents walked toward the first wind turbine in what seemed like a never-ending field of them. Some turbines still stood tall, but most of them had been felled. Seeing small gatherings of trees in the distance, it was amazing how the turbines dwarfed them. The turbines were scattered throughout the land, making one think the giant fans were what created the wind rather than the machines that once harnessed its power.

The turbine in front of them was lying on the ground, rusted and covered in wheat. Its base was hollow, which allowed the agents to enter it.

As soon as they were inside, the wind stopped. With flashlights in hand, they had to manoeuvre around the spiral stairs, which now lay horizontally with the turbine.

The shade made it cooler inside. It was amazing how walking from light to pitch dark could change a person's mood. It was so healthy and vibrant outside and then dead inside the turbine, with no light. It was similar to how Ryland had felt over the past few weeks: dead, lost, and without purpose. He was the one who started all this.

He thought about the times when things just changed. He would be sitting in a bad mood and then something just changed, not in the environment but just in his head. Something would shift, like cracking an aching knuckle and getting instant relief. He wished it could happen now. But this was all too big, and his despair was too deep.

Searching the turbines didn't take long. They were huge, but they were straight and narrowed toward what would have been their tops. Ryland thought it was strange to search a wind turbine. What could they possibly find there? But a few years back, agents found a few different turbines with things of value in them. Ryland didn't mind looking; the scenery around the turbines was amazing. There were never many buildings around them, and they were always in a clear area. No trees or mountains, always calm and open land. During the day it made Ryland feel open and free. At night it was something different entirely, like the change in emotion from the absence of light. Nighttime in an open field made Ryland feel smaller and more vulnerable, albeit that was before he became an agent. Now he was at the top of the food chain. Not only the top but the top of the top, especially with the new armoured suit enveloping his body.

"Sorry about Liz," Fred said as they reached the end of the turbine, they turned around to walk back.

"Why are you apologizing to me?" Ryland asked.

"I was close to Liz too. She thought of you as a brother." Did that mean she told Fred about her and Ryland's talks? That would be a break in confidentiality.

"What did she tell you? Why?" Ryland asked.

"Because you and I were working on something together, to watch out for you. Especially because it directly involved you," Fred replied. His comment made Ryland think back to what Liz had said at the little diner about him needing a partner. "The Venusians have never done anything like that before," Fred continued, referring to the trap that had killed Liz. "You couldn't have known."

"I found out, just not quick enough. And another agent died because of it."

"Agents are always going to die, Ryland. We're in the business of death, whether we're causing it or affected by it."

They were walking back toward the light, but Ryland couldn't fight the emotional change anymore; the conversation was keeping him in darkness. He wanted to run toward the bright open field, though not necessarily away from the conversation. At the same time, Ryland knew that Fred was the best person to talk to. It was what Liz had wanted for him, someone who knew Ryland well enough to challenge him.

"Neither death was your fault," Fred said. "Your god is omnipresent, not you. You can't always be there for everyone."

"You had an apprentice die, right? How did you deal with it?" Ryland blushed, realizing he might have said it a little too carelessly. "Sorry."

"It's okay. It was hard. He was my responsibility. But like you, we ran into something new, and I couldn't save him." As he emerged from the darkness of the turbine, he squinted in the sunlight. "For a while I couldn't do anything. Then I took my anger out on the Venusians. Soon after that, I was able to gain a new perspective that allowed me to let go, move on, and concentrate on not letting it happen again."

"What was the new perspective?" Ryland asked, hoping he could gain it himself.

"I don't know how to explain it. It was just a moment of clarity. I was thinking about Tom's death, feeling sorry for myself, and thinking about the torturous things I did to the Venusians in my anger. Then I thought, 'None of this is me. I'm here for the people of Earth, protecting them from harm.' I don't know, man; it was a perspective about protecting the entire planet. It's impossible, but it's a huge privilege to be trained and be part of the Sentry program."

Ryland understood how Fred felt. It was a privilege to be a Sentry agent. But Ryland also knew that perspectives weren't the same for everyone. He could never borrow Fred's experience. He had to arrive at his own.

Whenever Ryland thought about how perspectives were different for everyone, it made him frustrated. If he described a perspective to someone, and they said they understood it, they might be telling the truth, but if he had them explain it back to him later, it would be different. Things felt different to everyone. Ryland hated the fact that no one ever fully knew what he was feeling. People said they understood, but they never fully did.

"Right," Ryland said after a short pause. "I'll have to get my own perspective. Thank you."

"I'm here for you, and so are the other agents."

Ryland could have made a comment about Dom, but that would have been a deflection.

"What else did Liz tell you?" Ryland asked as they walked across the field of wheat, which was knee high. A little house was located a hundred metres from the turbine.

"Nothing personal. But I know she made you think about a partnership."

"Good," Ryland said, having wondered about just that.

When they reached the house, they realized it was more of a storage unit, probably used for the turbines. The door had a rusted lock on it that Ryland broke with one blow from his armoured fist. From the doorway they could see the entire room, excluding what was behind the door. The wall across from them was full of shelves holding tools, most of which neither agent had ever seen before. Ryland peeked behind the door and saw a broom and dustpan. *Can't imagine what that's for,* he thought.

Both agents heard something coming. Fred moved to the back of the shed, and Ryland stayed just inside.

A few seconds later, elephants came into view over a hill fifty metres away. The agents relaxed, and Fred came to stand in the doorway. They watched the elephants walk across the field, not even noticing the agents.

Before the war, elephants looked different, but these were normal to the post-war world. They were covered in hair.

"You know, there were animals called mammoths before the war," Fred said. "They had hair just like those elephants and huge tusks, but they were larger than elephants today." He liked nature and animals. He enjoyed how peaceful they were and how vicious they could be when required. Elephants fit that description perfectly, so calm and peaceful yet so big and powerful.

"Oh yeah?" Ryland replied. "I guess Earth has its mammoths back now."

They watched the beasts parade across the golden field as if they were out on a Sunday walk, their hair bouncing and swaying with each step.

"You got your priorities figured out for this next mission?" Fred asked as they continued toward the next house five hundred metres away.

"What do you mean?"

"Are you ready to kill the aliens?"

Ryland paused, his eyes narrowed, his jaw clenched, and his lips pressed into a thin line. "Yes," Ryland replied.

"Even though this Vaul guy has had his second chance, there are at least two more," Fred said.

"These aliens are coming to kill me and expose their existence," Ryland replied. "That may open a slew of problems, putting all of humanity in danger."

"Good. I've been trying to think of all the possible scenarios that could happen tomorrow, such as more than three aliens coming, no aliens coming, aliens coming and offering to make peace, us being unable to stop them, or you and Keira not being able to bring yourselves to kill them." He looked at Ryland and raised his hands in surrender. Fred had a tendency to think through every possibility, whether he dismissed them instantly or not.

"I can't let them do any more harm, not Vaul or any other Venusian who comes after him," Ryland said. "I just hope we'll be able to continue to stop them. I'm afraid that once the war on Venus ends, more will come."

"We'll just continue to train more agents and leave such possibilities to the Circle of Generals to sort out," Fred replied.

Ryland thought for a moment and then nodded. "Right."

Once they were done with the second house, they decided to head back to headquarters. The next turbine was a kilometre away, and they already checked three others and a house. The looting never promised success, but it was nice to get out in the wilderness, whether alone or with someone else, looking into the past.

"Thank you for the looting mission," Ryland said. "I needed a break, and this was a good way to get away from everything for a while."

Fred smiled, then nodded in approval.

THIRTY-TWO

"YOU DON'T THINK I know how to run my city?" the mayor of Scandal Town said, licking his lips and tilting his head in accusation toward General Finch of the Circle of Generals. They visited towns as frequently as possible, gathering information for their reports to the Circle of Generals when they met every month or so.

"Your town is known as Scandal Town, not Marshville," Finch replied. "You didn't do a good job of covering your so-called alliance with the original Marshville." They were meeting in the mayor's office with the doors locked and the window shades drawn.

"What are you here for?" Ezra asked. He hated Finch's harsh personality, but he was offering help and power that Ezra could not get himself.

"To ensure you're doing your end of the job," Finch replied. He was younger than Ezra, which made things worse. It was only a matter of a few years, but still, Ezra had run this town for ten years now, helping it grow and balancing allies with enemies as he expanded his reputation, all while devising his conquests.

"Of course I am," Ezra said. He wanted this. Needed this. If he went against Finch, he would be destroyed, especially since Finch knew his plans. Even if he didn't, the Circle of Generals was a hurdle Ezra could not overcome.

"I have a team in Mount Horizon. They're searching for the contents of the castle and preparing for the siege. They will infiltrate without being seen and ensure easy access for the rest of the weapons and raiders. We will force the mayor of Mount Horizon to listen and make it seem like it's his idea. If they still refuse, we'll start the incursion. They're making a route to the west. There's a path through the mountains, and they'll be ready for the siege when the second group arrives." He knew how to plan. His city was running smoothly enough. Trade was going well, and his citizens worked hard and were paid well. No one knew his intentions for Mount Horizon, and soon after that, Laketown. He even had a circle of men and women who could take over for him if the worst happened.

"How are you avoiding being seen?" Finch asked.

Does he think I'm a child? Ezra wondered, bristling. *He's a general, but I'm not in over my head. Just because he's in the Circle of Generals. Arrogant prick.*

"Do you think I'm incompetent?" Ezra asked. "No one in Mount Horizon even knows the castle is there."

"How do you know that for sure?" Finch asked, trying to fluster him. It worked. Ezra leaped to his feet.

"I know what I'm doing, General. I have run this town for ten years, and no one has found out my plans for Mount Horizon." He had no idea the Sentry agents were aware of his plans. "Don't act like I'm a little child who needs to be questioned to ensure I think of everything. My men are skilled and can handle their mission, including the augmented animals around the castle."

Finch had smiled throughout Ezra's rant, but at the mention of the augmented animals, his smile disappeared.

"Don't underestimate those animals," Finch said. "But if you think your team can do it, I'll leave that up to you. Do not fail; we need that serum to combine with ours. Then this world will be ours. Nothing will be able to stand against what we create."

"What are you creating?" Ezra asked.

"Humans think they're the top of the food chain, but I am not so arrogant."

Right, Ezra thought, barely holding back a sneer.

"The dragon has caused great problems for us. I will create the most impressive beasts on the planet and set them against the Sentry agents and Specialists."

"Specialists? What are the Specialists?"

"Nothing for you to be concerned about," Finch said as he turned and peeked out the window. "I'm not sure I have full confidence in your side of the plan. I will focus on my plans but also keep an eye on your progress. But it causes enough stress as is."

"What does?" Ezra asked, genuinely confused.

"Supervising you."

"Don't. I can handle things," Ezra said, his frustration growing. He licked his lips to wet them. His mouth was running out of saliva, just like his patience. He wanted to kick the general out, but Ezra knew the void sucker had more information than he did.

"I don't believe you can," Finch said, causing Ezra to clench his jaw in anger. "Do you have a plan to overcome the river between here and the mountains?" He said it to make the mayor more like a child, like his subordinate.

"There is a narrow section of the river on the west end before the lake. They will build a small bridge," Ezra said. *Why do I keep answering? Get rid of him.*

General Finch hesitated, then sighed, looking at the window shades. "Inform me when you have the serum." With that he went out, leaving the door wide open behind him. Ezra could hear his employees working away: people talking and papers being shuffled, stacked, shredded, or stuffed into files.

The mayor's secretary popped her head in as Ezra sat slumped in his chair, releasing his stress in a lengthy sigh. "Sir, your clique is here," she said as Lucy, Travis, and Ryan entered.

"Thank you, Melissa."

Ryan shut the door, and Ezra motioned for them to sit. "Did Finch see you come in?"

"He only saw us waiting," Travis replied.

"So, what's the plan?" Lucy asked. She was a rough girl and seemed to lack empathy. She was as big as Ryan although slightly shorter. Travis was bigger than the two with light brown hair that matched Lucy's.

"Same as before. You will lead the group into Mount Horizon and seize the town one day after you arrive. Send the serum back when you have it. Just surround the town. We don't want to frighten them. The incursion is only a backup. We need this to be quiet, and make it look like a mutual partnership."

"And if the town doesn't comply?" Travis asked.

"Once we have the serum, we can take the town over and force the mayor into meeting our demands. The town will benefit from the agreement and be happy with it, and we'll make the entire thing seem like their idea."

THIRTY-THREE

THE DAY OF the alien's supposed return had finally arrived. The agents had been training and getting to know each other and their new member, Keira. She was good at using her opponents' strengths or gadgets against them. She once pulled the pin of a dummy grenade that was on Fred without him realizing it. The only thing he felt was when she drop kicked him through a door. When he recovered, he whirled toward her, his gun at the ready. But before he could fire, the grenade exploded, the explosion of super condensed air sending him flying for ten feet. Keira even set off one of Marcus's traps with confetti. She would have defeated Marcus as well, but Dom took him out first. Keira wound up engaged in hand-to-hand combat with Dom, which she lost, but even so she had made remarkable progress.

The agents slept extra hours the day before so they wouldn't have to sleep from 12:00 to 6:00, like they usually did, in case the aliens came at that point.

As the sun rose, the agents went and sat in the warp helicopter. It was a sleek matte-black chopper with thrusters that enabled it to go faster than any other helicopter. The agents were wide awake and eager to go.

Ryland was standing outside the helicopter, leaning against the side door, reading the journal. He hadn't had any time to read it after the last entry when he found out not only that the author wasn't from the pre-war times but also that his father was still alive.

The next entry had nothing more about his father. The author described how he had tried to get a better look at the weapon they were meeting at, but it wasn't possible. The entry after that claimed that he had been caught. He said, "the untrusting servant of the government captured by the untrusting government."

Of course he doesn't write more about my father, Ryland thought. *He doesn't know I'm looking for it, and it's not important to him.*

Ryland skimmed through the next few pages where the author talked about the Blood's Shadow, but he didn't find anything of interest. The whole world fell for rumour that the Venusians were augmented humans. Ryland closed the book as Marcus approached.

"Find anything new?" Marcus asked, nodding at the notebook.

"Nothing," Ryland replied, shaking his head in defeat.

"You ever meet any nice aliens?" He rolled his ankles, as he usually did. It was a habit they were all familiar with.

"No, they're all pretty aggressive," Ryland replied.

"Then why would you let one have a chance to come back?" Marcus asked.

"Honestly, I wasn't sure how they fit in with my beliefs or if they're part of God's plan."

"Isn't everything part of his plan?"

"Yes. God would have known about them and all that's about to happen. But I'm not sure if they're included in the salvation part. I don't know. I thought that with how badly I beat him, he would rethink what he was doing."

"Don't underestimate your opponent, Ryland. You know that. But hey, we got your back, and we need you too."

When the pilot came out, he was in awe that he was carrying around these mysterious armoured beings. When Dom looked at him, the pilot almost forgot they were on the same side seeing as Dom's mask had a white skull painted on it.

"You Tom?" Jovian asked. He took off his helmet so the pilot could recognize who was speaking. "You're a good pilot. In fact, I've heard the best." Fred liked to know who was on his team.

"The best, eh? I'm flattered, sir. But there are a lot of great pilots here. I don't think there is a *best*." Tom had worked hard to reach his skill level, as had the other pilots.

"My name is Fred, but call me Jovian in the field." Fred wanted to make Tom feel respected as an equal. "I read your file, and I'm glad to have you as our pilot. Thanks for letting us into your aircraft."

"We all share the aircraft, Fred," Tom replied. "I'll do my best. I just hope it's enough considering the situation." Tom and the other agents knew the situation was anything but normal and would require some unique tactics.

As Tom prepared the helicopter for takeoff, Nick was back in the building with an engineer and the rest of the global analysts surveying the new warp detector they had built. All of them hoped the tech would detect the aliens' arrival. If Zhelm had been telling the truth and hadn't hidden anything from them, they would be able to detect the ships coming. The room was tense. It seemed like everyone in the world was holding their breath while waiting for the machine to detect a warp, but the truth was, no one but a handful of people knew what was about to happen.

The warp detector was part of a new satellite. It also had a camera watching for any ships to appear. Nick hoped that if the detector missed the ship's arrival, the cameras would detect it. It seemed like an impossible situation. They had to keep an eye on the entire world, with only a handful of people in place to protect thousands more.

Finally, an alert popped up on each screen. The analysts started typing. They pulled up another tab and examined some calculations. Nick had no idea what was going on.

"Yup, this is the aliens," an analyst confirmed.

"Where are they?" Nick asked, ready to give the order to the pilot and the agents.

"They haven't come out of warp yet. The warp detector watches interdimensional space." The analyst pushed a few buttons on the keyboard. "And now the aliens have entered that space and are in range of the warp detector. We should be able to figure out where they will warp back into normal space." The analyst typed a few commands and then a location was circled. One hundred kilometres above Earth's surface and approximately one hundred and fifty kilometres from their position. That meant the agents could be there in about twenty minutes,

"How long till they come back into normal space?" Nick asked. He understood a bit of the physics but was having a hard time picturing inter-dimensional space. "And you're positive they'll come out there?"

"Yes, sir. And they'll be there in about fifteen minutes."

Nick grabbed his radio. "Tom. Head north now. The exact coordinates will be sent shortly."

■

The agents strapped in as Tom started the helicopter, the rotors spinning and the engines it had for extra speed roaring to life. The noise was deafening, but the agents' helmets dampened it.

The helicopter lifted off the roof of the HQ building and headed north. They were so high they could almost see the curvature of the Earth. Ryland thought about all the times he had gone hunting or travelling under the red sky with the sun just above the horizon. The view was even more beautiful from on high than it was on the ground.

The agents' nerves about the current situation disappeared for a moment as they sank into deep thought. Then a voice over the comms brought them back to reality,

"The nearest town to the aliens' point of entry is Martin Valley," Nick said. "I'm sending you a schematic of the town and the surrounding area." His voice was calm and assertive. He was in control and confident in his agents. They looked at the schematic. Martin Valley's streets were shaped like a backwards E with tall buildings in between. On the south side was a giant hill, and there was a row of buildings between the spine of the E and the hill.

Fred strategized where each agent could position themselves for maximum efficiency. The other agents searched for their strategy of attack, defence, and evacuation.

The helicopter made a slight turn, now flying straight toward Martin Valley. With a little more than five minutes left in the flight, Ryland glimpsed a flash of light high in the sky. It was bluish white, almost like the blue sky itself got mixed with a white substance that faded after the two were mixed. Then Ryland saw three small ships, smaller than jet fighters, fly down into Earth's atmosphere.

"They're here," Tom called back to the agents. The agents checked their equipment one last time as the helicopter sliced through the air. The agents were antsy for the fight, thinking back to all their other encounters with the Venusians.

Tom aimed to land about fifty metres from the hill. Eager to get rid of the invaders, Dom and Ryland jumped out of the craft before it touched down. As soon as the helicopter touched down, the other agents jumped out. As the helicopter lifted off again, the five Sentry agents were on the ground, ready to enforce.

THIRTY-FOUR

"SET UP IN ninety-degree angles in relation to the east target," Jovian said. "Hunter, go into the office building and get level with the target."

"Got it." Hunter ran into the building.

"Thief, get ready for a tackle," Jovian said. "Sentinel and Banshee, go on the east and west sides of the target."

"Got it," Thief replied, then ran to join Hunter. Banshee ran behind the same building to flank the first target. It was hard to stay in silence as the aliens toyed with the civilians. The aliens were strong enough to lift cars with ease. None of the agents had ever noticed such strength before, and they started to feel the same as the civilians, like this attack was unlike anything they had seen before. They had to respond, but they also had to get into a strong position to oppose them.

"These people look terrified," Hunter said.

"They probably know this is unusual for the Blood's Shadow," Ryland replied.

"No one has seen so many Venusians all at once," Fred said.

The Venusians caused chaos in Martin Valley as they waited for their opponents to arrive. They were like teenagers calling out a classmate to meet them in the parking lot to fight after school and trashing the classmate's car as they waited.

"This building has every organization renting a floor. Pretty cool," Marcus said, still exasperated from running the stairs.

Hmm... that's interesting, Keira thought as she ran by signs for different companies on each floor. It was such a small town with tall buildings still standing from before the war that they shared the buildings. For a small town, it had a lot of paved streets, but they were narrow with only a few vehicles scattered throughout the town. The place was so small it didn't seem to make sense to have a vehicle.

Hunter and Keira got to the floor that was level with where one of the aliens was hovering. Keira cleared a path of desks and chairs while Hunter set up his rifle on a desk. Keira went to stand beside him. The sun was shining on the alien, making his black skin easy to see. Keira thought it looked like a shadow hanging in midair. *That would be something that would tip the civilians off that this isn't just Blood's Shadow.*

"Ready," Banshee announced. The other agents echoed his call.

"On my mark," Jovian said. "Two... one..."

Keira prepared to run; she was only needed if the first assault failed. A stun grenade appeared, then stopped midair as if something had caught it. Then it went off with a small puff of smoke but a bright light and a loud bang. It shattered a few windows in Keira's building.

"Mark," Jovian said as the alien clutched its head.

So that's where its senses are, Keira thought.

Hunter fired, as did Banshee and Sentinel from different directions on the street level. The alien stopped Ryland's bullet, but the other two were too much for the alien to concentrate on while stunned, and they pierced the Venusian's skull. Three more shots were fired, and all three hit their marks, ripping through the alien's chest. Keira was not needed this time, which was a good thing, as it would keep the other aliens ignorant of all the agents' locations.

As gravity took control, the alien fell, tumbling head over foot until he smacked into the street. Deep red blood oozed from his wounds and crept toward the nearest storm drain.

The other aliens, who were occupying other intersections, watched as their comrade fell. Filled with anger, they flew toward his body, but Sentinel and Jovian walked into the middle of the intersection. The aliens stopped, both teams at a standstill. The entire town was silent now. Even the civilians were remarkably quiet, realizing the first attempt to resist the invaders had been a success. Unfortunately, it also gave the civilians the impression that they might not have to leave. If the agents were this skilled against the Blood's Shadow, they thought the fight might end soon.

One of the aliens grabbed a car and sent it tumbling toward Sentinel and Jovian, but Sentinel did a side flip over it, and Jovian dove out of the way. When they landed, they fired their rifles at the alien who had thrown it. Banshee and Hunter opened fire as well, but none of the bullets made it to their mark, all of them stopped by an invisible wall.

Thief charged through a broken window and attempted to tackle the alien, but it sensed her coming and used its telekinetic power to send her flying into the roof of a school at the corner of the intersection.

Thief rolled back onto her shoulders and flipped onto her feet. She looked at her enemies, two aliens floating in the middle of a civilian-filled town facing off against four humans dressed in suits of armour. The sight was surreal, and for a few seconds, Keira couldn't believe she was a part of it.

She snapped back to the present when she saw a car fly into the alley where Banshee was standing. She hoped he got out of the way in time.

Jovian and Sentinel split up on either side of the street to divide the aliens, who were slightly angled from each other, one farther down the street from the other. Hunter, still in the office building with the shattered windows, threw a thermos through the far window in front of the second alien. Distracted, the alien watched the thermos fly through the air, almost missing Hunter as he leaped toward him. Hunter went to stab the alien, but the alien stopped him with his mind and threw Hunter down to the street, then flew down after him and rammed him into a van. The impact left a huge dent.

How much did the armour protect him from that? Thief wondered.

The agents were scattered. An alien threw a car in Jovian's path, then floated down to the ground to face off against Sentinel. He forced Sentinel into the air, holding him completely still.

The alien who was fighting Hunter threw him across the street, back toward the office building. Thief ran to Hunter's aid but stopped as a white noise grew louder. The helicopter appeared on the west side below the buildings, and its guns lit up, firing straight down the middle of the street. The aliens flew down the street to escape, throwing anything they could between them and the helicopter. Meanwhile, the agents dove out of the way as cars, garbage cans, mailboxes, and even the asphalt were shredded in the barrage of bullets.

This town is going to need some serious repairs, Thief thought.

"Everyone okay?" Sentinel hadn't seen Banshee for a while, and he had seen Jovian get hit by a car. Thankfully, Jovian was the first to respond.

"I'm good, went through a window, though."

"All good," Hunter and Thief replied.

"I'm good. Just flanking them." Banshee said.

"Hunter, did you feel how still the air is around them when you tackled that one?" Thief asked.

"Yeah. Feels weird. They can sense anything coming because they control even the air around them. It's like walking into a vacuum."

"We need a good distraction and something big to hit them with," Sentinel said.

One of the aliens threw a car at the helicopter, but Tom dodged it and moved behind the buildings.

"Thanks, Tom," Jovian said, appreciating the few seconds he had bought them, which allowed everyone to get back on their feet.

"I have an idea for a distraction," Sentinel said as he walked out into the middle of the street, his weapon down. Once he got halfway to the aliens, he took off his helmet. Vaul, the alien that Sentinel had spared, focused on him, recognizing his face.

Thief wasn't sure how they saw him without eyes, but they did. *Maybe through telepathy,* she thought as Vaul floated down to the ground.

You beat me once, but you have no chance now, Vaul said. *You're weak; you're all weak. You don't deserve this planet.* He pulsed the idea throughout their minds. It came to them in a chanting tone, like he was addressing a crowd.

"You're right," Ryland said. "We don't deserve a lot of what we get. But we were put here on this planet, and you have trespassed and caused way too much trouble, including killing civilians." Hearing the anger in Ryland's voice, the other agents thought back to all the different aliens they had faced and all the trouble and destruction they had caused. Ryland thought only of this one alien and all that it had led to, this threat to all of humanity.

Banshee made his way around the back side of the buildings. Hunter and Thief were standing on either side of the street behind Ryland. Jovian had set up a sniper perch in the southwesternmost building. Everything seemed still but tense as Sentinel and Vaul continued to converse.

If we killed all of you, your rules would cease to exist, the other alien said from behind Vaul, *and we could take this planet for our own. We were the first to travel to another planet, and we are worthy of your planet.*

"You think just because you can take and kill whatever you want, you have the right to do so?" Hunter asked as he walked into the middle of the street.

Banshee had had enough of the conversation. He pulled the pins of two grenades and threw them high above his enemies. The first grenade blew up two metres above his target. The second exploded next to the second alien. Sentinel put on his helmet as Vaul lunged for him. Hunter shot and then jumped at Vaul. They smacked into each other and fell to the ground. Vaul kicked Hunter off of him, then flew into the side of a building. The second alien threw a phone booth at Hunter. The glass shattered, and Hunter gasped, but neither Hunter nor the booth fell.

"No!" Thief ran across the street to Hunter, shooting at the aliens. Jovian also shot a few explosive rounds at Vaul. They exploded in midair, but Jovian hoped they would still stun Vaul.

Ryland, Thief, and Vaul looked up at the last second as a car that had been thrown six storeys up into the building beside them a few minutes earlier fell toward Vaul. Vaul tried to stop it, but it had too much momentum, and it crushed him. Then something came from where the car had come from. It looked like an agent, but its armour was thicker. It landed on top of the car, crushing Vaul even further. Two more of the human tanks came out of the hole in the building, and several came from every direction. A total of seven humans appeared with armour at least two inches thick, three of whom jumped out of a six-storey hole without hesitation or even a roll to soften their landing.

The agents and the last standing alien were surrounded. Thief was still working on getting Hunter down, but it was no use, Hunter was slumped and stuck, part of the building now with no sign of life. Then a flash of light high in the sky blinded the agents and the alien, another alien ship.

"Crap," Jovian exclaimed. The ship flew straight down, and an alien emerged from it as the ship flew by. He grabbed the remaining alien, slammed him into the south building, and yelled something that none of the human witnesses understood. All guns were trained on both aliens. The new arrival turned to the humans.

They should not have come, he said. *I apologize.*

THIRTY-FIVE
Six years earlier

"**DO YOU KNOW** the story of Thael?" Ryland asked Nat.

"Yeah. He was the one who led Elo's people from what is now Lunatia to Mesania," Nat replied. To this day a huge river still flowed through the two countries, which looked like they were once one unified country. Elo, through Thael, walked them through the water, fully submerged to avoid attack from the Lunitians, and they never had to come out of the water for a single breath. Most people knew the story of Thael, even those who didn't accept Elo and called the stories myths or fairy tales.

"Exactly. Thael resisted his call to lead those people."

"But he was the strongest believer." Nat didn't see any resistance from Thael through any of the stories she knew about him.

"At first he didn't want to do what Elo asked," Ryland explained. "He made excuses and didn't want to do it. His people were slaves, and he would have had to oppose the Lunatians."

"But he still ended up doing it," Nat replied.

"Yes. After Elo showed Thael his power."

"Ah, right. He showed him miracles." As obvious as it was for a god to show his subjects miracles as proof of their superiority, miracles had to be used because, well, they were miracles. If the god showed something within the natural realm, it could be explained away. Something outside of the natural world would show that the god was also outside of the natural world, able to control it.

"Yes, a series of miracles that affected the kingdom."

"Why? Seems like a lot when it had nothing to do with getting the people out," Nat observed.

"Elo shows his power to show who he is. Going up against the king's magicians and sorcerers, Elo showed he was more powerful than the dark powers that the magicians and sorcerers claimed to use," Ryland explained. "Elo chose Thael to be the start of his people, and it was time for Thael to free them so Elo could set them apart from the rest of the world. Then Elo himself came centuries later to set them free, not only Thael's descendants but everyone throughout time."

"So why would Elo choose Thael to have his own separate people in history?"

"To show the rest of the world what it looked like to follow the one true God. He wanted to unite the world by showing them that all other idols and gods were fake and then coming down into the world and wiping our sins away."

■

The body lay in the dark, rocky cave, mangled. Bruises covered the body, rendering it unrecognizable. Ryland's heart stopped at the possibility of who it might be.

■

"So you think the aliens can't be saved the same way we can?" Natalie asked.

"I'm not sure, but it stands to reason. Elo came to us as a man to save man. Through the first man came sin, but through the second man, Elo, comes life. 'For by man came death, by a man has come also resurrection of the dead.' So, if he was to save the aliens as well, he would have to be a descendant of them." It took a while to see that that verse could mean that only humans could be saved. He had never thought about it from another species' perspective.

Their phones rang, breaking their train of thought. An alien had arrived. They checked their devices and saw that a Blood's Shadow member was a few kilometres from their position. They geared up, grabbing weapons and proper clothes. Natalie also grabbed her field kit, which contained medication and analysis equipment. They wanted to understand their opponents instead of just killing them and then studying them. They were good partners; they both questioned the Venusians' reasons for invading Earth.

This Venusian gave them no discussion. As soon as it arrived, it attacked. Natalie dropped her field kit and joined the fight.

∎

The cave was damp and hard to find. Ryland only found it because there was an odd formation above the small descent into the cave mouth.

∎

Sliding past the intruders' knees, Ryland sliced his knife through its tough skin. Nat punched its face, both of them running in opposite directions to make it hard for the alien to follow. Natalie drew her pistol, but the alien knocked it out of her hand. Ryland jumped and swung on a tree branch to perform a 180-degree turn, coming right back at the alien while Nat threw a rock from the opposite direction. The Venusian couldn't focus on everything that was happening, allowing the agents to continue to pummel their opponent.

Natalie shoulder charged the alien, but he threw her off to the side, sending her sliding across the dirt and into a building. Ryland came in close to the Venusian, trading punches and kicks. He admired the Venusians. They could just throw him into things, but they typically fought hand to hand when their opponent did the same.

The Venusian held his own against Ryland, showing adequate skills. But Ryland had a partner, and it wasn't long before Natalie returned. She went to elbow the intruder in the head, but the Venusian slowed the blow with his telepathy. It wasn't enough to stop the two agents from landing multiple hits, hindering the alien's concentration.

Natalie was knocked back, but she saw the pistol to her side. She grabbed it and then attacked. She jumped and did a spin kick. As she landed, she fired at the alien's head. The bullet travelled through the thick skin of the Venusian's neck. Ryland punched the alien's head and ripped the hole bigger, causing more thick red blood to pour out.

■

He entered with caution and looked on in horror. Between the bruises, the body's skin was pale and covered with red cuts. Blood ceased to ooze, for it had dried long ago and there was no more to bleed. The blood had pooled on the ground and was now motionless, like the body. Tears formed in Ryland's eyes, and he clenched his fists in anger.

■

"I wish we didn't have to kill these things," Natalie said.

Ryland looked at her. "You wish we could be friends with them?"

"Well, at least be able to live with them. They deserve to live, don't they?"

He shrugged. "Maybe not. There was a species before that was an abomination that was wiped out by Elo. I feel the same as you, though. I want to understand them and live with them. But Elo makes it seem that we're the only ones he meant to create above all."

Ryland looked at Natalie's collar, where a necklace hung. It consisted of wood, rock, glass, metal, and bone beads. She had gathered them herself as she researched different interests. Ryland admired her deeply. She always wanted to understand animals, Earth, humans, and now the aliens. He loved her, and she looked up to him for his knowledge, integrity, and strength.

■

"If my mind is unfaithful, my body may soon follow," Ryland argued, hesitation in his voice. He didn't want to have this conversation. Tears were running down her face. They had been on a relaxing week with no aliens, civilians needing help, or terrain to be monitored in days. They had done so much together since their training, but they had these recurring thoughts.

"You don't know that," Natalie said. "Just stay with me and I can help." Her voice cracked from the tightness inside.

"I can't trust myself. And you can't trust me either."

"Well, I do trust you, Ryland," she replied. "You sound like you have no choice."

"This is my choice. I may hurt you more if I stay. I admire other women. I love you, Nat. But I... I lust after others. I'm sorry. I don't want to hurt you."

"You're hurting me now!" she yelled, then closed her mouth, regretting her tone.

Ryland wanted to take everything back. He wished he could stay, but he would only hurt her more. He wanted to be honest, but that would involve telling her his desires. Even if she didn't need to know his lusts, he would feel fake and disrespectful. He wanted to treat her the way she deserved. Ryland's dad had always said his mother was the daughter of the king of the universe. Ryland didn't fully know what that meant, but his father was a good father and husband, and Ryland wanted to be the same. Now he just couldn't obtain that status.

Ryland noticed that in addition to her necklace, she was wearing his wooden cross with a metal frame. He gave it to her as they started to read Elo's story, which he carried with him. He gave her his book with that cross, which came from his father's study. Ryland took it after his father passed. Now he had to leave it with her and leave her.

■

He walked up to the corpse and knelt beside it, his knees soaked in blood. He placed his hand on the corpse's cold, dead wrist. Her hair was still so pleasant, her face elegant. Then he saw the necklace. Beads of wood, rock, metal, bone, and glass. He pulled it off the floor to see the whole thing. The cross was intact, but the glass was broken in half.

THIRTY-SIX

Present day

WHO WERE THESE new armoured humans? Was it their suits, or had something been done to them that made them strong enough to throw a car? Was the serum still around? Had it been perfected? Their armour was all similar, grey and bulky with squared-off edges. However, each suit had different markings carved into it in different places. They all stood close to seven feet tall. The alien was less of a surprise at that point. Being a top-secret agency to keep alien traffic a secret, one would think they knew about most other secret agencies and companies, but these human tanks, "Specialists" they called themselves, were indeed humans and were as secret as the Sentry program, if not more.

The agents were sitting in a room together with the seven Specialists, a distinct line between the two groups. A clock on the wall ticked. It was now 4:36. They all had to be debriefed after the situation in Martin Valley. Apparently the newcomer alien was there to collect the alien trespassers. He was different from the others. Instead of a red glass-like material on their biceps and thighs, the glass was white. He had the same build but was more powerful, both physically and in terms of his rank.

The group of them had been in that room for an hour or so. The Specialists had been nice enough to give them some info on who and what they were, but a lot of that time was spent in silence as the agents processed Marcus's death. They stood around uneasily, wanting to talk but not in front of the strangers.

"Sorry about your loss," a Specialist said. She was a female, as evidenced by her voice and her posture. The armour for male and female Specialists was more or less the same. Only smaller at the waist for the females.

"Thanks," Ryland said. "He was a good agent and a good friend. We've all trained together since the beginning." He looked into the Specialist's visor but couldn't see anything but a reflection of himself.

Dom stared at the floor. He didn't feel comfortable sharing information with this new agency, not knowing what they would do with it. Were they from another country?

"We've lost some friends in our program as well," another Specialist said, connecting with their pain. Another Specialist spun his helmeted head toward the one who spoke as if to say, "What are you doing?"

"And what program is that?" Dom asked, seizing the opportunity to get more information. No one replied. Then the door opened, revealing a man in a black suit.

"Everyone, follow me," he said, then turned to walk away. The Specialists walked out first. Their armour sounded heavy with each step.

How do they stay quiet in battle? Ryland wondered.

They walked down a hallway that opened into a large foyer with marble floors, thick pillars and railings, and long staircases on either side. Across the foyer was another door that led to a room with a giant wooden table with ten seats behind it. Down the centre of the room was an aisle with rows of empty chairs on either side. It was a military courtroom.

The two aliens stood wearing reinforced handcuffs and electric collars around their necks. Four marines with guns stood with them, two on either side. The Specialists and agents spread out into a line facing the table, at which three men were sitting. Their name tags read, from left to right, Corporal Mitchell, General Finch, and Sergeant Morrison.

The door behind them opened. They heard some commotion but couldn't make out what was said.

Then they heard Nick thank someone and walk down the aisle. The door shut with a quiet click behind him.

"Agents," Nick said as he stopped and stood beside them, filling in a space between them and the Specialists.

"Alright, let's get this started," Finch said. All that was visible of the men sitting behind the table were their shoulders and heads. "Ryland, please step forward." Ryland did as he was told, putting himself in the centre of the room.

"You had first contact with the alien," Finch continued, shuffling through some papers. He was bald and in his mid-fifties. "The alien's name was Vaul. Is that correct?"

"That is correct, sir," Ryland replied.

"And how did that end?" Corporal Mitchell asked.

"We fought, I won, and then I gave him two options: to die or to return to his planet."

"Why did you think it was a good idea to let him go?" Corporal Mitchell asked with a hint of resentment, clasping his hands on the table in front of him.

"Because he cares for his enemies too," Fred said as he stepped forward beside Ryland.

"Stand down, soldier," General Finch ordered. Nick put his arm on Fred's shoulder to pull him back. The agents were a brotherhood. Even though they were separated most of the time, they were not going to be stopped by the formal walls and rules of a courtroom. Some who knew that about the Sentry program thought the agents were arrogant.

"He's right though, sir," Ryland said. "We're to love those around us."

"You caused a big problem and an even bigger threat," Sergeant Morrison said.

"With all due respect, sir, we neutralized the immediate threat and just have to let the public know."

"We'll decide what has to be done," Mitchell replied. "You just follow orders!"

"He made a mistake, and they fixed it, sir," Nick said, rising to his feet. "And now we no longer have the burden of trying to keep the Venusians' presence a secret."

"So this was your plan all along?" Morrison asked.

"No, sir," Nick replied. "I reprimanded Ryland for his actions, and we prepared a plan to keep the Venusians a secret."

"You forced the Specialists to deploy early for backup, Nick," Morrison pointed out.

"And we thank you for the backup, but who exactly are these Specialists?" Nick asked, trying to keep the focus off his agents.

"They are part of the Sentry 2 program," Finch replied.

Nick and the agents were shocked to hear there was a second Sentry program. How did they not know? Who made it? The agents didn't even know who had made their Sentry program.

"They are trained with performance-enhancing augmentation and armour," Finch continued. "They are also trained in threat analysis and combat."

"Sentry 2?" Nick asked in surprise. "So it's an upgraded Sentry program? Why was I not informed?"

"Because you didn't need to be informed. It's a top-secret program, and no one knows about them. But now you have nullified that."

"Sirs," Fred said, standing up again. "Ryland was kind to his enemy. These are all first-case scenarios. He gave them a chance, and now we know how they will act. And we also have this alien who came to take the rogue aliens back."

"We can't trust this alien, just like Ryland shouldn't have trusted Vaul," Corporal Mitchell said, staring at Ryland.

"I do regret my actions, sir," Ryland replied. "I gave him a chance and trusted God."

"These are aliens, Ryland. Your God does not apply," Corporal Mitchell said.

"I disagree, sir," Ryland said, although he had to admit Mitchell might have been right in one sense.

"This is not a religious debate," General Finch declared, stopping the conversation before it got more off topic. "Ryland, you and Keira will be reassigned to desk jobs. As for the two aliens, Zawn and Xelk," he looked at the aliens, who had been so quiet the others would have forgotten they were there if not for the soldiers surrounding them, "they will be publicly executed." The announcement was met with commotion amongst the agents.

"You can't do that!" Ryland protested. *How are you going to control their reaction when you execute one of their own, especially one that came to stop the others?* Ryland thought.

"Stand down!" Finch said, standing to his feet. "You have made a disgrace of this courtroom with your interruptions!" He sat back down and collected himself, "Specialists, do you have anything to add?" When the stoic human tanks didn't respond, he nodded. "Alright. They will be executed tomorrow at noon, with the event broadcast live."

Neither the Specialists nor the aliens reacted to the news. Nick lowered his head with disappointment. Dom didn't seem to care too much. He didn't want to get involved in whether alien life should be valued on Earth.

"And Nick," Finch added, "teach your agents to think of the bigger picture."

THIRTY-SEVEN

"WHERE IS HE?" Alek asked his brother as he walked into the room where Anton and General Leonid were standing. His wife was crying, unsure what was going to happen. Alek saluted his superior. The general nodded, and Alek lowered his arm but didn't relax. He didn't know why the general was there. He glanced at Anton, who looked scared, which he should have been.

"Your nephew has a skill set that may be useful to the Circle of Generals," Leonid said. Alek's mind flashed to the AI that Anton has been developing.

Did he finish it? Alek wondered. *Did he place the AI in a system he shouldn't have?*

"What skill set is that, sir?" Alek asked.

"I'm sure you know, soldier, or I would be dealing with his parents at this moment and not you," the general replied.

Alek's eyes twitched. "Yes, sir. May I ask how you found out?" He wanted to see what the general knew before admitting to his own knowledge of the circumstances.

"Please, take a seat." Leonid gestured to a chair beside the couch where the general and Anton were sitting. "He has tampered with high-security mainframes."

Alek glared at Anton, who recoiled from the look.

"Don't worry, Alek," Leonid continued. "We shut him down, but his young age is impressive, and it's the reason I'm here." He asked for Anton to go into the other room. His mother went with him as the men talked.

"I can't take him away from you," Leonid said, looking at Anton's father. "But we would like to test him. He could be of value to us."

"What are you planning to station him as, sir?" Alek asked. Before Leonid could answer, Anton's mother returned with three cups of coffee and a jug of water with glasses. After she placed them on the table, Leonid was the first to reach for the coffee, thanking her. Alek poured himself a glass of water as well, thanking his sister-in-law.

"Analyzing electronics," Leonid continued. "He seems to enjoy that. Someday he might make some important advancements for us." He sipped his coffee, testing the temperature.

Leonid and Alek were careful about the words they used around the civilians. Anton and his parents knew that Alek worked as security under the Circle of Generals, but they didn't know it was for the Sentry program or that they often dealt with alien trespassers.

"But he's only a boy," Anton's father said, trying to keep his emotions in check.

"That's why I'm here talking to you and not him directly," Leonid replied. "With me he could help the Circle of Generals protect and strengthen the globe."

"Strengthen it against what? Other humans?" Anton's father asked.

Alek tensed. There were, of course, human conflicts, but the main problem was the Venusians.

"There are stories of the pre-war world having eyes around the world. Anton could help us with having screens and cameras watching elsewhere," Leonid replied.

Anton's father considered this in awe, although he didn't fully understand it.

Alek knew how hard it was to get something like Anton's computer. Not many towns had TVs, radios, or cameras. It was tempting to have Anton help the Circle of Generals and the world. Alek knew that Anton was working now; it was the deal he made with his father if he wanted to quit school. Alek wanted Anton to follow through with his work.

"Anton may be able to help us with that," Leonid continued. "I don't know how he connected with our systems without directly connecting, so with our current knowledge and his ability to work around our systems or invent new ones, we can advance together. I am here to get your permission to bring your son for testing of his abilities. I'll give you a few days to decide whether you want your son to contribute to the world and make something of himself. I can assure you that we take care of our fellow members and strive to do the same for every human. Just ask Alek."

Alek knew it was true, but he also knew the general was only saying that to tempt his brother into letting Anton go.

After seeing the general out, Alek returned to the house with Anton's father.

"What were you doing?" he asked the boy. "Have you not learned to obey and respect the authorities?"

"I... they have an AI," Anton replied.

"Anton, you can't meddle with the authorities' systems."

"Sorry. I was just looking for a challenge and information. My AI's information processor was malfunctioning." He looked at the ground, ashamed to admit his failures.

"Why didn't you ask me?" Alek inquired.

"You were gone."

"Patience, Anton," Alek said. "I know this is important to you, but you must have patience in life."

"I know. It's just been frustrating that it isn't working."

Alek was quiet for a moment, processing his feelings. Then he looked up at Alek. "Can I ask you something, Uncle?"

"Of course."

"You said not to meddle with the authorities."

"Yes."

"Then why did you stand in the general's way?"

"I stood in front of authority to protect you. I didn't want them to punish or hurt you, so I had to try."

"So you can go against the authorities to protect others?" Anton asked. Alek smiled at the comment. He was a smart kid.

"As long as you're not hurting anyone else. And as long as you're willing to take the punishment."

"You were going to take my punishment?" Anton asked.

"I was," Alek replied, putting his arm around his nephew and pulling him close.

THIRTY-EIGHT

RYLAND DIDN'T KNOW there were so many cameras in the region. Maybe that was something the COG had. It made sense why everyone wanted the execution to be broadcast. Aliens were real and on Earth, and the human race was about to execute them to send a warning. At the same time, the Sentry 1 and Sentry 2 programs were being announced. It was a good way to do it. Bad news first, "There are aliens, and they have overstepped their bounds and threatened us," followed by the good news, "But we have these agents and super soldiers to protect you."

The air was still, as was the crowd, the sun beaming down on them, uninterrupted by clouds. Ryland, Keira, Fred, and Dom stood to the right of the stage, and the seven Specialists stood to the left. The two aliens stood at centre stage, still wearing their enforced cuffs and shock collars and escorted by the marines. The aliens looked calm, but without faces it was difficult to know how they were facing their imminent death.

General Finch walked up the side stairs onto the stage and then stopped, standing just in front of the aliens and off to the side. "This is an important day," he said, his voice confident as he addressed the crowd. "We now know we are not alone in the universe or in our solar system." He paused to let the news sink in. "These beings are not the augmented humans you think they are. They are not the Blood's Shadow. They are from Venus, our neighbouring planet. The bad news is, they're hostile." Finch let his head drop and took a few steps like he was pondering what to say next. "They have come here and damaged our cities and taken lives." His voice was more empathetic, but he raised it back to a powerful tone. "But today we are sending them and all other extraterrestrial life a warning."

The crowd cheered, but they didn't really know the whole story. They didn't know the one alien came to make peace and return to Venus with the others.

"We also have these soldiers." He spread his arms and signalled for the Specialists and the agents to come on stage. "These are the members of our Sentry programs. They are the ones who found these intruders and captured them."

The crowd applauded, but Ryland didn't accept the applause. He still felt this was the wrong decision. But he stood quietly in his armour. His visor was like a bubble around his face, his mirrored visor concealing his feelings.

"We shall send this message: there are penalties to causing trouble with Earth."

At that point, the four marines stepped back.

"Ready," Finch said without looking. "Aim." The marines raised their guns, pointing them at Zawn and Xelk's heads.

As Finch was about to say the last word, which everyone knew, a loud noise came from the buildings behind the stage. A dropship rose over the buildings. Then a flash-bang and an electro-magnetic pulse went off, blinding everyone. Panic ensued as everyone ducked and shielded their eyes.

The Sentry 1 agents sprang over to the aliens. Knowing the attack was coming, they weren't affected. They escorted the aliens into the dropship and then took off.

Ryland watched from the dropship as the people and the soldiers tried to collect themselves. The Specialists were the first to recover.

The EM pulse didn't do anything to their suits? Ryland wondered. *At least the flash-bang caught them off guard.* Their sight adjusted in time for Ryland to see the seven heavily armoured, enhanced soldiers look straight at him, making him their next target.

"Looks like we're good," Dom said, peering out beside Ryland and watching for a countermove as they flew away. The craft was a classified Sentry drop ship with two dual jet engines, four harrier thrusters, two afterburners, and a makeshift heat shield making it capable of space travel, which would be needed now. The ship had two-inch-thick titanium alloy armour, a fifty-calibre armour-piercing gun under the cockpit, and an auto turret on top of the ship with rockets as an explosive option.

"Why are we doing this?" Dom asked as they headed back to the passenger hold.

"They were doing the wrong thing," Ryland said, midway between Dom and the pilot's seat. There was a wall with a doorway separating the cockpit with four seats and four more foldable bench seats in it. The entire cockpit was able to eject in case of emergency.

"They're our superiors," Dom retorted.

"Dom, they were gonna murder them. It would have started a war with the Venusians," Fred said, having agreed with Ryland from the beginning. He was standing next to Tom, their pilot from their mission to stop the aliens and now to save the aliens. Tom jokingly said the agents were "going on strike." That reminded Ryland of his conversation with Liz.

"One of these things killed Marcus, and now we are saving them?" Dom asked.

"The authorities are too quick to kill our new neighbours," Ryland replied. "We need to start this right, even though the Venusians aren't." He looked at the alien captives sitting on the left side of the craft. "Marcus died for the right thing. But now we have a chance to save more lives in a different way."

These are the foreigners from the prophecy, he thought. *They are the ones we are to save.*

"This isn't about your religion, Ryland," Dom said.

"It's about saving more lives, Dom," Ryland shot back. *Which is what God wants,* he thought.

"Remember, not everyone believes in what you believe," Dom replied.

"I'm well aware of that," Ryland said. "I won't force you to do anything you don't believe in, Dom."

"Dom, you agreed to help us," Nick reminded him, speaking as a friend rather than a superior.

"I'm not backing out," Dom replied. "I'm just questioning why we're saving them." They all knew Dom didn't care as much, but they were a team and friends, and Dom would stay loyal to that.

They passed over the river that divided the meadows that lead to Scandal Town and the forest that lead to Mount Horizon. There was a bridge over the river.

When did they make a bridge? Ryland wondered. The forest was undisturbed from what he could tell, and the city looked busy. However, as they got closer, Ryland realized it wasn't busy; it was a raid, and the bridge was for the raiders to get over the river.

Shoot! Ryland thought. *Mayor Ezra started the raid!* The Venusian issues had blinded him to the possible war that the mayor of Scandal Town had planned. Ryland tried to think of how they could help, but they were on the run from super soldiers who had more resources than they did, and they had no time. Ryland saw smoke rising, knowing Keira probably saw it too.

"They're raiding Mount Horizon!" she exclaimed. "We need to help them!"

"We don't have time," Fred said as he peered through the front window.

"This is our home and our family," she said. Everyone knew she was talking about Earth and not just Mount Horizon.

"We're still wanted, Keira," Ryland said.

"We can hide again, run when we're done, fight them," she insisted, her voice full of passion and anger.

"We can't fight them," Fred replied. "The super soldiers are more numerous, stronger, and have more resources. If we help now, they'll arrest us within the hour."

"But my family is down there!" she said.

Everyone fell silent. Then Ryland stepped forward and put his hand on her shoulder. She shrugged it off as she opened the door.

"Keira!" Ryland tried to grab her, but she evaded his grasp. She was a fast learner. The other agents watched her body fall from the craft. She gained control of her free fall and angled toward the nearest mountain.

■

The sound of the wind was one of the coolest sounds. It reminded Keira of ATVing with her brother. But this time the sound came with a more in-depth feeling: fear. But she had gone through training, and she knew how to push past her fear now. Even before she met Ryland, she had pushed past it better than most.

She angled toward the mountain ahead, making her body like a spear to increase her speed. She had climbed that mountain many times before. It was small, and it took only half a day to reach the top. She would sit at the top for the rest of the day and look out over the town. It gave her perspective, and seeing the larger mountains behind her humbled her. It was odd how the mountain made everything else look small when she was on top of it, and now it looked small. But as she raced toward it, it was increasing in size. Once she was over it, she opened her arms and legs to slow down and control her descent.

When she passed the peak with the little ledge she used to sit on when she reached the top, she pulled out an impact grenade and pulled the pin, then held it, calculating when to throw it. There was a small quarry at the base of the mountain, filled with runoff. She threw the grenade straight down, then continued into a front flip and caught her spin to slow her descent. The grenade fell faster than her due to it having less air resistance, then disappeared into the water and exploded. At the last second, she straightened out and dove into the disrupted water, feet first.

She slammed into the water and it slammed back on her from all sides. It was cold too. A feeling of dread consumed her as she felt helpless to her sinking. Then her body slowed to a stop. She was still dry because of her suit. She took a cautious breath, knowing the suit's air holes would have closed when it made contact with the water. She started to swim upwards, surprised at how well she could swim in the suit.

When she broke the surface, she swam for the edge, the sounds of gunfire, explosions, and screams all around her.

She got out of the quarry and observed the mayhem, which was still a few hundred metres away. People were running on the outskirts of the town, and smoke was rising from within.

"Bastards," she whispered under her breath. She ran toward the buildings that signified her home, her beginning.

There were trees on the edge of town that she used for cover. The citizens used the trees as traps. Some of the traps had been sprung, with bodies left behind. Blood pooled around some bodies. Others had been deformed by blunt hits.

She slowed into a jog and then crouch-walked, moving alongside the small one- to two-storey buildings. Gardens had been trampled and blown to bits, full of craters. As she got closer to the centre of town, she saw citizens and raiders running, most toward the mountains or the forested valley to the south. Then Keira saw someone pointing and yelling orders.

Someone in charge, she thought. *Good.*

The person yelling orders backed behind a corner, continuing to issue commands. Keira pulled out her auto rifle and then walked toward the group, opening fire. Headshots took down five raiders before anyone else came from behind the corner.

When she reached the corner, she came at it wide, attempting to see if anyone was around it. A rock smashed a window over the street directly adjacent to Keira. She ducked, then realized she probably didn't need to do that due to her suit. When she stood up, someone tackled her from behind, knocking her rifle out of her hands.

Her attacker had a buzz cut with a five o'clock shadow highlighting his jawline. They both got up, and the man pulled out a short baton. He flicked it, and it extended. When Keira stepped into range, he smacked her with it. It would have broken her arm if not for the armour.

She moved in closer, but he backed away, Keira lunged and grabbed his collar. He lowered his shoulder and tried to bring Keira with him, but she wrapped herself around him and grabbed his neck, throwing him back. He flew a few feet and then landed with a thud on the brick walkway.

Other raiders stepped forward to fight. Keira broke the first guy's arm and then the next. The last guy had a pistol. Keira jumped toward him, grabbed his arm, then went under it and flipped him, dislocating his arm as she slammed him into the ground, knocking him unconscious.

A staff lunged at her face, but she maneuvered out of the way. Then she punched the man who had swung it in the abdomen and grabbed the back of his neck.

"What are you doing here?" she asked, squeezing his neck. In response, he shortened the staff and then extended it into her chest. Then he switched his grip, jumped up, and came down on Keira's helmet. She fell to one knee, and when she looked back, she saw the man running away from her.

You're too ambitious, Ryland's voice told her in her head. The man had gotten away, but gunshots rang out, and she knew she had to find cover in case the raiders returned.

As she headed toward the garden near the fountain, she saw her parents. That's when it hit her that she had left home and became an agent without telling them. Now she was standing only a few feet away, and they didn't recognize her as their daughter.

What was I thinking? she thought. How was she going to explain this? Then again, maybe she didn't have to. *They don't recognize me. I'll just make sure they're alright.*

She walked toward them, her rifle in hand. "Are you okay?" Keira asked. Next to them she saw a body, bleeding from three holes in the chest. It was her Uncle Connor. A lump formed in her throat. The man who had taken her hunting. The one who would make jokes and nag her whenever he got the chance. Her vision got blurry, and she realized it was from tears.

Shoot. Stop crying.

With her helmet on, she couldn't even wipe away the tears. She took a deep breath. "It isn't safe for you here," she said, thankful there was no trace of tears in her voice.

They went to their house and got some weapons. Then she led them into a cave at the base of the mountain near the quarry. Keira left her parents there without telling them anything.

Where is Ryland's god in all this? she wondered. He had mentioned that the timing of the augmented animals and the Venusians' arrival seemed to be orchestrated. It was a good point. No one knew the Venusians were aliens because of the Blood's Shadow theory. *But what about now? The Venusians assaulted Earth, then were almost executed even after one of their superiors came to stop them. Now the agents are fugitives on the run, and I'm here because the COG didn't see this raid happening. Plus, my uncle is dead! Where is the being I'm meant to put my faith in? Maybe he was juggling too many things and lost control.*

She made her way through town, taking out raiders whenever she could. She found a large group of them making their way to the mountains. *What do they want there?*

She followed the group by heading toward an adjacent mountain. Crossing over the mountain to get a higher vantage point, Keira realized they were heading toward the castle.

The serum, she thought. *They don't know it's gone.*

Keira crept along the side of the mountain above the raiders as they entered the castle. A group of men was standing at the entrance of the trail. Keira threw a rock to the other side of the trail. The sun would block the raiders' view if they looked up at her. The rock tumbled back down the rocky hillside. She took out her longbow and arrow and shot two arrows before the raiders realized the threat was on the other side. She shot the third man in the chest. Then she jumped down next to him, ripped the arrow out of his bleeding chest, and blocked the last raider's gun, stabbing the arrow into his neck. Blood squirted out, covering her hand.

Keira collected her arrows and then set some traps along the trail. The raiders would realize soon that the serum and NEO were not there, and then they would come to interrogate the townspeople.

As she went back to collect her friends and family, Keira tried to imagine what the raiders would do if they got the serum and NEO.

THIRTY-NINE

THE OTHER AGENTS watched Keira fall toward the base of the mountain.

"She's got more guts than I thought," Dom said. Ryland didn't know whether to order the pilot to land the craft or keep going. He was sure the other agents would say to keep going.

"We need to get her," Ryland said.

"We don't have time," Dom replied.

"She's your apprentice," Nick said. "Do you think she needs help?"

"Against the raider, no. Against the Specialists, yes."

"Ryland, she has made her decision," Fred said. "She may get captured, but she won't get killed."

Ryland didn't know how to feel. Keira was his apprentice, which meant he was responsible for her. But this was her decision in a dire situation. She had her family, but she also had a mission. While she had chosen to abandon her mission and her team, Ryland still felt pulled to follow her, not wanting to leave her behind.

"Let her go," Fred said, seeing Ryland's struggle. "We need you here with us."

"This isn't about love," Ryland replied. Then he remembered what the prophet had said: "Let the thief go." *This is the right time,* he thought. As much as he still wanted to stop, he let her go.

"She can handle herself," Dom said. "They're only raiders, and she has been trained for worse." He nodded toward the aliens to explain what he meant. There was a silent pause while everyone awaited Ryland's decision, every second the aircraft, moving further and further away.

This was her decision, Ryland thought, *but she could use help. If any of us go to help her, though, we'll all get caught by the Specialists sooner or later.* That was it. He decided to keep going.

The ship flew undisturbed for the rest of the flight, then landed on the roof of the headquarters building. The agents were tense, keeping an eye out for their enemies. Nick and Fred went inside to get a file that was downloading all data on the Sentry 1 program, after which they would delete all other files pertaining to the program.

The sky was clear as Ryland and Dom waited on the helipad, watching for incoming ships while keeping an eye on their captives, who were abnormally quiet. *Could they direct who hears their speech?* Ryland thought.

"How long will this take?" Dom asked.

"The file should be downloaded. I just have to grab it and delete the rest while sending another warning."

"How long?" Dom asked, his patience thinning.

"Five minutes?" Nick said.

"I don't think we have five minutes," Dom replied as he watched a dot in the distance turn into a helicopter.

"Contact," Ryland said over the comms. "Ten kilos out." They would be at the HQ in one minute.

"Once they get within range, hit them with an EMP," Nick said. "We don't want to kill them."

"Roger that," Ryland said. He went back to the dropship and pulled out a grenade launcher, loading it with an EMP grenade.

"Don't try anything," he said to the Venusians.

This is your war, Zawn said. Ryland paused at that then walked back to the edge of the roof and waited as the helicopter got closer.

Accounting for the wind, Ryland took aim, then fired two grenades. The first exploded near the helicopter's rotors, and it dropped into a tailspin. Ryland watched intently, hoping the crash didn't kill his fellow soldiers. They had gone rogue, but they were not murderous.

When the chopper was about ten storeys off the ground, the pilot regained control and went into a controlled descent. When it touched down, five Specialists leapt out and ran into the HQ building. There had been seven of them earlier. Did that mean the other two were in the helicopter, or had they seen Keira jump out and sent two Specialists after her?

"They're going in the front door," Ryland said over the comms.

"Roger that. I'll shut down the elevators." Nick replied. Dom walked toward the door. "Coming your way."

"You guys gonna be out in time?" Ryland asked.

"Should be," Nick replied. "I don't want to underestimate our foes, but they have to climb a hundred storeys using the stairs."

Ryland watched as the helicopter took off and flew away from the building. He assumed they were going to hover just out of range, ready to swoop in for a quick pickup if needed. He watched the helicopter through his scope, looking for any sign of a Specialist inside. Then he went back into the dropship, not wanting to get sniped, if that's what they were planning. He also had to keep an eye on the Venusians.

What kind of mess have I made? Ryland wondered. *Aliens are now publicly known, two of my friends and fellow agents are dead, and now we're fugitives. And at the same time as becoming fugitives, we find out that there are super soldiers, and they're the ones sent to get us. I can't believe I left Keira behind.*

Ryland peered out of the dropship to confirm what the camera showed: the helicopter still hovering in the distance. He switched his comms to a channel where the recipient was the only target of the message.

"Thief, I don't blame you for your decisions, and I hope you don't blame me for mine." Ryland knew the Specialists might be able to hack it, so he tried to make it sound like he was talking to Keira face to face. Then they wouldn't know she had separated from the group. "I know your goal is to protect humanity. I'm trying to do the same. I hope we can both keep our methods and our respect for each other. We're on the same team. Remember your training, and don't forget about your team."

He switched back to the regular channel, only to hear Fred's voice. "I get you're just following orders, and I respect that. But your superiors are wrong," Fred said. Ryland realized he must be talking to the Specialists. "This is not how you retaliate against a new alien species." Ryland could only hear one side of the conversation. "That's the objective," Fred admitted.

After a while of silence on the comms, Nick's voice rang in their ears. "Jovian, Banshee, let's go. Sentinel, you better be at the ship. Tom, get ready for a hot extraction."

"Roger that," Tom said.

Ryland went to the cockpit to make sure Tom had the aircraft fully ready. "I'm here," he said. "And their chopper is waiting out of range to follow."

A few seconds later Dom and Fred appeared from the stairs. Then Fred stopped and ran back down.

"Jovian, what are you doing?" Ryland yelled.

"Just go! They're too fast." Fred said, sounding defeated. "Go!" An explosion sounded in the background.

"Nick? Where are you?" Dom asked through the comms, but there was no reply. "Nick!" Dom shouted.

"Get us off the ground, Tom!" Ryland demanded.

As the ship took off from the roof, Ryland watched for any sign of Fred or Nick. Three Specialists came out onto the roof, and soon after that, Fred was led out in handcuffs with the fourth Specialist. *Maybe they got Nick too*, Ryland thought as the building became smaller in the distance and the Specialists' helicopter flew in for pickup.

FORTY

"SO, WHAT HAPPENS if I surrender?" the agent hiding in the forest asked. He had speakers surrounding the Specialists. He had heard they were now hunting the Sentry 1 program agents when Nick sent out a warning two days earlier.

"That's for our superiors to decide," Elias, the leader of his crew, replied. His team spread out, looking in every direction. The forest was thick, with trees and bushes every three metres. Elias thought it would be perfect to build a house there, even knowing he would never get the chance to do so. He couldn't think like that; he was a trained super soldier and the objective at hand had to be top of mind. That and his team. The daylight shone through, reflecting off the green vegetation and creating a green glow that the Specialists' enhanced eyes could see.

"You know my superiors let us in on decisions because they trusted us." The agent's voice came from six speakers spread out fifty metres from each other.

"Destiny, find the source. Fujita, find a vantage point. Mirra, Cameron, Malik, Chris, form on me, and drop some traps as we go," Elias ordered through the team comms.

Destiny found all six speakers within seconds with electromagnetic scopes. Now she had to backtrack and find the microphone.

As soon as he got his order, Fujita ran up a tree. Even with a heavy power suit, he moved with ease and soon disappeared.

"Your program has been shut down," Elias informed the agent, as if he didn't already know.

"So you go straight to hunting us down? Just like trying to execute those aliens."

"Your fellow agents created that problem," Elias replied.

"And your superiors went straight to execution. How does that make things better with the Venusians?"

"Why are you indulging him, Elias?" Malik asked over the team comms.

"He knows everything already," Elias replied. "If I get him talking, he'll be more distracted. Just find him."

"Elias, behind us, five o'clock," Destiny reported. "A cluster of trees, twenty metres up."

"Fujita, got that?" Elias asked.

"Roger."

"We'll deal with the Venusians when they come," Elias said to the forest.

"I don't think that's your actual answer," the agent retorted.

Fujita found the agent waiting in a different location than the one Destiny reported. Unarmed, the agent surrendered. Fujita came out of the trees with the agent in restraints,

"He was waiting for us," Fujita said. The agent had a trimmed dark brown beard, thick eyebrows, and golden-brown eyes. He had a fairly big build and was wearing a fitted brown coat and jeans that were spray-painted with forest colours and tattered at the bottom. An empty holster hung from his hip. Elias wasn't sure if the agent had removed his gun or if Fujita did.

"Waiting?" Elias asked. The agent was surrounded by super soldiers, which didn't seem to scare him, or if it did, he hid it well.

"I wouldn't be able to run from all seven of you," the agent said, looking at his seven almost identical captors.

"Most of the others saw it as a challenge to try," Chris remarked.

"Alright. Let's pack up then," Elias said. They marched their captive back to their waiting helicopter.

"So, Derek, AKA Predator, we're searching for a few of your fellow agents," Sergeant Morrison said. He was in charge of interrogations in the Sentry 1 program. The room they were in was small, with one table and two chairs. It was soundproof too, the walls absorbing every syllable.

"You mean Nick and the agents who were present at the execution?" Derek asked.

"Yes. Where are they?"

"I don't know. They sent a warning message three days ago, and I haven't heard from Nick since. Banshee, Sentinel, and—"

"We know their real names," Morrison said.

"Yes, well Banshee, Sentinel, and Thief went silent four days ago. It was probably part of their plan."

"What do you know about their plan?" Morrison asked.

"Nothing. They were called together to stop the aliens. I had no need to know. I back them up, though. It was a bad idea to execute the Venusians, you know."

"Yes, I know your opinion on it," Morrison replied. "Will you help us find your friends?"

"What's in it for me? Do I get to escape the gallows?"

"You're not going to the gallows," Morrison replied, "but you'll get a better deal."

"Deal?" Derek laughed. "I'm not looking for a *better deal* for me. I'm speaking for the rest of the agents. We aren't the enemy."

"And what do you propose?" Morrison asked.

"To be what we're supposed to be. A team, on the same side, working together." This was all crazy. A new program hunting down the former just because they disagreed about killing a new alien race.

"Well, that has a nice feel to it. But your fellow agents went against orders and betrayed General Finch, and he controls this situation."

"So, orders are above morals? Sounds like the pre-war world," Derek said with a wink. That was going to have consequences.

■

"They got away?" General Finch exclaimed. "How? You're elite, augmented super soldiers!" His voice echoed in the empty room.

"Sorry, sir," Elias said.

"That doesn't change anything!" Finch replied. He was pacing, thinking of what their next move would be. His super soldiers weren't doing such a super job.

They were in a small courtroom, and everyone was standing at the front in the space between the judge and the attorneys' seating area. One of the Specialists was standing at the back of the group, leaning against the jury bench.

"Yes, sir." Elias said. "We're scanning for their ship now, and we have one of the agents in custody for interrogation."

"What about Nick?"

"We couldn't find him."

"Couldn't find him?" Finch exclaimed.

"The building was clear, sir," Malik replied. "We have no idea where he went."

The courtroom doors swung open,

"General Finch, I am relieving you of your duty," General Ambrose said as he entered. Now there were two generals in the same room, which never happened in public. Only when they had their General meetings were they all together. The Circle of General were spread out across the world to manage their agents and ensure no elevated human conflict ensued.

This is going to be interesting, Elias thought.

"You have abused your power. And in the midst of your plan, you have made trusted people very upset."

Finch bristled at the accusation. "You don't have the authority to relieve me—"

"The other generals and I are in agreement that what you're doing is treason," General Ambrose said. He stopped in front of his target, not even acknowledging the Specialists. "Some new information has come to our attention about your plans."

At that moment, Alek walked through the doors with a few folders in hand. The Specialists were surprised and confused, though their expressions were concealed by their helmets. Their current orders were to arrest agents. Now an agent had just walked into the dark, tense courtroom.

General Ambrose leaned in toward General Finch, "We brought you into the Circle, you, being the youngest ever. Now you have shown your true colours. You no longer represent what the Circle is supposed to be." He stood back. "Specialists, arrest him."

Without hesitation, the Specialists moved in. Elias took it upon himself to handcuff Finch. Not because he wanted revenge for his earlier comments but because if more conflict between generals ensued and the Specialists listened to the wrong general, it would be Elias who was to blame and not his team. But he knew General Ambrose would protect them.

"Well done, Specialists. Sorry you had a corrupt commander."

"How was he corrupt, sir?" Chris asked.

"Alek has that information," Ambrose said, nodding to him. "Alek."

Alek placed the files on that table where the defence attorney would normally sit. He spread out the papers, revealing multiple plans from General Finch. The majority of the plans consisted of using his military power to control the government and the COG. He had blueprints of the houses of each general and the military bases in each country.

"Alright, soldiers, you don't have to worry about these plans now that General Finch is in custody. Dismissed."

The Specialists filed out of the room. But when Destiny passed the general, he reached out to stop her. "Destiny, have you seen Ryland?"

FORTY-ONE

"RYLAND? AS IN my brother? You think I've talked to him? Reunited with him? It's been twelve years. I have to find him. General—Dad," she said, calling him that for the first time in years, "may I go find him?"

He heard her confidence, followed by her soft daughterlike tone. "Go with Elias and bring your brother home."

As Destiny walked out of the courtroom, she approached Elias.

"Elias," Destiny called to him. "We have a mission."

"I see that. What are we doing?" he asked as he stepped away from the rest of the team.

"Looking for one specific agent: Ryland Ambrose."

"Ambrose? You mean your brother?"

"Exactly."

Just then, Alek walked past.

"Alek," Destiny said, turning to him, "do you know where Ryland and his crew went?"

"Over the last few days, I've only heard their emergency broadcast but nothing on where they are. A safe house is a good guess." Alek had no judgment toward the Specialists. He knew they were serving under a corrupt commander. "You have Fred in custody. Maybe he knows." He smiled, realizing he wasn't supposed to know that. "Here." He handed Destiny a microchip.

"What is this?" she asked, taking it from him.

"*He* is NEO, a Nano Electronic Organism. Ryland found him, and he might be pleased to get him back. You can plug him right into your suit, he might help run your suit and can help in the battlefield."

"Thank you, Alek," she said hesitantly looking at the chip in her hand. "How long did you know about Finch?"

"He was ambitious when he finally got into the Circle of Generals, and arrogant. He wanted to eradicate the peacekeepers and was aggressive toward the Venusians.

"I looked into his history. He suffered trauma that could account for aggression toward the Venusians. He went to a psychiatrist, who labelled him as mentally disturbed. After a few weeks of digging, I found those plans." Destiny plugged NEO into the back of her neck.

"Whoa, this is high-tech!" NEO exclaimed.

Destiny felt a small electric shock travel through her body. The sensation faded into a dull ache and then disappeared.

"What was that about?" Destiny asked.

"I was interfacing with your suit," NEO replied. "Familiarizing myself with your systems."

"Oh. That's comforting," she said, sounding nervous.

"Don't worry; we have gotten to know him. He won't try any funny business," Alek said. "He'll even help you run your systems."

"Hmm…" Destiny said, still not liking it. She didn't like needing help from others. What if she became too reliant on it?

"I'll stay relatively quiet to help you adjust," NEO said, trying to help.

"Yeah, okay," Destiny replied.

"You know, I'm plugged into your—"

"Okay. You should probably get going," Alek said.

"No. What are you plugged into?" Destiny asked. "I need to know what all my equipment is capable of."

"I'm plugged into your nervous system," NEO said. "I can feel your pain and hear and sense what you sense."

"Really? Can you read my mind?" Destiny asked, wondering if NEO was hiding something.

"No. Brain waves are hard to predict and, therefore, hard to read and understand," NEO replied.

The Specialists departed with their new equipment and crew member, reaching their helicopter in under a minute.

"Where are the others?" the pilot asked as they entered the aircraft.

"They aren't coming. We need to get to the base of operations," Elias said.

"Roger that," the pilot confirmed, then lifted off.

As they flew over the ocean, the waves looking like rolling hills, Destiny wondered what the world was like before the war. She had heard stories of how the scientists thought it wasn't going to be habitable for five hundred years. An older man once told her that his grandfather told him that Earth now seemed even stronger than before.

They passed over the Centre Islands, which showed the beauty of what the man was talking about. It went against how Destiny felt now.

She turned away from the window and thought about what it would be like when she found Ryland. Her long-lost brother, stripped from her when she was eight years old. Would he run when they found him? Did he know that the contract was void? Did he even know she was alive?

"So, what is he like?" Elias asked, breaking into her thoughts.

"My brother?"

"Yeah."

"When we were little, he took care of me and my mom. After our dad faked his death."

"General Ambrose?"

"Yeah. Ryland blamed himself, but our father taught us to be strong and caring. Ryland aimed to be the man of the house when our mother couldn't take it anymore." Destiny's voice had a shameful tone. The man the Specialists followed had left his family and made his children grow up too fast.

"Wow, I didn't know that," Elias said. "The last time you saw him was twelve years ago?"

"Ryland left when he was ten to join the Sentry 1 program, which I just found out about." She was angry that her father hadn't told her that and that she hadn't thought to ask. It had been so long that she was used to not knowing. "Our father 'died' when we were on a family trip. Ryland was chasing a lizard and nearly went off a cliff, but my dad grabbed him and ended up falling himself, or so it appeared." She stared at the floor, listening to herself tell the story as she watched events replay in her mind. "Our mother was destroyed and couldn't continue looking after us. Ryland and I ended up in an orphanage for two years.

"I found out later that my father was the one who took Ryland out of the orphanage. Then a few years later, I was taken into the Sentry 2 program. I grew up feeling alone."

Destiny wasn't acknowledging Elias; it was more like she was talking to herself. She didn't realize she was telling him her darkest griefs. "Having my dad taken away. Watching Ryland act like my father. They were both great men. The third family I was a part of never measured up. My morals were stronger than theirs even though I didn't always follow them and just kept to myself." She felt Elias's pitiful gaze through his visor.

"It's pretty amazing that your brother is a successful agent now, though," Elias said. It was true. He had become something special. Something legendary.

The helicopter landed in front of the single-storey base for the Sentry 2 program, and the Specialists hopped out, feeling at home.

Finally, some comfort, Destiny thought.

The facility was built at the base of a small cluster of mountains. The sun was just about always hidden from the base, making it cooler until the sun was at its highest point in the sky. It was no problem for the Specialists, though; their suits regulated their temperature.

The reinforced doors slid open once the soldiers got close, and Fred came out.

"Fred," Destiny said in greeting as if he were an old friend. She was careful not to offend since they had just arrested him and taken him away from his crew. "We could use some help."

"What do you need?" he replied, smiling. He had his helmet tucked under his arm. Was his tone genuine, or was he just playing along?

"We need to find Ryland," she said.

"Why are you interested in Ryland?" he asked.

"He's my brother."

Surprisingly, Fred didn't react. *Did he already know?* Destiny wondered. *If so, does Ryland know too?*

"I don't know where he is. They had the Venusians with them, and they acquired a warp drive."

"A warp drive?" Destiny said, puzzled. Was the human race that close to space travel? Wouldn't the Sentry 2 program be the first to have access to warp drives?

"The Venusians helped build it," Fred explained. "That's how they got to our planet without us detecting them."

"Hmm. So, they could be anywhere right now," Destiny said.

"Yes, I assume so. Go to Sur, the Archive. You should be able to find out where they went. All records go through there."

A map popped up on Destiny's heads-up display from NEO. A safe house blinked. The Sur safe house. The Archive.

FORTY-TWO

DESTINY REMEMBERED STORIES from her foster grandfather that he heard from his grandfather about how the world was uninhabitable. The weapons they used in the war caused mass destruction and poisoned the planet. The poison had infected the air and would kill humans if they were exposed to it for long. Each country was almost entirely destroyed. Of course, some cities survived because they weren't heavily populated or didn't have a military presence. That was where most cities were built now, using the buildings that were left.

Luckily, the scientists were wrong, and the planet healed itself somehow, though not without side effects. The animals that were exposed to small doses of the poison changed in terms of their physical appearance.

She looked down from the aircraft and watched the ground move past like a treadmill.

"I've done more flying today than most people do in their entire lives," Destiny said.

"I did a little travelling in my life," Elias said, looking down at the green-covered land of Sur. "My family moved from south of Sur."

"Oh yeah? I only travelled short distances in the same country with my family," Destiny replied.

Elias asked about the scenario they were about to enter. This was her mission, so she was in charge.

"I don't know if the agents there will know we're coming or if they know we're not hunting them anymore," Destiny said.

"Even if they know the contract is over, they might think differently when they see us walk in," Elias replied.

"Right, so we still need to exercise caution," Destiny said.

The pressure didn't change for the Specialists as the helicopter descended, their suits compensating for it. When the helicopter landed, the Specialists got out quickly in case the agent tried to flee.

"Sentry agent, we are not here to harm or arrest you," Destiny said as she entered the building. Two rows of six pillars lined the room. Destiny walked down the middle while Elias went to the right, neither of them carrying weapons. Destiny felt vulnerable but confident in her ability and her reaction time.

"I wouldn't go any further," a voice said from all directions, the same trick the agent in the forest had used. The Specialists did as they were told. They looked around the room and saw barred windows to the left and a countertop beside a wall that formed a room to the right.

"The trap in front of you is one of many," the voice said.

Shoot, Destiny thought. There were lasers that she hadn't noticed on the first pillars. *How did I miss that?*

"I can attempt to scan for the other traps," NEO said. His voice scared Destiny. She had forgotten about NEO.

"We aren't here to arrest you. We need info," Elias said.

"Why should I believe you?"

"Alek Rauz and Fred Williams sent us. We're looking for Ryland. General Finch has been arrested for treason."

"What do you want with Ryland?" the voice asked. The two Specialists still could not figure out where he was. Destiny thought the logical spot was the small room in the corner to her one o'clock.

"He's my brother," Destiny said. "My name is Destiny Ambrose. Our father is in the Circle of Generals and is the head of the Sentry programs."

"I'm not sensing any real traps here," NEO said. "That laser isn't connected to anything, and I don't see anything else." Destiny stepped through the laser. NEO was right; nothing happened.

"Hey!" the voice said, but this time it came from in front of them. "The first trap was a bluff, but there are others." An agent stepped out of the room that Destiny thought he would be in. He was bald with a thick but well-trimmed dark beard. He was wearing a white undershirt with a green open dress shirt. His shorts and rolled-up sleeves revealed his muscular build.

"We know there are no traps. Thank you for coming out," Destiny said, curious why he would show himself unless he was serious. The agent walked to the pillar to his right, entered a code into a keypad, and a metal wall slid from pillar to pillar in the blink of an eye. It had an explosive on it too.

"NEO, why didn't you see that?" Destiny asked. The wall slid back into the original pillar, the agent still there.

"I don't know," NEO replied, deeply puzzled.

"How do you know about the Circle of Generals' names?" the agent asked.

"Let us show you," Destiny said. Elias saw a laptop on the counter near him. He grabbed it and started working on it.

"If you thought you were still being hunted, why didn't you leave a while ago?" Destiny asked. She was trying to be friendly, which was hard considering she was a super soldier wearing tank-like armour who had been ordered to hunt down the Sentry 1 agents just a few days earlier.

"Well, you just confirmed my hypothesis of you being a top organization, since you're Sentry program. I know your minimum equipment and authorities and that you'd be able to find me almost anywhere. I also wanted to see what you were, and I had a plan to escape. I'm already packed."

Elias was done with the laptop. He set it on the floor and slid it over to the agent. The agent picked it up and saw what Elias had pulled up: the names of the generals in the Circle, the politics associated with each general, and the records of the Sentry programs with the candidates' names, Destiny's name was at the top.

"What's your name, agent?" Destiny asked.

"Bruce," he replied, looking up from the computer.

"Well, Bruce, do you know where my brother is?" Destiny asked.

"I don't. But I know a few agents got pulled to where he was for support." Bruce was still holding the laptop, moving his fingers across the screen and the keys. "Hmm... Okay. Follow me."

He went into the room he had come out of. Destiny nodded at Elias, and they followed Bruce. He was standing near the far wall with a book in his hand. Destiny saw a screen on the page he opened. It scanned his hand, then entered a code, and a section of tiles on the floor slid open. Bruce motioned for them to follow.

"Let me show you another reason why I stayed," he said, then kept walking. It was dark, and he was engulfed in darkness. Destiny, or maybe NEO, activated her night vision, revealing a long, wide stairway. It wound in a large circle downwards.

They came to a door, and Bruce tapped a few keys on a computer, after which the door opened into a large room, revealing pillars of computer towers scattered around the room.

"To keep this safe. This is the Archive."

The room was dark and cold with dim yellow and brown lights on the ceiling and blinking computer lights. The ceiling was six metres high. A layer of mist floated just above the floor.

"Fred mentioned the Archive," Elisa said. "What is it?"

"There must be so much information in these!" NEO said on team comms.

"This is where all agent info comes through and is stored. It's backed up at another location." As Bruce walked through the aisles of the computer towers, he rolled down his sleeves and buttoned his shirt.

"So, will we be able to find out where Ryland went?" Destiny asked.

"Should be able to, yeah. The ship they used, even the new suits they have now, I should be able to track them all. That has been logged for a while as a new project. Here." Bruce stopped at a terminal and started typing, causing files to pop up. One file showed a picture of a helicopter. "This was the form for their modded aircraft."

"Yeah, they put a warp drive on it," Destiny said. Another picture came up of the mods they did. It no longer had a propeller, and it had an airtight cabin. There was a device on the bottom of the tail, which must have been the warp drive. Small wings had been added on top of the sliding doors with thrusters on them. It didn't make sense to Destiny, but she didn't know much about warp drives or what they could do.

"Now we go into tracking it and the systems records," Bruce said as he typed in more commands. "Hmm... they have taken some precautions to hide it."

"Can you find it?" Destiny asked.

"One sec," Bruce replied.

"All their records are here?" NEO asked. "We could learn so much from the Sentry 1 program."

"You could learn the same thing from the Sentry 2 program," Destiny said.

"I'd love to," NEO replied.

"There," Bruce said. "Oh."

"What?" Elias asked.

"They... they went to Venus."

"They what?" Destiny cried. Then she realized the answer to her own question. *The warp drive. It's how they were getting on our planet without us detecting them. It's space travel. Duh.*

FORTY-THREE

SPACE TRAVEL IS *weird,* Destiny thought. They didn't have enough time or a large enough ship to create a gravity generator, only a warp drive thanks to the Sentry 1 program agents. The pilot and the Specialists had to stay in their seats or they would be floating around the ship's cabin. Still, their organs didn't have seat belts to keep them in place. Destiny felt like she was going to throw up several times. She was thankful the trip only took fifteen minutes.

Venus appeared like a rock thrown and then put on pause. The planet turned a deeper orange and red the closer they got.

Once they entered the atmosphere, gravity started to return, lighter than Earth's but better than the zero gravity of space. The planet's multilayered cloud system made the ship shake. They hit dense clouds, which created terrible turbulence. Destiny had to hold on to the ship's safety bars to steady herself. The clouds whipped across the planet at 320 kilometres per hour. The ship was pushed so hard that the pilot decided to let the clouds take them instead of fighting them. It didn't reduce the turbulence much, though, making it feel like the ship was being tossed and twisted in the wind.

Once the turbulence slowed, they looked outside to see the new planet that no human had ever been, apart from the agents they were there to find. All they saw was a second layer of dense, fiery clouds. The window was covered in rain, which NEO analyzed as sulfuric acid. They had to grab the safety bars again as the turbulence continued, though thankfully not as hard.

The surface looked like a desert with rivers of lava running through it. Smoke rose like pillars holding up the clouds. Destiny hoped their armoured suits would allow them to survive in the new atmosphere.

"So, what's the play, Destiny?" Elias asked.

"We have to be careful," she replied. "All we're doing is finding the agents and then leaving. We need to make that clear. No weapons unless absolutely necessary."

"Roger that," Elias confirmed. He must have been thinking the same.

The soldiers prepared their weapons and equipment, knowing a new environment meant new problems. Was Ryland even still alive? Could their suits endure the environment? Maybe this could just be a wild goose chase to find dead bodies and find out that humans can't live on Venus. How did the Venusians live on here?

As they descended, they tested their radar, crew member vitals, communications, and the new electromagnetic shielding to protect them from the environment. Their pilot found a landing spot near some buildings. As they touched down, everyone was quiet and tense. What was going to happen?

"Walk out with your hands raised," Destiny told Elias, who nodded with confirmation.

When the door opened, the two Specialists were met with a blast of heat and humidity. It was dark too. The sun never shone there due to the dense atmosphere. Their suits worked overtime to cool them down in the immense heat. The gravity was noticeably weaker than that on Earth.

As Destiny and Elias walked out with their hands raised, a few Venusians walked toward them. Destiny assumed more were in the buildings, which had a rough, grainy texture and looked like they were made of rock. The air was more dangerous than Destiny had anticipated. *Good thing we have the shields,* she thought. The sulfuric acid was deadly. There was a noticeable sizzling every time a large raindrop hit the shield. The shields polarized the acid and split the molecules on contact. The main problem was the suits had only a small supply of oxygen. Destiny and Elias would have to return to the ship and get the extra oxygen tanks they brought.

How did Ryland and his team deal with the oxygen and atmosphere? she wondered.

The five locals circled the foreigners.

How did you get here? someone asked, the question popping into their heads. It was hard to understand the aliens with such little experience. They were taught how to communicate with them, but they had no experience in the field.

What are you doing here? another asked. This question had more authority to it and seemed to nullify the former.

"We got here on our ship, which was rigged with a warp drive that was made by the agents we're here to find," Destiny said, her and Elias's hands still raised as they faced the aliens.

Ah, the agents. They said they weren't expecting any others of their kind, the lead Venusian said.

"They didn't know we could follow them," Elias said. "We're not hunting them but seeking to take them back home."

The image of one of the aliens, the one from Earth who was with the agents, appeared in the Specialists' heads standing next to the alien who was now communicating with them. Then a betrayal of the agents toward the Specialists. It was like a picture book inside the Specialists' minds. With only limited contact with the Venusians, it was hard for them to understand that the images that formed in their heads were not their own thoughts.

"The leader we followed was corrupt," Destiny explained. "The bounty for the agents has been terminated."

Well, you're both on my planet without permission, the alien replied.

Destiny felt a surge of panic rise within her, knowing how alien trespassers were treated on Earth.

You can resolve this on your own. You will find a base to the north. The Venusians there will not cause you problems if you don't cause any problems for them.

Good, she thought. *They're just going to leave us alone.*

"Thank you," Destiny replied. The Specialists grabbed their extra oxygen tanks. Then the Venusians showed them a map of where they were to go. No Venusians escorted them.

They either don't care, or they have some other issues to tend to, Destiny thought.

The wind was almost nonexistent on the surface, unlike higher in the atmosphere, where the clouds were constantly in motion. The ground was soft from being so hot. Venus didn't have tectonic plates, but the planet was so warm that its crust was one big bending, shifting plate. Rivers of molten lava flowed through the land like rivers of water on Earth. Rocks, hills, and mountains covered the land.

"This land looks violent on its... like it's going to... alive and attack us." Static broke up some of Elias's speech. The assault from the atmosphere on their magnetic shielding disrupted their communications.

"I agree," Destiny replied. "Let's get off this planet as fast as we can." In her mind, she ran through all the things that could kill them there: Venusians, any hostile creatures that lived on the planet, sulfuric acid, and lack of oxygen and water. It made her feel so out of control. At least two of those things she could not stop. As for the other two, they could be outnumbered easily. At least they had a water pouch on their belts.

Destiny started running, and Elias followed. The land was empty of life, and according to the map they just needed to get over the next hill.

Once they reached the top of the hill, they saw the base. Most of the buildings were dome shaped and made of dirt. Others were made of metal. To the far east was a massive volcano spewing lava like an overflowing cup. Heatwaves rose up toward the clouds.

They seem so close, Destiny thought. *If the volcano exploded, it would overtake the base. But it's already spewing lava. Maybe that stops it from exploding.*

The two Specialists started down the hill. The heat was exhausting despite their suits' cooling system and with the weaker gravity, but soon they reached their objective. At the bottom of the hill, they ran into more locals. Destiny and Elias hoped the first Venusians had told the base of their arrival. It was impossible to tell if the aliens were surprised or if they knew they were here. *Humans rely on facial expressions for so much,* Destiny thought.

The east building is where your kind are, one of them said. As a picture of the building formed in Destiny's mind, the Venusians returned to their work.

Destiny and Elias made their way east of the camp. The buildings were made from a mixture of materials, including rock and metal. The rock seemed to originate from the middle of the camp. *Were they the first structures built?* Destiny wondered.

All the cloud cover made it dark. The Venusians didn't need light; they just controlled and felt the molecules around them.

The building they were searching for was a bulky, one-storey structure.

"Enter cautiously," Destiny warned. "We don't know if they know the contract is nullified."

When they entered, they saw a hallway that ran the length of the building with two doors on either side. They moved slowly and quietly, keeping an eye out for traps. The door closed behind them with a hiss.

"Eyes open, but don't draw your weapon," Destiny said.

"Roger that."

As they searched the first rooms, their hands rested on their weapons in case it was a trap. On top of the agents not knowing they had come, the Venusians might try to kill them or have other plans to kill Destiny and Elias.

"The building's atmosphere contains oxygen," NEO informed the Specialists.

Out of the shadows at the end of the hallway, three figures appeared, two agents in their armour and a man in a jumpsuit, the pilot.

Destiny was overwhelmed with relief. *I found him,* she thought. Then she remembered he didn't know it was her and that they were there to be allies. One of the agents and the pilot had their weapons raised. The other was holding his at ease. The Specialists raised their hands in surrender.

"Ryland," Destiny said. She reached for her helmet, twisted it with a hiss, and lifted it off, revealing her face. Her dark brown hair fell just past her chin. Her cheeks were soft and round, like the rest of her face. Her eyes were deep brown, matching Ryland's. "We aren't here to hurt you. Or to bring you in."

The pilot looked at Ryland, who must have been shocked. That was Destiny's guess at least. Dominic kept his weapon trained on the Specialist.

"Destiny?" Ryland asked, revealing his shock. The pilot lowered his weapon. "You're a Specialist?"

"Yes. I didn't know you were a Sentry agent," she replied.

Ryland took off his helmet as well. "Dom, lower your weapon," he said.

"She's here to bring us in," Dom replied. "I'm not moving."

"The contract for you has been voided," Destiny said. "The general we served under was corrupt. He has been arrested, and the Sentry programs are merging."

Elias pulled out a USB drive and tossed it to Ryland, who plugged it into a nearby laptop. It had a document on it signed by Nick. Ryland skimmed through the document. It voided the contract and united the programs, as they said. Dom took a few steps back and glanced at the signature. Then he lowered his weapon because he knew that no one could make Nick do anything he didn't want to do, especially if it involved his agents. With the tension subsiding, Destiny threw a chip to Ryland.

"It's NEO," she said.

"Why are you giving it to me?"

"Alek said you would appreciate it."

"Alek? Alright." Ryland accepted NEO. There was a port in his suit for updates that NEO could fit in. Ryland plugged him in now that he trusted the Nano Electronic Organism.

"Once I found out it was you, I had to come find you," Destiny continued once the others left and went into one of the side rooms.

"How did you become a Specialist?" Ryland asked.

"Uh, it's a long story, but I got chosen."

"Is it true that Dad is the head of the Sentry 1 program?" Ryland asked.

"And the founder of the Sentry 2 program, the Specialists," Destiny said, seeing the pain on Ryland's face. Didn't he know any of this?

"So you were chosen by Dad?" Ryland asked.

Destiny nodded. "Yes."

"How long have you been in the program?"

"Four years." Saying it made Destiny feel like she was bragging. Ryland was a Sentry 1 agent. They trained hard to get to the top; Destiny knew that much, but she had just been trained and augmented, and she surpassed them already. It wasn't her fault she got the best and newest technology, but she felt sympathy for Ryland.

FORTY-FOUR

RYLAND FELT BETRAYED. He couldn't figure out why his father had kept his own existence and the Sentry programs a secret from him. And now his sister had shown up as a super soldier. *She has been a Sentry 2 program soldier for four years!*

"Did you ever search for me?" Ryland asked. "I found out about our father only a few days ago. I thought looking for you was a dead end because you were part of the Sentry 2 program." Ryland was trying to justify himself, although he knew he could have searched for her once he became an agent.

"Yeah, it was the same for you," Destiny said.

I was in the Sentry program before her. She wouldn't have had the clearance to find me. Destiny didn't comment on how he would have had the clearance to find her.

"Why didn't you ask Dad, or why didn't he tell you about me?" Ryland asked, knowing she wouldn't be able to answer the second question.

"I... I don't know. I guess I felt that asking him as my general—"

"He's your father!" Ryland said. "Does family mean nothing to you?" *I was right to think family is temporary,* he thought.

"You left as well, Ryland!" Destiny said.

"I got chosen for it. They chose me. It was probably Dad who did it. You were with the Harolds," Ryland said, referring to the family friends who took them in.

"Like that matters." Destiny turned away, unable to face her brother. "You were the one I looked up to. You followed Dad's instructions even better than he did. Then you left. Just like he did."

Ryland went silent. He had always felt alone, and then he felt betrayed when he found out his family was still alive. *I guess that's how you feel too, Destiny,* he thought, looking at her. She was so grown up. A super soldier, faster and stronger than he could ever be. And they both were standing on an alien planet. Destiny finally turned back to him. The silence lingered for a few more seconds.

"How was Mom?" Ryland asked.

"She got better, but after a few years, she went downhill. I put her into a home where they will take care of her."

"Good," Ryland said. "How did you get chosen for the Sentry 2 program?"

"Since I was taking care of Mom, I didn't feel the whole purpose of life thing that Dad talked about so often." She paused, thinking back to the day the candidates were brought together. "Apart from being chosen because I'm his daughter, he chose young candidates who didn't know what their purpose was." She was the only one who knew anything about the program. "They were people that were suicidal."

Ryland looked at her as if it was his fault. He had left after taking care of her and their mother, then never searched for her again.

"It wasn't your fault," she assured him. "I mean, it might have been different if you were there, but I had family, and they didn't mean much to me."

"I'm sorry I didn't find you after I left. I had all the resources in the world."

"I know, but now things are different," Destiny said, referring to both of them being in the Sentry programs.

"Do you know why Dad kept this from me and didn't tell you about me?" Ryland asked.

"No, I don't. I rarely see him in person. I only get orders from him."

Ryland understood what she was saying, but he still felt alone and betrayed.

"I hate to break up the family reunion," Elias said as he walked in. His appearance was still daunting, bulky tank-like armour in the shape of a human. "But what's the plan now, Destiny? Why are you all still here?"

Destiny looked back at Ryland. "What are you guys doing here?" she asked. The room was dark, and there was no way to create a light.

"We were planning to stay here since we had a bounty on our heads," he said as Dom and Tom joined the group. "We were going to see how we could help the war here. But now we have a decision to make." Ryland and Destiny sat on the benches that had been quickly made in the few days that Ryland and Dom were there.

"Yes, you do. We all do. My mission was to bring you home," Destiny said.

"When you found out it was me, what did you do?" Ryland asked.

"I asked if I could come to find you now that there's no bounty."

"So then it's not an official 'get back as soon as possible' mission?" Dom asked. "They're figuring everything out with the two Sentry programs," he added.

"Dom would rather stay here and fight," Ryland said. "Tom?" he asked, turning to him.

"I'm your pilot," he replied, leaning back against the wall.

"Looks like you guys can do whatever you want," Ryland said, addressing the Specialist in the room.

"Elias?" Destiny asked.

"We should be heading home, back to command," he said, "but we can't do that empty-handed, leaving the agents on this planet. So let's see how the united Sentry works."

"It's settled then," Destiny replied. "So, what is this war about?"

"It's just for power," Ryland replied. "One side wants to rule, and the other is defending its ground. Then there are those who want to leave and go to Earth."

"Hmm... There's a bigger picture here too," Destiny said. "If we help and lose, the other side will hate us and potentially continue the war with us. If we win, we will make a treaty with them and let them come to our planet, which would take a long time, and some of our people won't like that causing tension."

"Also, if we die here that could look like they trapped us, and that could start a war between humans and Venusians," Elias added.

"We aren't prepared for a war like that," Tom added, thinking of how they had just made a ship for space travel. Earth did not have many factories available to make more quickly, but the Venusians did, or at least it seemed like they did.

∎

The united Sentry forces had been on Venus for a week, learning about their new friends and their foes and learning about the planet's safeties and dangers. While being sent on missions, the Specialists learned to work with the agents, Tom flying them where they needed to go. They were sent to volcanic valleys, sulfuric mountains, and dark and dense tunnels that extended deep within the planet. On their latest mission, the United Sentry travelled as one. They snuck behind enemy lines underground to determine the enemy's plans. It was so much hotter under the planet. Volcanic activity underneath heated the crust, so it never cracked like Earth's. The planet's mantle just got hotter the deeper one went.

"Anyone else find it hard to differentiate between the sides in this war?" Elias asked. He had begun to open up as he learned more about his new teammates.

"Yeah, I find it hard," Tom replied. "They all look the same, besides their ranks and they have no uniforms to differentiate." He had been given a makeshift suit so he could survive the planet's harsh environment, albeit he was suffering the most from the heat. The ship they used included a suit for pilots on high-altitude missions. The Specialists and agents made adjustments to accommodate the atmosphere. Tom had to sit out of many missions because his suit wouldn't let him survive long outside. The Specialists helped rig up more electromagnetic shields for each of the Specialists and Tom.

Ryland nodded as well, agreeing with the conversation. Dom was still wary of the heavy super soldiers. He was jealous of their skills, which surpassed his just because they got augmentation shots. It unsettled him.

Ryland and Destiny led the walk through the dark tunnels underground. The air was thick and dark with heat waves rising in front of them, but the Specialists used flashlights to illuminate the path.

They ran into no opposition on their way to the enemy lines, sneaking in to find their foes' plans. The sentries got to the surface on the far northeast side of an enemy base.

"Whoa," Tom said, turning to look at the mountain behind them. The rest of the sentries also turned to look. The mountains reached up to the burning clouds. Sometimes the clouds glowed, reflecting off lava rivers or volcanoes.

"Let's get back to the mission," Dom said, bringing everyone back to reality.

"Right, let's go," Elias said, and everyone followed.

"Hey, Sentinel," Destiny called out. "What do you think of all this alien stuff?"

He knew what she meant. *What do you think Father would have taught us about it?*

"I don't know," he replied as they advanced on the base. "My only guess is that God made the Venusians as well, dying for them too. The Son of God dying for another species doesn't make sense seeing as he was human. He would have had to be a Venusian as well to save them."

"It's because God doesn't exist," Dom said. There was no response. Destiny and Ryland would have this conversation later.

Once they got within five hundred metres of the base, they stopped. Elias and Ryland pulled out grenade launchers and aimed at opposite ends of the base. They all had learned that at a big enough base, the Venusians would have a field around it that allowed them to sense anything that entered the field. By controlling every atom around the base, they knew of every change. It was as if the aliens could link their telekinesis and build off each other's abilities.

Ryland and Elias shot their frequency grenades, then left their bags and continued toward the base. The other sentries spread out in different directions. The frequency grenades ebbed ad flowed frequencies to change the movement of atoms in the air, making it more difficult for the Venusians to control and therefore see.

As Ryland ran for the first building at the centre of the base, the ground felt soft beneath his feet due to the heat radiating from the planet. It was a single storey with a slightly angled roof. He slowed down as he approached and went into a crouch, then moved to another side of the building. The Venusians didn't have many windows, so he didn't have to worry about being spotted.

A few Venusians roaming around the base were alerted by the distraction and turned the other direction, giving Ryland the opportunity to sneak into the building. Sometimes the Venusians focused their telekinetic powers on one region.

I guess they still have a sense of front and back with sight, he thought. None of the buildings the sentries had been in had chairs or furniture for the aliens. *I guess I'm the alien now*, Ryland thought.

The locals could levitate, so there was no need for beds, chairs, or the like. Luckily, their way of communication was similar, a form of writing with symbols, like ancient times on Earth that agents had uncovered while looting, which they wrote on dense rock. But another way was a telepathic message held within a device. Like a voice recording, it held onto the message and released it when activated. Ryland found a few stone tablets hanging on the walls like pictures. One stood out with the symbol for the human race or inhabitants of Earth. He also swiped one of the recording devices.

When he came out of the building, one of the Venusians had found a frequency grenade that could create a high and low pitch, disrupting the Venusians' ability to sense their surroundings. Ryland also saw Destiny sneaking through a few smaller buildings.

"They found the north disruptor," he said over the comms.

"Roger," Tom replied as he waited outside the base for his teammates. Ryland had done his part, so he ran back into the shadows with Tom.

"I'm back," he informed his team. Once they regrouped, it didn't take long until the Venusians found the disruptors even if they had distorted their senses.

■

What did you find? Zawn asked, pushing the question into their heads. They brought forth items from their base. The Sentries had been getting better as they did more missions. They had only been gone for two hours this time. Zawn was impressed with their efficiency on every mission. The group's trust in Zawn deepened, and they all became good warriors together. The humans and Venusians could become cohabitating species. Zawn read through the slates and the recordings. Suddenly, the Sentries felt great fear and anxiety, but it wasn't from them.

"What is it?" Ryland asked, getting good at communicating with the Venusians.

Look here, Zawn said. *This symbol.* He pointed his finger. *It's for "Earth."* They had been getting used to the symbol. *And this is for "invade." This other tablet has two coordinates for "entry." And this tablet has a treaty signed by both leaders of the war.*

The Sentries shared his fear and anxiety now. Dom pulled his weapon and pointed it at Zawn. "Why should we trust you? You're one of them. Telling us this could just be a trap."

I don't share this treaty. These leaders are not mine, Zawn replied, refusing to raise his hands in surrender. It wasn't something the Venusians did. It was almost threatening, but Ryland reminded himself that Zawn was Venusian, not human, which meant it could go either way. Zawn could be preparing to attack, or it could just be doing what it thought was less threatening.

Elias had moved to the windows and looked out in case Dom was right, but he saw no one around, which meant there was no trap, at least not yet.

"What do you mean? You're in this war," Ryland said, confused by the statement.

I only joined this war because you would have been able to unite our species, Zawn explained. *I was once a rogue Venusian, not wanting to be a part of this war. But then citizens like Vaul went even more rogue and invaded your planet.* Anger rose in his voice. *I wanted to stop it and keep any conflict on our planet and not involve any other species.*

"Then help us," Tom said.

"He won't help us. His allegiance lies only with his species," Dom said, his weapon still trained on the alien.

"No," Ryland said. "He's been helping us this whole time—us, not them. Zawn found the missions from them to help the conflict. He wants the war to end."

Ryland's heart stopped. *He has been helping us. We teamed up after Jovian, Hunter, Banshee, Thief, and I saved them. The prophecy was about the Venusians and us! The prophet was right.*

Then Ryland remembered the incident that he and Hunter had run into when returning to Mount Horizon. The company that had investigated was dead, and the only one missing was the prophet. Ryland needed to find that man.

"It infuriates me that my species will join the rogue agenda," Zawn said. "We must deal with our problems at home and not involve others. We must leave now."

The sentries gathered the remaining tablets and recorders and then left for home, hopefully in time to warn the rest of humanity.

www.ingramcontent.com/pod-product-compliance
Lightning Source LLC
LaVergne TN
LVHW021530090325
805522LV00003B/264